CALCULATED DECEPTION

CALCULATED DECEPTION

THE CALCULATED SERIES: BOOK 1

K.T. LEE

VERTICAL LINE PUBLISHING

K.T. Lee

www.ktleeauthor.com

Publisher's Note: This work of fiction is a product of the writer's overactive imagination. It is not intended to be a factual representation of events, people, locales, businesses, government agencies, or propulsion engineering. Names are used fictitiously and any resemblance to actual people, living or dead, is completely coincidental.

Calculated Deception/ K.T. Lee - 1st ed.

ISBN 978-1-947870-00-0

Book cover design by The Book Design House

The Calculated Series

Calculated Extortion (Prequel Novella)
Calculated Deception (Book 1)
Calculated Contagion (Book 2)
Calculated Sabotage (Book 3)
Calculated Reaction (Book 4)
Calculated Entrapment (Book 5)

For my family

1

Dr. Matt Brown raised a hand to cover his yawn as he shuffled into Kelvin Hall, the home of all things mechanical engineering at Indiana Polytechnic. When he passed through the doorway to his office and flicked on the lights, his muscles tensed. The open cardboard box crammed into the crowded lab space next to his office hadn't been there when he left yesterday. A shipment of parts was innocuous enough, but if this one was like the others, he needed to call it in. Matt checked the recipient and peered inside. Damn. After walking the perimeter of the lab to ensure he was alone, Matt closed the door and dialed a long series of numbers from memory. He tapped his foot impatiently until a voice at the end of the line answered.

"Matt. What's happening?"

"There's been another package."

"Good work, Matt. Lay low and keep your cover. Our colleagues will take it from here."

2

Dr. Ree Ryland's practical black pumps clipped against the concrete sidewalk, breaking through the quiet of the early morning. She made a beeline to the civil engineering building to buy a coffee from the student-run lounge, filled her insulated mug exactly one inch from the top, added milk and sugar, and popped on the lid. After making small talk with the cashier and paying for her morning energy boost, she resumed her efficient pace until she reached her office. Ree dropped her purse on her desk, took a long pull of fortifying caffeine, and pressed the power button on her computer at precisely 7:15 a.m.

Ree lowered herself into her chair, swiveled ninety degrees, and plonked her heavy bag into the bottom drawer of her file cabinet. She locked the drawer and gave it a quick tug to make sure her things were secure, even though Indiana Polytechnic wasn't exactly crawling with criminals. While Ree wasn't worried about a student stealing her things, she didn't want someone to come across her small handgun by accident. Ree quietly exploited the lack of a policy on concealed weapons on campus by carrying her secured Glock zipped into the front pocket of a purse designed for that purpose. Despite chiding herself for her paranoia in the busy daytime hours, she drew comfort from knowing she could defend herself when she worked in the building alone at night.

Ree placed her earbuds in her ears and selected a playlist on her phone before retrieving the thick pad of graph paper from the corner of her desk. The cheerful, fast beat of her favorite song served as the perfect complement to the calculations that needed to be finished by the end of the week. Bobbing her head as she worked, she pulled open her desk drawer to pluck out the pencil and ruler that were stored next to her "break in case of emergency" chocolate and high-powered calculator.

Holding the ruler steady, Ree drew crisp lines and arrows on her diagram, making sure she'd made the right assumptions before plugging the problem into her 3D stress analysis software. She nodded in satisfaction and turned to the keyboard. Her fingers danced across it, tapping to the rhythm of the music that drowned out her surroundings. Ree looked up from her computer to check her diagram and realized, too late, that she wasn't alone. Her focus was broken by the sound of her own shriek.

When she realized that the cause of her alarm was waving a piece of paper and not trying to kill her, Ree slapped a hand to her mouth and felt her cheeks flush. Grinning, the man said, "Dr. Ryland? I'm sorry to sneak up on you...but do you have a moment?"

Ree's heart pounded as she rummaged through her mental file to work out who was standing in front of her. While students were most often the people that visited her office at odd hours, the man in front of her wore dress pants and a polo instead of the typical uniform of a sweatshirt and jeans. He was tall and youngish, with short, dark blond hair, but looked too old to be one of her students. His eyes darted around her office, which meant that either she had scared him or he was in a hurry. Ree tried to remember if there had been any gossip about new professors starting this week but came up empty. Powers of deduction at a loss, she gathered up her dignity, smiled pleasantly, and confirmed, "That's me. What can I help you with?"

. . .

Parker returned a smile to Dr. Ryland with practiced ease. She wore simple but trendy clothes, had an athletic build, and her brown hair was pulled back into a neat twist. At 32, he couldn't count on his looks to fool the professor into thinking he was an undergraduate student and had planned accordingly. Parker was playing the part of a college student interested in starting a new career after spending several years working as an electrician. This alias was easier than most. Parker worked as an intern for an electrical contractor for a summer in college and had graduated with an engineering degree before getting recruited into the FBI. That the FBI recruited engineers wasn't a secret, but it also wasn't widely known, which would come in handy when he tried to convince the young professor that he was just another student.

Parker placed the form on her meticulously organized desk and explained, "I'm Parker Landon, and I was wondering if it wouldn't be too much trouble to transfer to your section. I'm completing most of my school work after my day job and your 6 p.m. section would really help me out. But, your class is already full and I have to get your permission to attend. Can you sign off on an extra student? I promise not to be too much trouble."

When the professor stared past him instead of answering the question, Parker tapped a finger on the paper, keeping his face even as he watched for signs that she had somehow seen through his façade. While unlikely, the possibility was ever-present in his line of work, and he forced himself to appear relaxed as he waited for her response.

Ree envisioned her classroom and the students in it to determine if she could take on an additional student. She should try and help him – working full-time and taking courses was hard enough, and coming into the university in the middle of the workday was a major inconvenience. She mentally reconciled the number of empty seats against her enrollment estimates and looked into the air past him, biting her lip and tapping her pencil against the desk. They were only a week into the semester and she had a few no-shows after the first class, a fact which both concerned and annoyed her since hers was a specialty, and her classes were nearly always full. Realizing her train of thought had run on for nearly a minute, she refocused her attention on the student still standing in front of her desk, watching hopefully for her response. "I'm sorry. I seem to have completely forgotten your name, but…"

"It's Parker. No problem, Dr. Ryland."

"Yes, Parker. You are welcome to join my class if you've taken the prerequisites and are a third-year mechanical, materials science, or physics major." He nodded. Ree signed his slip, placed her earbuds back in her ears, and turned the volume down a few notches to prevent future heart attacks. She returned to her sketches and calculations before her newest student even left the room. Scrunching her nose and pulling out her big white eraser to change a detail on her diagram, she was oblivious to Parker's scan of her desk, lab equipment, and computer program. When she finally looked up from her work, he was gone.

After a few iterations of calculations, Ree's eyes began to blur. She blinked hard and leaned back in her chair to stretch. An hour had passed, and students were starting to shuffle past her open office door. Dr. Kenneth Moran walked in and gave her a wave. While Dr. Moran's name was on the door as the lab manager, he spent much of his time traveling to conferences as a keynote speaker and working with the management at the college. As a result, Ree did most of the actual work in the automotive safety lab. However, Dr. Moran was an easy man to like when he was around. He always had a smile on his round face and loved telling stories about his grandchildren, pictures of whom formed dense wallpaper around his desk. She greeted him with a quick hello and undocked her laptop to take it to class. Her schedule this semester included a dynamics course, and she had a herd of sophomore undergraduates to teach. She would have to make time to catch up with Dr. Moran later. He was still her boss, if in name only.

Later that evening, Ree was setting up for her automotive safety engineering course when the angry growl of her stomach disrupted the silence of the empty classroom. She'd forgotten to eat. Again. She pulled a protein bar from her purse, placed her laptop on the large desk at the front of the room, and plugged the cord into the projector. Leaning into the computer screen to select the correct presentation, she heard a noise in the hallway. It was likely just someone coming to class early, but her students typically arrived with just seconds to spare, not fifteen minutes.

She slowly turned around to assess the situation. Her newest student, Parker, stood just outside the door. His eyes darted to his cell phone as if to check that he was in the right place. She gave him a wave and took a bite of her snack. Overthinking a simple arrival time was a good reminder that if she wanted a clear head, she shouldn't skip lunch. There was no crime in arriving early.

Ree tried to focus on her materials, but a tingling sensation crept up her neck, and she couldn't reconcile the feeling that everything was not as it seemed. Maybe it wasn't all in her head after all. Whatever it was, it was best to face it head-on. She made eye contact with Parker as he dropped his bag on top of a desk and leveled his gaze in return. It wasn't threatening, but there was still something different about him that she couldn't place. Fearing that this was another case of a student trying to hit on her, Ree measured her next steps carefully. While it didn't happen often, Ree had learned the most successful approach was to stare them down while feigning ignorance. It was a delicate balance to avoid hurting feelings without appearing as if she was flirting with a student. If she successfully navigated the minefield tonight, some chocolate and a glass of wine would be in order.

WHEN PARKER LOOKED up from his phone into the observant and suspicious eyes of his new professor, he forced himself to appear sheepish. Clearly, she was nervous to see an unexpected guest. Interesting. Parker said, "Hi, Dr. Ryland. I know I'm early, but I was hoping you could catch me up on Monday's material, to make sure that Dr. Knight covered the same material that you covered."

Ree put her hand on her heart and let out a sigh. Parker looked behind him to try and decipher the cause of her alarm. His attention was drawn back to Dr. Ryland as words began to tumble out of her mouth. "Of course, no problem. I don't think you missed much. We really just covered the syllabus and my expectations for homework. As a third-year student, I have high expectations for the work you will accomplish. I'm counting on you to do your own research, cite your sources, and make assumptions, just like I do in my lab every day. With any luck, you'll fall in love with the subject, just like I have. In some cases, my work has been used to demonstrate that a client is injured and not faking pain. In other cases, by determining where forces are transmitted to passengers of a vehicle, large automotive manufacturers have been able to design better crash protection systems. I think this is a subject worth getting passionate about, and I therefore expect the best from my students. Do you have any questions?"

Parker wasn't expecting a follow-up question, but Dr. Ryland was looking at him expectantly, poise regained and eyebrows raised. He improvised the second question that came to mind since he couldn't exactly ask if she was committing felonies on a regular basis. "So, with all of your experience, are you planning on writing a textbook or anything?"

Dr. Ryland paused for a moment, and then replied, "Right now, I'm focusing on my work and my lecture materials. If anyone ever thinks I'm smart enough to write a book, they know where to find me."

Okay, so she had a little spunk. While that fit the profile of their suspect, Parker didn't get any negativity from her, just a healthy dose of the self-deprecating humor that he'd seen in his good friends in college. Too bad she could be smuggling weapons in her free time, instead of writing that textbook.

Parker nodded at the professor and settled into his desk. He pulled out a pen and a notebook and prepared to make some professional observations of her character without any more small talk. He had a sneaking suspicion she was clever enough to realize when she was being bullshitted, and even with a solid cover, he didn't want to get too friendly and take chances. Dr. Ryland was clearly capable of pulling off the crime, but then again, so were a number of her colleagues. However, the packages had been addressed to her lab, and every time they were delivered, her boss was conveniently out of town. Dedicated surveillance would be the best way to determine if she was a suspect or an innocent civilian lucky enough to have the FBI watching her back.

3

"OKAY, PARKER, WHAT DO YOU THINK?" MIKE MORETTI, PARKER'S longtime friend, poker buddy, and partner asked, as he made himself comfortable in the faded green chair next to Parker's desk. The two agents worked out of the FBI's Chicago field office. Like every other government building in the country, it was filled with utilitarian furniture. Mike had been conducting surveillance at Indiana Polytechnic for a few days, but Parker was the one who had face-to-face interactions with their suspect. Mike's carefully cultivated air of carelessness served him well in the field but didn't fool his friend, who knew Mike was eager to get right to business.

Parker said, "First impressions? She's a young, eager academic who has no idea what is going on. Second impression? Being a young, eager academic is a great cover for someone trying to smuggle weapons to earn a little extra cash. She's smart, driven, and a little jumpy. I have a hard time believing this could be going on right under her nose without her having a whiff of it. Background check turned up a concealed carry permit and third degree black belt in karate."

"Hardly a crime, but she's awfully prepared for one."

"Exactly. The thing of it is though, her record is squeaky clean. She shows up at work the same time every day, she gave me a long speech about why she cares about what she does, makes sure her students understand the material, packs up after her last class and goes home. I haven't caught her doing anything wrong, but I've been at this too long to believe it's that simple."

"Anything else show up in the background check? Grudges? Homicidal tendencies? Gambling problem?" Mike and Parker had worked together for years, and when they were talking shop, neither saw a point to sugarcoating the realities of the people they investigated. They both figured it took less time to get to the answer that way, and most of the time, they were able to rein in their bluntness around anyone who wasn't an agent or a cop. Mike had been fortunate enough to marry a profiler from the FBI who found his honesty endearing. As a result, his brain-to-mouth filter was now nearly nonexistent from lack of practice.

Parker shook his head. "Nothing. No personality traits that scream sociopath, terrorist, or drug addict. Nah, if she's doing it, it's got to be for the money. But she lives in a modest house, drives a modest car, walks almost everywhere. Works all the time, seems to get along with people okay."

"So, she makes decent money, and she doesn't seem the type, but our intel says she's still getting missile guidance system components shipped to her office when her boss isn't around. That doesn't exactly help us. Guess we need more information?"

"Yeah. Unfortunately, we need to do a little digging, see if we can find evidence or motive. I already filled out the paperwork to search her office and want you to come with me when we go. It'll take a couple of days to go through, but that'll give us some more time to see if she's up to anything." Parker slid a piece of paper across the desk to his partner. Paperwork or not, they weren't planning to get caught. Nothing would save them from the ridicule from their fellow agents if they got busted by an academic. Even if they could talk their way out of it, they'd never live it down at the Bureau. Per protocol, they treated her as armed and dangerous, even though Parker hadn't seen Dr. Ryland armed with anything other than the barely-drinkable beverage they called coffee from the student lounge.

. . .

Before the week was over, two FBI agents wearing Indiana Polytechnic sweatshirts and carrying shoulder bags arrived at the mechanical engineering building at 8:55 a.m., just before Dr. Ryland's first class. If their intel was accurate, her colleague had left for a conference the previous day, and Dr. Ryland's shared office would be empty inside of five minutes. While Mike and Parker preferred to perform the search at night, when the risk of being caught was lower, Dr. Ryland wouldn't be careless enough to leave anything important behind in the evenings. Since Enterprise, Indiana, wasn't usually the epicenter of FBI investigations, this part should be straightforward. Still, Parker had been in the business long enough to know that things often went sideways when you least expected it, and saying anything was "straightforward" was one of the best ways to invite disaster onto your investigation.

Parker and Mike both wore earpieces so they could talk freely without too much notice, even though Dr. Ryland's office wasn't on a busy floor. There was no sense in being careless just because there weren't many people around. Mike edged into the lead position as the two men changed their respective paces to put some distance between them. When Parker caught up to his partner, Mike had positioned his back in a corner. This spot would give him visibility down both hallways that led to the automotive safety lab while his phone would stream the surveillance feed from adjacent hallways. Parker would depend on Mike for defense, and a camera embedded in Parker's glasses would collect evidence without him needing to extract anything physical during his search. It was as good as it was going to get, considering they were conducting a covert search on a busy campus in broad daylight.

When Parker reached Dr. Ryland's office, he eased the door shut behind him and began to work. Given the time constraints, he kept his search localized to the office space.

Mike waited a few minutes before giving in to his curiosity. It was impressive, considering Mike didn't have a lot of patience and was used to watching a live feed. "Finding anything, buddy?"

"Nothing yet," Parker said, as he flipped through the files in Dr.

Ryland's desk drawer. Fortunately, the weather was cool, and it looked as if Parker just hadn't removed his leather gloves upon coming inside, rather than his more calculated motivation of ensuring he wouldn't leave fingerprints behind. The lab was lined with windows to the hallway, but there was a door separating the lab and the office. He had closed it upon his arrival to minimize exposure, noting the position so he could open it back up again before he left. Parker lifted stacks of papers on her desk and flipped through them. He took a few minutes to read the contents of the papers but didn't find anything outside of a lot of calculations and diagrams. He carefully arranged them back into the neat, color-coded pile he had found them in. It took a few extra moments, but his attention to detail would ensure he left no evidence of his visit. He pulled out his lock picks and went to work on the only locked desk drawer, briefly glancing at the clock to note the time he had left. The simple lock clicked open and he began to examine the contents of the drawer.

"Shit." Parker's body tensed. While he had been reminding his brain that she might be guilty, his gut thought they were chasing the wrong lead. However, he had misjudged the seemingly good-natured Dr. Ryland. "Mikey, she brings the gun to work." Parker carefully lifted a gun with the muzzle pointing at the floor from Dr. Ryland's handbag so Mike could see it on video later.

"What is it?"

"Small Glock with a trigger lock."

"A criminal that locks up her piece out of her possession near the scene of the crime? Too easy, Parker. Keep looking." Since Mikey was occasionally right, Parker bit his tongue instead of telling his partner that not all criminals were masterminds, and sometimes evidence was easy to find. Parker placed his hand back inside the bag, and his shoulders relaxed a fraction as his mood flipped from angry to amused.

"I just found her concealed carry permit. It matches her purse. Did you know you could buy a purse with a gun pocket and matching concealed carry case?" Parker quipped. Dr. Ryland wasn't off the hook, but in his years at the Bureau, he hadn't found a lot of hardened criminals who kept the appropriate paperwork in a stylish case next to a secured weapon. He placed the weapon and paperwork back into the handbag and fiddled with the inexpensive drawer lock until it clicked back into position. Checking his watch, Parker quickly mounted a small surveillance camera in the vent over Dr. Ryland's desk.

"Class lets out in five minutes, P, and the hallways are about to get busy. You need to get a move on," Mike's voice reminded him. Parker opened the door between the lab and the office to precisely the same position he had found it in and took one last look to ensure her office showed no evidence of his visit. It would be nearly impossible to know he'd been there, and while he didn't have the information he needed, they had a surveillance camera in place. It was a start.

4

After her class, Ree dropped into her chair, and the air hissed out of the old cushion in response. Teaching could be both exhilarating and exhausting. She swiveled the chair, then placed her feet on the floor to come to a sudden stop. Something was off. Straightening the stack of papers in front of her, she did a quick scan of her lab and made a mental note that she needed to find a lab assistant this semester. Yes, something was definitely off – the lab door usually swung back a bit from full open, no matter how hard she pushed it, but it didn't seem like it was in the same spot it always settled into. Maybe maintenance had worked on the door or something. Besides, it was just a door, and it wasn't off by more than a fraction of a degree. Between almost hitting the ceiling when a student came to talk to her several days prior and thinking that the same student was trying to hit on her, her internal radar was off in a big way and obviously could not be trusted. Shaking her head to clear it, she opened her laptop and started checking emails when she heard a tap on her door.

"Ree! A pleasure to see you again, and looking beautiful, as always." Steve Huff strode into her office and graced her with his presence without preamble. She stepped around her desk to shake his hand, and he pulled her close to kiss her cheek.

Ree fought the urge to wipe her face like a petulant teenager. Reining in her behavior and words around this man was always a struggle, especially when he insisted on putting his overly affectionate lips on her cheek. While she had been successful in keeping their interactions professional, Ree couldn't help calling him "Skeezy Steve" in her head. She'd been trying to break the habit, not because it wasn't true, but out of the fear she would say it out loud someday when she was tired or not paying attention.

Steve was a lawyer in Chicago, and Ree had a terrific working relationship with several of his partners at the law firm. They regularly contracted with her lab when they needed additional information for their cases. However, Steve had been a little too attentive ever since they worked together on a motorcycle accident case. He was frequently as close as was appropriate, always pushing the limit but staying just on this side of professional. She'd never seen him act unethically but suspected his motivation for doing the right thing came from the fear of getting disbarred rather than a strong moral compass. Regardless, she worked with his firm regularly, and it was important to treat him with the same respect she'd treat another colleague. It wouldn't kill her to be friendly to the man. Probably not, anyway.

JUST OUTSIDE OF THE BUILDING, in a nondescript black van, Parker watched the video feed from Dr. Ryland's office with Mike. Mike leaned forward and pointed to the monitor. "Now, isn't that interesting?"

Parker squinted at the screen. "Is that the sleazy lawyer from that firm a few miles away? What's his name? Huff, something. Seems pretty friendly with our suspect."

"Steve Huff. Very sleazy, and yes, a little too friendly."

"What is he doing in Dr. Ryland's office?"

"Maybe he's our missing link. Let's see how this plays out."

. . .

"STEVE – what brings you all the way down to Enterprise? I'm afraid I'm short on time today. I can set something up with one of your associates for next week if you have a case you'd like to discuss with me. I'll be up in Chicago for an unrelated meeting." Ree invented a scenario so that Steve could get what he came for and find someone else to bother.

"Ree, while I enjoy our time together and would absolutely love your help on all of my cases, that's not why I'm here." Ree wrinkled her nose as Steve slipped out of his suit jacket, slipping it over his arm before adjusting his tie. Wonderful. He planned on staying awhile.

"I actually need to pick up the evidence your lab was kind enough to examine for me from the John Doe case in Rockford. It looks like they will settle out of court, but loose ends, and all of that. I was here meeting with the provost and thought I would stop by."

It was unlikely the provost would take time to meet with an out-of-town lawyer unless his firm was making a large donation to the university, but Steve loved nothing more than sounding important. Silencing her childish side, Ree indulged him in order to be rid of him as quickly as possible. "Of course, I'm happy to help."

Ree walked briskly over to the lab cabinets, unlocked them, removed a large box, and handed it to Steve, thrilled to be getting rid of him so easily. As a bonus, his hands were occupied, so he couldn't get any grabbier. Steve, arms full of a large box, still managed to let his gaze linger then drift up and down. He paused and looked around the office, but Ree grabbed her jacket and ushered him out the door by sheer force of will. She picked up her laptop and keys, locked the door behind her, and waved a quick goodbye before making her exit from the building.

"WELL, THAT WAS INTERESTING," Parker said. He leaned away from the video feed of Ree's empty office and tapped a pen against his palm.

"You're telling me. Did you get a chance to look inside those boxes while you were in there?" Mike asked.

"Negative. I only had time to plant the camera and search her desk.

We have no excuse to stop Steve. Her handing him a box is purely circumstantial, even if we have it on camera. But all the missile parts we've tracked are small enough to fit in that box, and she sure wanted him out of her office in a hurry." Parker narrowed his eyes at the unchanged video feed. Her actions made her look guilty but didn't prove anything. Parker pushed himself to think of a reasonable explanation for her strange behavior but came up with nothing.

"Be right back," Parker said over his shoulder as he hopped out of the surveillance van. "Gotta grab a cup of coffee, and then we can head out," he called over his shoulder for the benefit of anyone who might be listening. What he was about to do fell in the gray area of investigation at best and absolutely wouldn't be upheld in court. However, he couldn't risk the sleazeball lawyer getting his hands on dangerous weapons. He had friends who were lawyers. He respected them and their job, but this guy wasn't anything like them. And he didn't like doing nothing while a man like Huff crossed paths with his suspect.

Jogging across the street to reach the campus grounds, Parker warred with himself as to how to strike up a conversation to find out what was in the box. He sped up to ensure his path would intersect with anyone leaving Dr. Ryland's lab and heading towards the main parking garage. Out of the corner of his eye, he spotted his target and adjusted course. When he passed a slow-moving student, inspiration struck, and he pulled out his cell phone as if texting. Parker corrected course one last time and, once he was perfectly positioned, he tripped, throwing his body into Steve.

"Whoa! Sorry, man!" Parker grabbed Steve's arm to keep him from falling as the box he was carrying tumbled to the sidewalk. The flimsy cardboard lid popped off of the box, revealing a bound report and a couple of plastic bags with damaged metal and plastic parts, neatly labeled in large red block letters as "EVIDENCE."

Steve glared at the mess on the sidewalk and dramatically wiped the dust from his suit. When he made eye contact with Parker, he slowed his hands and softened his scowl. He raised his hands in the air and said, "No harm, no foul." Steve picked up his box, replaced the lid, and grumbled before resuming his walk to the parking garage.

. . .

"WHAT THE HELL was that about, P?" Mike asked when Parker jumped into the van several minutes later. Parker handed Mike a coffee, placed his hand on his chin to pop his neck to the left, then right, and took a satisfied sip from his own coffee.

"Clumsy me," Parker said. "I ran into that lawyer that was in Ryland's office while I was grabbing us some coffee and he dropped his box of parts. Good thing nothing got damaged. Looked like he was carrying some pretty important samples with a case number on them."

Mike rolled his eyes and started up the van. Parker didn't usually bend the rules, but the information on this case in the analysts' reports had them all on edge. They knew that someone was acquiring high technology capable of directing missiles to a target but knew little else. Their team was charged with searching the university for a target, a motive, and a killer who had gone to great lengths to stay invisible. Usually, they would know at least one of the three, but all they had was one suspect who wasn't giving them enough to work with. While Parker's behavior was a little reckless, it had gotten results. They had just observed their only suspect interacting with a known asshole but saved themselves the trouble of following up and wasting time on the wrong lead. Mike began the long drive back to the office to meet with their unit chief for an update.

5

"You did what?" Patrick Sandhill clenched his teeth and glared at Parker. Known as Sandy to just about everyone in the Bureau, he had been Parker's unit chief for over five years and knew his people well. Sandy was average in height with a build that had been drilled into him in basic training and had not slipped with middle age. The dark hair at his temples had begun to gray, but he otherwise did not look his 50 years. His eyes narrowed as he stared down one of his best agents. "I don't recall approving you engaging with any suspects outside of Dr. Ryland, Parker."

Parker's voice was pure reason. "Sir, I simply ran into him this morning and took advantage of the opportunity to look inside the box that had opened during our purely incidental interaction. I don't believe that's against the law, is it, sir? I was only out to grab some coffee since we had a break in surveillance, and Agent Moretti was covering Dr. Ryland's office. It could have happened to anyone. However, given the opportunistic nature of my observation, as well as Steve Huff's interactions with Dr. Ryland, I felt it was my duty to report the mishap in order to provide the details needed to solve this case, sir."

Sandy crossed his arms and glared at the two men, allowing an uncomfortable silence to settle into the space. Mike shifted in his chair and Parker kept his poker face even. He projected a disapproving look for another few moments but didn't overdo it. He wasn't stupid enough to believe Parker's story – no one on his team believed in accidents when it came to interacting with suspects. However, he wasn't in the habit of punishing people for results when no laws were broken, and he wisely left the matter alone.

"Okay, now that you guys have had some time with the suspect, what are your impressions?"

Mike spoke first. "Look, I know we've only been at this for about a week, but if this woman is involved in a multi-million-dollar weapons smuggling ring, she's the best actor I've ever seen. Her habits are predictable, she's friendly when she doesn't have to be, and she hasn't broken any laws in the interactions we've observed. She's not hurting for money and doesn't have any addictions or gambling problems. After a few days of surveillance, something usually slips, but we aren't seeing it. She's carrying a weapon, but it's registered, and she has the proper permits for it. She's a single woman who works odd hours, and our background check shows her dad is in the security business. If she was my sister, I'd have her packing too. The only problem is she's the perfect person to commit a crime without suspicion."

"You realize if she isn't behind this..." Sandy started, and Parker finished.

"Yeah, Chief, we get it. She's in deeper than she has any clue. The problem is, sir, we don't have proof, and every one of those packages has been addressed to her lab. She works for another professor who's never there, which is the perfect cover. We found out from the background check that Dr. Ryland has proven in the courtroom that she has more backbone than most people give her credit for. Worse, she is smarter than most of the criminals I have chased down, which makes me think that if she wanted to hide it, she could. For all I know, she knows we're on to her and is behaving differently because she knows we're watching."

"You think she is onto you, Parker?" Mike asked.

Parker let out a breath. "Not sure. But I think if she's guilty and she knows I'm a fake, she's playing it cool. She watches me pretty close any time I show up. And she's been a little jumpy whenever I talk to her."

"Parker, you have an engineering degree. I'm not sure you qualify as a 'fake.' You flunking her class, son? I could have one of the rookies that just graduated help you out. I think we just got one fresh from school," Sandy goaded Parker.

"No, sir. I'm getting by just fine."

"Maybe it's time you started flunking so you can get some extra help from your teacher." Sandy leaned back in his chair and continued, "You been talking in class and letting on what you know?"

"No, sir. Been keeping my mouth shut and eyes open."

"Good. Gonna need you to go play dumb, son."

"Yes, sir." Parker looked at his watch. "We better get going. I have some homework to screw up before I visit Dr. Ryland tomorrow."

6

"SERIOUSLY?" REE SAID TO HER EMPTY OFFICE. SHE DROPPED HER head back against the top of her chair and stared at the ceiling as the pain from the hot coffee soaking through her white sweater subsided. She had just finished her morning class and was more tired than usual. Over the past week, she had been having trouble sleeping. She was normally a champion sleeper, but her brain kept chewing on a problem that she couldn't quite articulate. As a result, she'd felt like something was just...off.

"Irina! How are you this morning?" The always cheerful Ivan Nobelkov gave three quick taps on her door and poked his head into her office on the way to his lab. Ree had been given her great-grandmother Irina's name from her mother as a nod to their distant Russian heritage. While everyone else called her Ree, Ivan had always called her by her given name. He ran the propulsion laboratory, and she had long called him her favorite rocket scientist. His wife, Joanna, was a few years younger than he was and also Ree's best friend.

Pointing at her stained shirt, Ree replied, "Ivan! I am a mess today. I barely got through my first course, have a full day of work ahead, and have already spilled very brown coffee on my very white shirt. I am hopeless, *nyet*?" Ree lifted her shoulders in an exaggerated shrug and smiled despite her rocky start to the day. Ivan always had a kind word for her, and she was glad to see a friendly face on an otherwise frustrating morning. While her Russian was atrocious, she often tried to slip in a word or two when talking to Ivan. If she were away from her home country as he was, she would miss her mother tongue, butchered in its delivery or not.

"You are fabulous, as always," Ivan said theatrically. "The coffee spill makes the rest of us feel as if you are human. A little water to wash it out, and your day will be better in no time." She chuckled and waved to his retreating back as he rushed back into the hallway.

Ree looked down at the spreading coffee stain. She needed to run to the ladies' room to wash out her sweater. Fortunately, she had a brightly colored scarf she could use to cover up her clumsiness, but a quick trip to rinse out the splotch was unavoidable if she wanted to wear the shirt again. Completely focused on her own problems, she rushed through her office door, turned on her heel, and bumped right into a very solid wall. On her journey to the floor, she realized the wall was one of her students. Landing on her backside, she braced herself on her palms, resigned herself to being hopelessly uncoordinated, and took the hand offered by Parker Landon to heave herself and her dignity back to a standing position.

"Thanks for the hand," Ree said sheepishly. "I'll be right with you, Parker. Have a seat in my office. I'll be back in five minutes." And before Parker could reply, she darted off.

PARKER EASED himself into her guest chair and scanned the room. He pulled his homework and pencil from his bag. With no sounds of Dr. Ryland returning, he started tapping the pencil against his notebook and turned his head to look around her office.

"Don't do it, Parker." Mike's voice crackled into Parker's earpiece. Mike was watching the video feed in the surveillance van, and he often had a sense for what people would do before they even knew. However, in this case, even Parker was fully aware that if Ree Ryland was gone much longer, snooping was inevitable.

"I won't," Parker drew out the word. He slowed the tap of his pencil against his notebook and leaned across her desk to peek at her open file drawer. It was hard to tell if there was anything new since the last time he'd rifled through her office. Maybe those cabinets in the lab would be unlocked.

"Parker! Seriously. Knock it off."

"Just sitting here, Mikey. You have eyes on the hallway, right?" Parker asked, knowing that his friend would have the surveillance feed in the hallways up and running.

"Parker, no."

"Eyes on, or not?"

Mike sighed. Parker jumped up from his chair and walked through the doorway separating the lab and office. A fatigue test machine was hammering on a complicated metal component that, if he had to guess, he would say was part of a car bumper. He turned towards the cabinets. One quick pull told him that the doors were, frustratingly, locked. He didn't think he could pick them open and relock them in time, but still, they beckoned. "You will have company in ten seconds, Parker. Get back in the chair and look studious."

BY THE TIME Ree returned to her office, her white sweater was see-through in one spot, and her newest student was sitting in the chair across from her desk. Without turning around to greet him, she grabbed the scarf draped across the back of her chair, dropped it around her neck to cover the spot as gracefully as possible, turned to him and asked, "What can I do for you, Parker?"

Parker gestured to his homework and began asking questions. Ree didn't mind helping a student, but something about him had her on edge. He was asking the right questions and seemed genuinely interested in the material she was teaching, so that wasn't it. He was nice to look at, but that was a line she would never cross and, therefore, irrelevant. She began to work on forgetting that she even had the thought.

. . .

PARKER WATCHED Dr. Ryland closely during their interaction. Sure, she was easy on the eyes, but there was something else just below the surface he couldn't put a name to. Her eyes sparkled as she explained the homework, regularly checking with him to make sure he understood the material. Her short fingernails and the tiny amount of grease lodged beneath them suggested that she'd be equally happy working on the lab equipment as she was teaching him about the physics of the human body in an accident.

It was hard to imagine the enthusiastic professor as a criminal, but she had earned a black belt in karate at a young age and returned to the sport in adulthood. Between that and the gun hiding in her purse, it wouldn't be wise to make too many assumptions based on her appearance. As the minutes passed, he caught her eyes darting to the clock with increasing frequency. There was no way he could discreetly tell Mike to keep track of who walked by the office, but it was probably unnecessary anyway. The guy didn't miss much.

Parker realized she had asked him a question and quickly recovered. He improvised. "I apologize, Dr. Ryland. I was thinking about part a of question one and the rotation of the passenger's neck and limbs. What did you say?"

REE SUSPICION that something wasn't as it seemed with Parker shifted into certainty when he apologized. He didn't seem like the type to lead with "I'm sorry," or gentle his approach unless he wanted something, and she hadn't a clue what that was. It was probably a research internship. That would explain the odd behavior. She hated playing games, had a headache, and needed to get lunch before she forgot to eat again. "I was just making sure you were comfortable with the polar coordinate system, so you aren't completely off-topic," Ree answered. "If you're good with that, I'm afraid I have to cut our time short."

Parker said, "Of course. Are you expecting someone else? I don't want to monopolize your time."

Ree explained that she had lunch plans and ushered her eager student out of the room so she could get back to work. His behavior was odd but not threatening. Even though he was clearly bright, he asked a lot of softball questions. It was as if he was trying to engage her in conversation, rather than actually struggling with the material. She should have been uncomfortable with the attention, but she wasn't. Ree especially didn't like that. She rushed to the cafeteria to get some food before they shut down for lunch and before she blew the non-situation entirely out of proportion.

After Ree finished her meal and returned from the cafeteria, she saw her best friend and Ivan's wife, Joanna, peeking in her office door. "Joanna!" Ree called, and Joanna popped back into the hallway when she heard Ree call her name. As usual, Joanna wore perfectly tailored clothes on her compact frame with dangling earrings. Her curly blonde hair was pulled back into a neat bun. Dr. Joanna Nobelkov couldn't wear much jewelry, as a result of working in healthcare and not wanting to snag her gloves or stethoscope on large necklaces or bracelets. Still, she wouldn't leave the house without her earrings, even if they had to be tucked into her purse as soon as she arrived at the office. Joanna gave Ree a kiss on the cheek and placed a memory card in her hand, explaining, "I finally uploaded the pictures from our girls' weekend and forgot to send them to you. I had the camera in my backseat and was in the area. Do you mind downloading these and then getting it back to me? I'm at the end of my lunch break and need to get back to the office."

Ree agreed and placed the small storage device in her pocket. Joanna had probably been in the building to see Ivan. They had been happily married as long as Ree had known Ivan, and they were lucky enough to have the type of marriage where they still looked forward to seeing each other.

In the surveillance van, Parker raised his eyebrows and looked towards his partner. "You get audio on that exchange, Mikey?"

Mike studied his equipment and fiddled with the settings. "Negative. They were out of range. The only mic we have is above her desk. Do you want to go back in?"

Parker cracked his knuckles while staring at the video feed. "Don't think we can, Mikey. I've already been there once today, and if I show up right after she's received a pass from another agent, my cover is blown. If the intel is right on this one, we're worried about a lot more than just a data transfer. I'll call in a background check on the other potential suspect, though. Let's see what gets churned up and go from there."

MIKE HAD WORKED with Parker long enough to know not to push the issue. Parker appeared laid back, but once he made a decision, it wasn't easy to change his mind. Parker was probably right, and they didn't have permission to be stealing things off Dr. Ryland's person, but damn. It went against every instinct he had to watch someone pass intel and just sit and wait because it could blow their cover. Mike looked over at his friend's clenched fists and realized Parker was angrier than he was letting on. Parker always relaxed his eyes and jaw, a product of intensive training, but occasionally he let his frustration show in his fists, a fact no one else seemed to notice, but Mike happily exploited on poker night. Parker twisted his neck to pop it, arched his back, and unclenched his fists. "We better go have another talk with Sandy."

"And I get to do more paperwork. Lucky me."

The camera would still be recording in their absence, which allowed them to leave immediately. Mike jumped into the front seat and started up the van. Neither of them was looking forward to the next conversation with Sandy.

7

Chief Sandhill sat in his desk chair, writing yet another report and trying not to grumble out loud. His hands typed clumsily on his keyboard, and he alternated between glaring at his fingers and squinting at his screen. He was of the generation that didn't grow up with home computers and wasn't quite as quick as his agents when typing up his case summaries. However, his typical reports were brief, so it had no other impact on his job other than to annoy him on a regular basis. Focused on the task at hand, he barely noticed Parker and Mike at his door until they walked through his doorway, shut the door, and sat across from him before he could greet them. The report could wait.

"Problem, gentlemen?"

"You could say that, sir. This happened a few hours ago." Mike slid a device across the desk to the Chief.

Because the video was less than a minute long and the women seemed to be in a hurry, it wasn't long before Sandy looked at his team. "When was this?"

Parker answered, "About 1300 hours, sir. We got back here as quick as we could without lighting up the van." A mere two and a half hours had passed between observing the interaction and their return to Chief Sandhill's office.

Sandy nodded. "Who is the woman passing information to Dr. Ryland?"

"We're working on that, sir," Mike replied.

"Do you know what they were exchanging? Is there audio?"

Mike and Parker shook their heads simultaneously. Parker said, "No, sir. The only audio we have is in Dr. Ryland's office. Sir, if this is what we think it is, we've got more than just weapons to worry about. We're going to need more help to keep an eye on Dr. Ryland and her accomplices."

"I can give you Alexis."

"Awesome," Mike said. "You can spare her?" Sandy nodded. Alexis was a little newer to the FBI than Mike and Parker, but there was no one better at reading a room and improvising accordingly.

"She's been working with the analysts trying to untangle the knots on this one, but she's eager to get back into the field. I'll route your request for the additional background checks, and she'll be on your field team at 0800 hours tomorrow. In the meantime, I want you two to stay close. I acquired a condo by the university for you guys in case things started to heat up. I want you on-site until this case is solved. You can keep me updated via phone, or I can come to meet with you."

"Perfect, sir. Anything else?" Parker said.

"Keep attending Dr. Ryland's classes and stop in as much as you can without tipping her off. I want a game plan in two days. I'll keep the analysts busy trying to mine more data once we know the name of Dr. Ryland's associate. We need to get that memory card, but I want you out of it, Parker. I need your nose clean since you're closer to her than anyone else, and I'm not going to risk your cover. I'll get you some additional folks on silent surveillance. I don't want them interacting with the suspect, but you're going to need backup if Dr. Ryland is working a team. Give me two days."

. . .

Alexis Thompson pulled up in a taxi several blocks from where Mike and Parker were parked, paid for her ride, and took in her surroundings. The quiet university neighborhood was pretty and unassuming. Her job was to catch the bad guy or girl behind this so it remained that way. She hoisted a large backpack over her shoulder and walked to the van's location. When she got close, a door on the van popped open. She ducked inside and tossed her bag on the floor.

"Boys." Alexis nodded at the two men. Mike reached over to give her a hearty thump on the back, and Parker pulled her in for a bear hug.

"Good to see you, kiddo." Parker and Mike's greeting was their equivalent to high school girls jumping up and down and screaming. She grinned broadly.

"Don't get carried away, boys. I was just getting used to not having to work with you." They rolled their eyes on cue. Despite the fact that she was only slightly younger, she happily embraced the older brothers/little sister dynamic that had developed shortly after they started working together. She grinned and continued, "Got some paperwork for you from the team back at the ranch. The other woman was a Joanna Nobelkov, wife of Ivan Nobelkov, a Russian who happens to work down the hall from Irina Ryland."

"Yeah, we've seen him. Scatterbrained, needs a haircut a week ago, booming voice...sound familiar?" Mike asked, raising his dark eyebrows. Mike had no trouble getting to the point, was as tall as Parker, and carried an extra 30 pounds or so of muscle. However, he looked and acted just like her oldest brother, and Alexis found him hilarious rather than intimidating. As long as you weren't committing a crime, Mike was as good as they came.

She rolled her eyes in mock exasperation and continued, "Yes, and happens to run a very successful propulsion laboratory. You guys know what that means?"

"Yeah, do you?" Mike asked.

"Sure do. I guess Uncle Sam wanted us to play nicely together again because they had me working the leads that pointed to Indiana Polytechnic. Several shipments were made to Dr. Ryland before we realized she was a source for missile control systems design and manufacture." Alexis pulled a folder out of her backpack and passed out copies of the analysts' research.

Mike flipped through the reports. "They've been shipping parts for almost a year. What took so long?"

"Truthfully? We had no reason to watch her. We typically monitor the propulsion researchers for this type of activity, but she's down the hall in a totally unrelated lab. Plus, she's been clever. She did a good job of disguising the parts as test equipment, and she hasn't stockpiled anything that goes boom. I'm not sure we would have realized what was happening at all if we hadn't received an anonymous tip a few months ago. This one scares the crap out of me. No one waits that long to blow things up unless they have something big planned. Does she look guilty?"

"Yeah. She does." Parker leaned back and crossed his arms.

Alexis noticed the shift in mood and immediately pounced on it. "You love catching the bad guy. Why aren't you happier about it? Not enough evidence?"

"Yes and no. I've got a feeling about this one, and I can't put my finger on it. When I'm around, I've caught her staring at me like she's trying to figure out if she can trust me. Who does that but a guilty person? But, she hasn't changed her actions, and she's not doing anything that screams criminal. The only thing we have is that memory card. So, either she's waiting us out, or she isn't guilty. She suspects me of something but hasn't called me out on it. Frankly, Alex, all the evidence points to her, but something isn't adding up."

Alexis raised an eyebrow. "What are you planning on doing about it, fearless leader?"

"Just keeping an eye out for now. I need to get that evidence, but Sandy already called me off, and he's right. We can't risk it. Doesn't mean I like it."

Alexis shrugged. "We can't. I can."

Mike interjected, "Alexis, you just got here. Literally. Less than five minutes ago."

"Yeah, but I've been thinking about this case and riding a desk for months. Don't worry, I'm not going to talk to Dr. Ryland, but let's see if there is an opening for me to borrow the memory card." She held up a device and waved it at them. "Won't take more than a minute, and I even have a permission slip. We'll keep an eye out this morning, and if there's an opportunity, I'll jump in."

Mike turned back to the surveillance feed and said to Parker in a stage whisper, "I wonder if Sandy realized while he had her cooped up with the analysts that he was creating a monster?" He didn't quite hide his smile when Alexis slugged his shoulder. "Nice to have you back, Alex."

REE DRAGGED her weary body into the office and thumped down into her chair. She'd spent another night trying to sleep with very little to show for it. When she pulled her computer out of its bag, a small piece of plastic tumbled to the floor. Well, crap. She left the memory card Joanna gave her in her laptop bag overnight and had forgotten to download the pictures. So much for Ivan being the scatterbrained one. She rubbed a hand down her face and slid the card into the slot on her laptop to save the pictures Joanna had taken. Once her task was complete, she placed it at the edge of her desk, where she couldn't forget about it. She'd catch Ivan on his way in.

"DID YOU SEE THAT?" Parker asked Mike, leaning into the screen.

"If I didn't, I should be fired. There are four total files, identified as jpegs. Could be a cover, though," Mike said as he froze the feed. He zoomed in on the image and scribbled down the names for Alexis, who was holding a small card reader. Without looking at her, he asked, "Your device isn't connected to a network, is it?"

Alexis scoffed by way of reply, and they bantered while they watched the feeds. It was nice to have fresh company in the van since the only thing more boring than tedious work was watching someone else do tedious work. Alexis and Mike began to argue about their respective alma maters' chances in a bowl game until a visitor passed by Dr. Ryland's door. They turned up the feed in time to hear a yelp come from their suspect. She'd smashed her knee into her desk when she leapt up to greet Ivan Nobelkov. Dr. Ryland limped over to the door with one hand on her leg and called after him.

IVAN WAS LATER than he'd intended to be that morning, and he was rushing by Ree's office when he heard a loud thump and a scream. He dashed inside and found his friend hopping on one leg. His panic changed to amusement, but years of training from his wife kept him from laughing out loud. He suspected that others didn't always share his appreciation for slapstick humor, and his wife had confirmed that hypothesis on several occasions. Ree was one of the brightest young professors at the university, but she often became so focused on the task at hand that she forgot to take stock of her surroundings, including furniture. Ree hobbled back to her desk, and returned to him holding a memory card. Before he could ask what it was for, she explained, "From Joanna. The files she wanted me to download?"

"Of course. Thank you. I'll make sure these get to the right place. Are you okay?"

"I'm fine. My pride took a hit, though," Ree said, and Ivan managed to reach the hallway before he let out a chuckle.

PARKER TOOK a sip of his coffee to hide his reaction, but his shoulders dropped, and he pressed his lips together in frustration. The gesture didn't escape Alexis's notice. She kept her mouth shut but made a mental note to keep an eye on her friend – he seemed uncharacteristically invested in this case.

"Please, can I go out and play?" Alexis asked, her voice dripping with false charm and real enthusiasm.

"Game plan?" Parker asked.

Alexis tapped her mouth with her pointer finger and replied, "Hmm...toss-up between looking for an internship and prospective student looking for the bathroom."

"Let's go with the first one. But don't rush this."

"You got it, boss." All business, Alexis grabbed a smaller backpack out of her pack. She threaded her ponytail through a visor with the university's logo emblazoned on it and threw the backpack over her shoulder. She had a bounce in her step as she headed towards the mechanical engineering labs to do a little research of her own.

IVAN PLACED his briefcase by the open door and surveyed his desk. Messy people rarely thought they had a problem, and he knew he certainly did not. While his desk and lab space were a bit crowded, he knew where everything was. Ivan moved a stack of papers from his chair to his desk before sitting down. He realized he was still holding the memory card Ree had given him. Ivan placed it at the edge of his desk, where his wife would be most likely to see it. His wife was accustomed to his scatterbrain and would pick it up next time she came through. Bless her. She thought his forgetfulness was because he was a genius, and he wasn't one to argue with a good woman. Moments later, he forgot all about it as he began to tackle the pile of paperwork that had accumulated over the previous week. As Ivan flipped through a report on his desk, his office door opened. An eager young student with bright eyes and a backpack slung over her shoulder walked in.

"Dr. Nobelkov?" the student asked. "Hi, I'm Alexis, and I was in your freshman engineering seminar a few years ago. I'm sure you remember me," she said cheerfully, sitting in the chair across from his desk before he could put down his report.

ALEXIS PLACED her backpack on the floor and gave Dr. Nobelkov a bright smile. "I was really encouraged by what you said in your class – oh, is that a new design for a rocket engine nozzle? Do you mind if I ask what you are working on?" Ivan redirected his attention to the 3D model displayed on his computer screen. Alexis discreetly located the memory card and slipped it into the reader.

Dr. Nobelkov's face lit up as he explained the science behind the design. Alexis would have had plenty of time to make several copies of the evidence, had she so desired, as he explained every detail of the design, down to the how the nozzle wall geometry was designed to optimally dissipate heat and direct the flow of hot gases to generate thrust. While Alexis half-listened to his eager description of the new technology, he was fully engaged in his explanation and oblivious to her response to it. He finally looked in her direction when she pointed to his screen to ask a question. As he looked back towards the monitor, Alexis put the small card back where she found it, although she doubted he would notice if she had taken it for hours. But, he also could just be a terrific actor, in which case, taking precautions was the right thing to do.

"That's fascinating, Dr. Nobelkov. Thank you so much for taking the time to explain it to me. I'm sorry. I got a bit distracted by your design. Originally, I came in to ask if you knew if anyone was hiring undergrads to work in labs this semester. It'd be a great experience for me, and you mentioned how hands-on experience is so important for students to prepare them for a career."

While asking for work in the lab went beyond getting information off of a memory card, Alexis had a good sense for when there was an opportunity to push her advantage just a little further. Dr. Nobelkov was a suspect, albeit of lower priority than Dr. Ryland, and she had done her research on the man. He was known for employing a large number of undergraduate students, and his proximity to Dr. Ryland's lab could be useful. She was pleasantly surprised when he said, "I can't take on any more students, but Ree – excuse me, Dr. Ryland – would like a lab assistant but can't seem to scrape together the funding. If you are willing to work pro-bono or for course credit, that's where I would start." He gave her a small smile before returning to his work.

Alexis thanked him, her enthusiasm genuine, as she strolled out of his office and back to the van.

"Don't get cocky," Parker said when Alexis tossed him the device with their data on it.

"And don't throw the evidence," Mike added.

"You're welcome," Alexis said victoriously.

They would get the files couriered back to the Bureau quickly so the computer team could figure out what had been hidden in the jpeg images. It would take some time to get answers, but they couldn't risk going into Dr. Ryland's computer – any decent spy or suspicious parent could install a key logger, and the techies capable of bypassing it without detection were up in Chicago.

"Any other news?" Mike asked.

"Looks like Dr. Ryland needs a lab assistant. Any volunteers?" she asked while buffing her Indiana Polytechnic visor.

"Alright, go in. But only because we've been keeping Mikey in the van, and I want to keep him out of the spotlight for now."

Alexis beamed. "You got it, boss."

8

THE FOLLOWING MORNING, REE WAS EXAMINING A SMALL COMPOSITE material sample that had broken during testing. She had just decided to take it to the microscope for a closer look when she was interrupted by a knock on her door. Ree looked up from the broken test piece to see a young woman, most likely a student, of average height with excitement sparkling in her eyes and a huge smile on her face. Ree was terrible with names but good with faces, and she didn't recognize the stranger at her door, so she asked, "May I help you?"

"Hi, Dr. Ryland! I asked Dr. Nobelkov if he knew of any opportunities to work as a lab assistant. He recommended I talk to you." Ree's face softened. She needed help but hadn't had time to get the word out. It was thoughtful of Ivan to direct students to her.

"Great. Have a seat..." Ree trailed off. The young woman stuck her hand out.

"Alexis Jenson. It is a pleasure to meet you in person. Dr. Nobelkov spoke highly of you, and I've read some of your research." Alexis sat in Ree's guest chair and pulled out a notebook and pen.

Ree rubbed her forehead as the smartly dressed girl eagerly told her how interested she was in mechanical and automotive safety engineering, and how she'd like to work for course credit. Maybe she needed another cup of coffee if she was considering turning down free help, but it didn't seem fair to give Alexis the opportunity without interviewing other candidates.

"I'm willing to work whatever hours you can give me," Alexis offered.

Ree sighed. "Alexis, I am absolutely thrilled to see someone so enthusiastic about the field, but I'll need to conduct additional interviews, in the name of due diligence. I'm going to need to get back to you next week. Will that be okay? If it's a good fit, we'll try and get you started on work you might be able to publish."

Alexis smiled brightly at Ree. "Absolutely, Dr. Ryland. I'm just happy to hear the position is still open since I think it could be a great experience for me. I hope that, if the job doesn't work out, we can continue to chat so I can learn from you?"

Ree nodded. "My door is always open, and I'd love to help you as I am able." It wasn't an empty offer. She was passionate about helping young learners, particularly young women, given the importance of female role models in a traditionally male-dominated field. The guys she worked with were great, but she ran into the occasional bad apple, and she'd long felt it was important for women to support each other. When Alexis forced a smile through her obvious disappointment, Ree said, "Don't give up hope yet. I will absolutely call you back next week with an answer either way."

ALEXIS GAVE Dr. Ryland her contact information, and before leaving, she leaned over to shake Dr. Ryland's hand. It hadn't taken long to understand Parker's reservations about their primary suspect. She had also connected easily to the young professor. Hopefully, it wasn't because Dr. Ryland was a card-carrying sociopath capable of manipulating those around her. Alexis hadn't had time to make a formal assessment, but she wasn't usually wrong about people. And Dr. Ryland didn't seem like one of the bad ones.

Unfortunately for her first impression, Alexis had done her research on the key players in this mess. It was hard to believe that Dr.

Ryland was oblivious to the fact she was being used as a weapons mule. There could simply be a more complicated motive that they didn't fully understand yet.

As she was leaving, Alexis stopped in Dr. Nobelkov's lab under the guise of thanking him for directing her to Dr. Ryland's office, but the only person there was a man she didn't recognize from the case files, most likely a student. He was fiddling with some complicated equipment but looked up when Alexis knocked on the door. "Excuse me, have you seen Dr. Nobelkov?"

The man narrowed his eyes but then responded with a beautiful African lilt to his English, "No, I am afraid you just missed him. Can I help you?"

Alexis shook her head. "No, I just wanted to thank him. He did me a favor. Good luck with whatever you're working on." Alexis gestured to his project, and he seemed relieved, probably because he didn't have to talk to her. It seemed most of the people she ran into in the engineering labs on campus were less than excited about talking to strangers. The man turned back to his equipment. Out of excuses to remain in the building, Alexis retreated to the van.

After the young woman left, Simon Kakra paced a now-familiar path around the propulsion lab. He pulled up an email account created just for this shipment and sent a request to his parts supplier to ship the parts he had carefully disguised as custom test equipment components the previous month. They always shipped with a tracking number, so he had a good idea of when the parts would come in, barring any extraordinary circumstances. He'd been concerned since school started up again that new eyes in the lab might want to know what he was doing, but no one in the lab seemed interested in his work.

Of course, working in a lab with a secure area and the associated government oversight was a threat to discovery, but the brazenness of his location was part of the brilliance of his plan. He hadn't been granted security clearance for the secure areas and would not appear to have access to anything dangerous. Now, it was time to get things moving before The General became impatient. Simon couldn't hide in America forever, and the window of time to get the parts he needed was getting shorter. It took no small amount of skill to hide his weaponry in plain sight, and no plan was without risk. The longer this dragged out, the more likely it was that some curious academic would figure out what he was up to, and he didn't need any additional complications. He checked to make sure the email had sent successfully and fingered the switchblade in his pocket before getting back to work.

9

After three days stuck in the van waiting for more information, Parker wasn't the only one growing restless. The FBI tech team had determined there was nothing detectable on the files other than pictures of Dr. Ryland and Joanna. Either she was better than their tech team or, more likely, she just wanted copies of the pictures. In the entirety of their surveillance, Dr. Ryland hadn't even broken a traffic law.

"We've got to do something. Either she's guilty, or she isn't. If she isn't it, I'm done wasting time." Mike broke through the silence.

Alexis nodded and said, "She doesn't fit the profile Scarlett worked up for me."

Mike quirked an eyebrow. "Scarlett was read in? She didn't mention it last weekend." Scarlett was one of their best profilers, and also Mikey's wife.

Alexis grinned. "Do I get to tell her you didn't recognize her work?"

"No way," Mike laughed. "She'd never let me hear the end of it."

Parker scratched his chin. "I don't know. That doesn't sound like a good reason not to tell her to me."

Mike rolled his eyes. "This is what happens when you work with your friends. Teach me to be nice to you guys."

Parker laughed. "Yeah, that's the problem, Mikey. You're too warm and fuzzy. So, we're in agreement. I requested that we do a full search of Dr. Ryland's house and the parts of her office we didn't touch and then get a move on if we don't find anything. Didn't want to throw you all under the bus if it was the wrong call, so officially, it just came from me."

"Any luck getting that approved?" Mike asked.

"Just came through. Let's get this over with and figure out where to go from there."

Alexis's phone buzzed, and she thumbed through the message. "It's about time." Turning to Mike and Parker, she continued, "Finally, some good news. The team back at the ranch did a little eavesdropping, and it looks like another delivery for Dr. Ryland is coming in tomorrow. So much for her not being involved. Normal deliveries occur at 11 a.m. to the entire mechanical engineering building. Looks like we'll finally figure out what she's doing with these parts."

Parker tapped a pen against his palm. "Since we have the go-ahead to search her house already, why don't you coordinate with the team at Dr. Ryland's house while I go in for homework help? Dr. Ryland teaches from 9 to 10, so I'll go in at 10:30. That should put me there when the package is delivered. You good with missing the drop to keep an eye on the search team?"

Alexis sighed in mock annoyance. "Fine, but I get to come in tonight for the office sweep."

Parker grinned at her. "Deal."

THE FOLLOWING DAY, Parker entered Dr. Ryland's office with a sense of purpose, notebook and textbook in hand. Alexis would be meticulously searching Dr. Ryland's house as Parker distracted her with homework questions. The team hadn't found anything in her office the previous evening. Depending on how she handled the imminent shipment, they would soon move onto the next suspect or determine if it was time to make an arrest. Parker thought he'd been doing a pretty good job not looking at the clock too frequently until Ree pointed to it. "Parker? I understand you need help with the material, but do you need to be at work? We can meet up another time that's more convenient for you."

"Actually, I have this morning off, but I do have a dentist appointment in an hour. I'm always paranoid about being late," Parker improvised, making a mental note to keep his thoughts on the task at hand. Parker managed to direct all of his focus to the homework, and after another two problems, he was unsure how much time had passed. His nerves were on edge as he waited for the package to arrive with his back exposed to the open office door. Complicating the situation, he was hitting a limit of how much of the professor's time he could monopolize without suspicion.

His reverie was interrupted by a loud thump at the door. Parker whipped around and shifted his body so that he was between the door and Dr. Ryland. Well, that was subtle. Even though they had some work to do for a formal all-clear, his instincts had made their decision that she wasn't involved.

"PACKAGE FOR DR. RYLAND?" The bored deliveryman held out an electronic signature pad. Ree rose to accept the box and squiggle a line on the pad, annoyed that it was necessary since they would have just dropped it off if she wasn't there. Parker's reaction to the noise was impossible to miss. Perhaps he was some sort of military veteran. It would explain his build and ability to focus on the task at hand. Hopefully, he wasn't having a hard time – coming back from a war always had a period of readjustment. She could look up some campus resources for him if she could work out a way to ask without offending him.

WHEN DR. RYLAND stared at him instead of bringing the package inside, Parker could practically hear the gears turning in her head. He tensed, waiting for her to make the first move. Several seconds passed until the silence became uncomfortable. Parker broke through the quiet.

"Do you need some help pulling that inside?" Parker hedged.

"I wouldn't turn it down, Parker. Although I may have you hoof it down to another lab for me if it's what I think it is and you're willing to help. I hardly ever have things shipped. It feels like the only packages I've been getting lately are actually for Ivan's students accidentally addressed to me."

"Do a lot of people mix up rocket parts and car parts?" Parker raised an eyebrow.

"You think it wouldn't be that hard, right? One of their suppliers seems bound and determined to send everything to me. One would hope they could tell the difference between crash safety systems and rocket engines. My guess is that they pulled the wrong office number since our lab information is right next to each other on the university website. It's been happening for almost a year and they still haven't fixed it."

Dr. Ryland dug into the package. The components were packed neatly in foam lined cases. She pulled out a large piece of metal and showed it to him, incredulous. "Does this look like a car part to you? Or a safety mechanism? Or anything remotely resembling an energy-absorbing design that I could test in my lab?" Not waiting for him to answer, she huffed out a breath and waved the cone-shaped part in the air. "No – this looks like a rocket nozzle, some scrap titanium, and a circuit board. Which would be perfect, if I were an engineer trying to test a missile, which, let's be honest, is really just a bomb with a map." She put the components back in the box and snorted at her own joke. "A bomb with a map. I've got to tell that one to Ivan."

Parker tensed. He scratched his neck and measured his words carefully. "A missile sounds serious. Should we call someone? The cops, maybe?"

Dr. Ryland laughed. "I don't think so, Parker. I'm right down the hallway from the propulsion lab, and this looks an awful lot like their stuff. That's what I meant when I said it was Ivan's lab – that's Dr.

Nobelkov. Electronics aren't really my forte, but my bet is it's a grad student project since bits and pieces have been coming in pretty regularly. I'd ask Ivan, but he's not into the nitty-gritty details of the piece parts his students are ordering, and all the good stuff is behind a locked door. But I'll just bet if we take it to his lab, someone will know what to do with it. Don't worry – you aren't the first person to panic over nothing. I knew an aerospace professor that nearly got arrested in an airport during a random search because he had traces of explosives from his last experiment on his pants. Good thing he had a business card or he might still be locked up."

She flashed him a quick smile and picked up the box. "You know that favor? Can you walk it down for me? I'm afraid with my track record, I'll drop it and cost a poor grad student thousands of dollars that neither of us have lying around to replace it."

"Of course," Parker said, keeping his expression even. "I'm afraid I'll have to ask you for some more help later this week since I have that dentist's appointment." Parker gingerly picked up the box and carried it out of the office. Once out of earshot, he mumbled, "Mikey?"

"Alexis just got back, and I'm on my way. No one in sight."

"We're gonna need a plan."

"Working on it."

"Detouring into the bathroom now. Meet me in here." Parker stopped in the bathroom and, upon seeing it empty, flipped the deadbolt. Carefully lowering the box to the floor, he peeled back the protective covers and took pictures of the contents. He used just his fingertips to pull out the small nozzle. It wasn't one of the parts he'd been looking for, but it was conceivable that whoever was ordering these parts might want small thrusters to course correct the missiles. They could also be using the extra parts as decoys. Parker and his team needed to figure out what mattered in the box and quickly, in case their actual suspect knew the box was in transit. It was time to recalibrate all of the information they knew in light of learning their perp had pulled a bait and switch. Damn, that was a smart way to stay invisible.

Parker pulled the circuit board from its protective covering and placed it next to the nozzles. He heard a faint tap on the door and Mike saying his name in a whisper through the earpiece. Parker unlocked the door. Mike eased into the room and whistled softly.

"That look like a missile to you?" Parker asked.

"Part of one." Mike ran a hand down his face. "If the counter-terrorism team caught everything, they've acquired some navigation equipment, and it looks like they could have the rest of the brains of the operation in that box. I've said it before, but we've got a problem here, buddy. Whoever wants this is taking their time and covering their tracks. They're planning something big."

Parker stared at the parts and made a decision. "The way I see it, Mikey," he explained, "we can take a couple of pieces out and see who gets mad that they've gone missing. However, that could put Dr. Ryland in danger if they think she's on to them. We could let it go and track the shipment, but I'm not willing to risk letting this stuff get out there. That leaves sabotaging the parts to try and get a reaction. Dr. Ryland will still have a safety problem, so we're going to have to stick to her pretty close and keep her in the dark as long as we can get away with it. Let's get this done so we can get out of here."

Mike held out a small tool. "I know how much you hated electrical engineering. How good were you at screwing up your circuit boards?"

"It was my specialty." Parker used the sharp edge to score an edge of the board and then snap it as if it had been broken in transit. If anyone looked carefully at the edge, they might be able to tell it had been scored. To complete the deception, he leaned over and scuffed the board on the grout on the tile floor. He then held the broken component underneath the faucet and let the tap water flow over it for a half a minute before patting the surface dry. In Parker's experience, water alone was enough to fry some of his electronics, and it was a decent back-up plan on short notice. Less than five minutes passed before the box was repacked to its original state, with the broken corner of the circuit board peeking out of its padding.

Mike grabbed the box and smashed one corner against the bathroom tile, just above where their broken board was located.

"That oughta do it." Parker gave a nod of approval at the final product. Mike left the bathroom, and Parker counted to sixty. Parker exited the bathroom, wiping alternating hands on his pants and switching the box from hand to hand as if he had skipped the dryer on his way to the propulsion lab.

Parker passed Mike in the hallway. He was leaning against the wall, probably watching the surveillance feed from Dr. Ryland's office on his phone. They had addressed the immediate threat, but now she would need 24/7 protection. Whoever was expecting the delivery was probably more than a little unstable and about to get very angry. If they thought the parts were sabotaged, the first person they would suspect would be Dr. Ryland. However, if Parker pulled the professor away from her position for her own safety, their covers would be blown. They might even spook their unknown perpetrator. This one was going to take a little finesse.

Parker brought the open box into the propulsion lab and almost walked straight into Ivan Nobelkov, who startled and grabbed Parker by the shoulders before they could fully collide.

"Excuse me, Professor," said Parker. "I'm just coming from Dr. Ryland's office, and she said this box was meant for your lab? Apparently, there's a rocket nozzle in it, which she doesn't have a lot of use for."

Parker placed the box on a table and Dr. Nobelkov followed him. Dr. Nobelkov pulled back the protective foam and winced when he saw the rocket nozzle and broken circuit board. "The wrong location again?" he asked. "And a broken part? Oh dear, I'm afraid if you hear an explosion from my lab, it'll probably be one of my students blowing their gasket. The nozzle looks fine, but the circuit board will be a problem."

Dr. Nobelkov picked up the board and tsked as he pulled the part closer to his nose to study it. "These things happen, I'm afraid. New boards can be ordered. It will just take time." Ivan placed the part back in the box and brushed his hands on his pants. "Do tell Ree that I am sorry about the mix-up. This seems to be happening far too often." He leaned down to scribble a note as Parker left.

Parker didn't need to linger to move Dr. Nobelkov to the top of their list of suspects. They had observed him and Dr. Ryland exchanging pleasantries, and Nobelkov's wife, Joanna Nobelkov, was Ryland's best friend. He had no family left in Russia and met his wife when she was a grad student from Nebraska and he was in his first year of teaching. By all accounts, it looked as if he had assimilated into America but retained a deep love for his country and history. That didn't make him guilty or innocent, but he was now in possession of cleverly disguised missile control system components, which meant they had some work to do.

Parker opened the passenger door to his team's black van and said, "Mikey, we have a problem."

"Just one?"

"We just set off a time bomb on a civilian and walked out the door. We need to get in touch with the Chief ASAP and get some coverage for Dr. Ryland. Within the hour, if possible."

"Ye of little faith. I already called, and we're going to take shifts and set up surveillance around the house for the time being. Witness protection is a no-go."

"Yeah, can't risk it even if we could get it approved. Hate to put her in the middle of things, but we don't have much of a choice."

"Can't win them all, P. Dr. Ryland has a donor's gala to attend tonight, and now you do too. I'll drop you so you can get dressed. Try and be charming. The gala starts at 2000 hours, and your ticket will be at the door."

10

Parker's phone beeped as he tightened the knot on his tie. He read Alexis's update, grabbed his jacket, and jogged to his car. The gala didn't start for an hour, but it was close enough that he could bump into Dr. Ryland at her office right after her class without too much suspicion. He'd been able to get a suit couriered to him from Chicago, but he'd had to skip Dr. Ryland's lecture that evening to get it. With anyone else, there was hope his absence would go unnoticed. However, Dr. Ryland would expect an explanation for why he missed her class. He added fabricating a reason for skipping her class to his growing to-do list.

Alexis sat on the floor in the hallway, less than fifty feet from Dr. Ryland's office, legs stretched out, and an open textbook in her lap. She had placed herself by an outlet and plugged her phone in as an excuse to explain her extended presence in an odd location. Parker would be arriving shortly, and her intent was to stay in position until she heard his footsteps. Dr. Ryland had waved to Alexis on the way into her office fifteen minutes earlier but had not left yet.

The mechanical engineering building became quiet as classes

ended. The students were mostly tucked away in computer labs, energy drinks in hand as their evening of homework, projects, and coding began. Alexis's phone beeped. *Here. - P.* She unplugged her charger, placed her book under her arm, and walked towards the footsteps, her hand resting on the Glock holstered at her waist underneath her loose jacket. Parker rounded the corner in a suit and tie. She bumped his shoulder. "Good luck," she quipped. "Try not to step on her toes at the big dance, Romeo. Sandy called, and she's cleared of all suspicion, so don't shoot her either." Parker bumped her back and shook his head while not completely hiding his smile at her ability to give him crap.

The FBI would send extra security to be in or near Kelvin Hall tomorrow, now that things were heating up. Their invisible allies couldn't get too close and had not been read in on all the case details to minimize leaks and exposure, but it was better than no help at all. If everything went as planned, the FBI would catch the bad guy, the extra security would disappear, and Dr. Ryland would remember Parker and Alexis only as students who spent a lot of time in the building until they dropped out of school due to the time commitment. The problem was, in her experience, nothing ever went as planned.

REE LOCKED the door to her office, slipped into the large storage closet in her lab, and locked that door for good measure, quickly changing into a modest but fashionable black gown. She hated galas, but the big donors expected the professors to come to hobnob and talk about the research their donations were funding. Since helping the university acquire funding was part of the job, she kept a formal dress and a pair of shoes in the lab closet behind boxes of equipment. That way, when she inevitably forgot about an event until she was at work, she never had to rush home for an appropriate outfit. A longtime fan of superhero movies, Ree tried to convince herself that she was like a superhero changing in a phone booth, although she couldn't recall a time when Superman had to wear a long dress and shake an endless stream of donor's hands in impractical, sparkly high heels. It was a good thing she wasn't planning on fighting crime tonight.

At least Joanna and Ivan would be there to ease the awkwardness. Skeezy Steve often showed up to represent his law firm, and she had to continue to be polite to him. Perhaps she could step on his toes, accidentally of course, if he asked her to dance. She let out a sigh. It was too bad she couldn't even be "accidentally" rude without feeling horrible about it later. She exited the closet and wobbled a bit on one heel while trying to clasp her necklace and walk at the same time. She unlocked her outside door and gasped when she saw Parker Landon lifting his hand to knock.

"We have to stop meeting like this," Parker said, his eyes twinkling as she tried to make sense of why he was standing outside of her office in a suit.

"Oh! My purse!" Ree turned on her heel and crossed the office to her desk. Parker had missed her class just an hour and a half earlier, which raised a prickle on the back of her neck. She grabbed her purse, and when she looked up, he had taken a few steps into her office. Ree was trapped behind her desk with Parker blocking her exit. It didn't make sense that he would be in her office so late when he missed her class, and the building was nearly empty. Something was definitely off.

Ree widened her stance for balance and slipped her hand into her purse. She had practiced unlocking her weapon quickly in case she was ever threatened, even though it seemed crazy at the time. But here she was, preparing herself in case she needed to use it. She pursed her lips for effect as if searching for lipstick and asked Parker, as casually as possible, "What are you all dressed up for?"

Parker looked at the floor before meeting her eyes. "Well, in addition to being a student," he said, "my company made a large donation to IP and asked me to attend a gala tonight. I was stopping through the labs to turn in my homework before it starts. I apologize, I missed your class because the same company who asked me to attend the gala didn't check to see if I had a suit. I had to do some last-minute shopping."

Ree's hand relaxed a fraction. The trigger was still unlocked but she released her gun. There was some scuffling in the hallway outside, which grew louder as the source of the noise came closer to her office.

It was probably some college kids horsing around, but Parker whipped his head toward the door. He closed the remaining distance between them with three large steps, a fierce expression on his face. "Get down. Now," he said. Ree didn't move, and Parker raised his hand to gesture for Ree to crouch behind the desk.

Ree stood a little taller, her tone confident even as her hands shook. "Parker, you are making me extremely uncomfortable, and I am not afraid to scream for help or keep you from walking for the foreseeable future. So, I am going to ask you once to back the hell away from me and get out of my office. In exchange, I'll pretend this little encounter never happened."

Ree reached back into her purse and grabbed her weapon without extracting it. While she was hoping that this would all be a misunderstanding, her dad had always told her that the best way to scare off a bear was to make yourself as large and scary as possible. The theory also held true with bullies and criminals. Probably.

PARKER DIDN'T MISS the fear in Ree's tone but compartmentalized it to address the more imminent threat outside. Parker kept himself between Dr. Ryland and the door for the second time that day as he tried to determine the source of the noise. He kept himself from fully facing the hallway since he wasn't willing to turn his back on a terrified woman with a loaded weapon. No one should be around this late, particularly since Ree's office was off the main thoroughfare. It was time to make a snap decision.

As he turned to face Ree, the depth of her fear became clear. He forced himself to relax his features and put his hand on top of hers to calm her. Barely above a whisper, Parker said as quickly and calmly as possible, "Dr. Ryland. Look at me. I'm FBI, and I'm here to help. We may have a situation outside. I'm going to slowly turn around and figure out what is going on, and I would very much like it if you don't shoot me in the back while I try to protect you. I know your weapon is unlocked and probably loaded. Reach inside my jacket in the inner pocket, and you'll find my ID. This noise could be nothing, but I'm wearing a bulletproof vest, and I'm willing to bet that you aren't." Dr. Ryland's eyes widened. She kept one hand in her purse while another reached inside Parker's jacket. "Some trust, please. I would like your hand off your weapon, now, or I will be forced to treat you as a threat."

THE URGENCY in his tone was real, but trust was a fragile thing, and it did not come easily to Ree. However, the noise outside worried her more than the man inside, and she had to make a call. Her hand loosened on her gun, and she pulled out a small leather wallet from Parker's suit jacket, with Parker's picture and FBI badge. She nodded slowly, and Parker slid her purse off the front of her desk, presumably to keep himself from getting shot. She couldn't muster the energy to be offended that he didn't trust her. Given her shaking hands, it was probably the right call. He walked towards the door, slipping his hand under his jacket as he approached it.

PARKER LOOKED out of Ree's office door and saw the back of a college student kicking a hacky sack down the hallway. He seemed oblivious to Parker's study and kept walking until he turned a corner, taking the same path Parker and Mike had taken hours earlier. It explained the noise but didn't explain why they had company this late in the evening. Once the threat was out of sight, Parker turned to face the situation at hand. Dr. Ryland was sitting in her chair with determination on her face and her phone in hand. Not sure what was suddenly more important than what had just happened, Parker said quietly, "Dr. Ryland, we need to talk."

Dr. Ryland wiggled her phone in the air and said, "I'd like to verify your story. Can you give me a moment in privacy, please?" The FBI "Contact Us" page was up on her phone browser. He nodded before exiting. She still had control of her weapon, but he made a judgment call that it would be better not to put her on the defensive again. Parker was almost sure that she wouldn't shoot him since she'd already had the chance and hadn't done it yet. Just in case, he pulled up the video feed from her office and clipped a headset into his phone so that he could hear her conversation. He smiled with appreciation when he heard her request to verify his identity and sent a message to the Chief to expedite her call.

Ten minutes later, Ree tucked her phone back in her bag and gestured for Parker to come inside. She pressed her lips into a line, steepled her fingers and raised her eyebrows at him. She was putting on a good show, and he almost didn't notice her hands shaking until she moved them from her desk into her lap.

"So, *Special Agent* Landon, is it? Apparently, a Chief Sandhill thinks I am needed for a federal investigation. Half an hour ago, I thought my biggest concern was getting to the gala without breaking my ankle in these ridiculous shoes so I could get back to my real job in one piece. So, I'm going to need you to make yourself comfortable because your 'Chief,'" Ree used air quotes, "said you would give me an explanation."

Moments earlier, Parker had received permission from the Chief to read her in. He had no desire to pull a civilian into this, but at this point, it wasn't his call. At least she was clever and didn't seem to be having a nervous breakdown. He'd been involved with some unusual cases, but this would the first time he had ever brought someone into one while she was wearing a gown and high heels. He looked at his watch. "You have time," she said. "Sit and explain. We can be late."

Parker sat and began, "Dr. Ryland."

"Parker, since you evidently are trying to keep someone from killing me, you can go ahead and call me Ree."

"Ree. We received intelligence that implicated you in illegal activity and have been monitoring you for the past couple of weeks. Those packages full of components for your friend Ivan's lab are not going to be used for a research project." Ree raised her eyebrows, and Parker decided against telling her the specifics of how many people had suspected her of corruption at best and treason at worst. "We believe that whoever is involved was using you as a decoy. We cleared you about an hour after the package was delivered. We don't know who ultimately received the parts. It's taken time to remove you from our suspect list, and that's time that we've lost in finding the person actually behind this."

Ree rubbed her temples. She blinked several times and shook her head to refocus, but still felt like an outsider to her own body as Parker's words sunk in. Parker studied her, his concern clear in his features.

"Ree, put your head between your knees."

"Excuse me?"

"Your head. Put it between your knees if you are feeling lightheaded. Trash can is in the corner if you need to puke."

"I'm not going to puke."

"You sure? For a minute there..."

"I was thinking. That was my thinking face. Seriously? Okay, let's start with the basics. Go back to the beginning. I have felt, I don't know, off-kilter these last couple of weeks, and that explains a lot. Were you snooping in my office last week? Or someone from your team? Wait, you know what, that's not important right now. Who is trying to smuggle what, and why are you involved? Doesn't this seem like overkill for a nozzle that's barely larger than one you can get from a decent hobby shop?" Ree stood and began to pace her office.

"Ree, we believe the parts you received were components our unknown subject is accumulating to build a short-range ballistic missile. We don't know as much as we'd like to, but we don't believe this is just an idiot trying to scare people without doing any damage. This is military-grade weaponry, and they are sending it piece by piece, mixed with off-the-shelf components, hoping you and anyone else looking would come to the conclusion that you did."

"It was just a small box..."

"It was. Yes, missiles are usually pretty big, but military-grade guidance and control systems aren't. They're not that easy to get since the government keeps a pretty close eye on suppliers. Our perpetrator is smart – they've done it a little bit at a time, using custom designs from multiple suppliers to avoid detection. Today, they received a circuit board that will be a part of a thrust control system. I wish I had more for you, but that's all I know right now."

Ree retreated to her chair and leaned back, ignoring the sharp pain of the tiny crystals on the strap of her dress pressing into her back. Several packages had come somewhat regularly and if she put them all together... "Oh no. I brought all of those packages to Ivan's lab, Parker. Every one of them. You don't think Ivan...?"

She put her hands on her cheeks, unable to finish the idea that her friend, mentor, and the husband of her best friend was involved in anything like this. Not him. That would wreck Joanna. And her.

"I'm sorry, Ree. We can't eliminate him as a suspect. There are a lot of people that work for him that could be involved as well. But we just can't clear him yet. So, we're going to need you to be careful but act as normally as possible until we can sort all of this out. And I'm afraid you are going to have some new friends spending time with you in the meantime."

Ree dropped her hands from her face. "Wait. You brought him the box? You knew, and you brought him the box? How could you take that kind of risk? What if someone gets hurt?"

"That's a great point. We may have, ahem, damaged the contents. We did what we could to make it look like the box had been dropped, but if anyone was watching the delivery, they'd know it happened after you touched it. So for all practical purposes, you're in this with us, without your consent. I'm sorry about that."

Ree let the truth wash over her. Of course, Parker's explanation fit the evidence, but she couldn't believe her friend was involved. But wasn't that what the friends and neighbors of the guilty *always* said when they were interviewed on the evening news? Wasn't someone in their life totally in the dark? Her overactive imagination kicked into gear, and she envisioned herself telling a news anchor how nice her friends had been, recalling the birthday parties they'd thrown and trips they'd taken.

Ree looked at the clock and said, "Parker, I have to go. They're expecting me..."

"At the donor's gala, I know. I'm now attending as well, so we can walk over there together." Ree swallowed, and Parker softened his tone. "I don't expect you to be instantly comfortable with this, but I need you to do your best to act as if you don't know what's going on. I haven't earned it yet, and I get that, but I am going to need you to trust me. And my team. If you see or even feel anything is out of the ordinary, I need you to let me know. Here's my cell phone number." Parker scribbled down a number. "It's on 24/7, and I'm renting a condo near your place. I'm sorry, I know that sounds creepy, but if it helps, Alexis and Mike are staying with me. Mike has been around, but if he's doing his job, you haven't noticed. You met Alexis last week."

Ree walked around the desk to grab her purse. Parker raised an eyebrow and she ignored it. "The eager student was one of you guys? I guess I have to hire her now, at least for a little while?"

"If it's not too much trouble."

"She's going to have to do real work, you know. After you guys leave, I still have papers that I have to publish." Ree turned to march out of her office indignantly but wobbled a bit on one heel. She had been doing such a great job of keeping it together in front of Parker, no, *Special Agent Parker Landon,* but as she regained her balance, her eyes began to well up. She straightened her back and took a deep breath. If she spoke, her voice would give her away. Ree walked past her friendly local FBI agent towards the gala that she was now dreading for a completely different reason. Every one of her colleagues, friends, and acquaintances were suspects in a federal investigation. How was she supposed to act like it was just another day at the office?

After a quiet walk over to the student union, Ree approached the ballroom with Parker at her elbow and plastered on a smile. "Act like you normally would," Parker whispered. She fought the urge to roll her eyes as his breath tickled her ear. Yes, just act normal, of course. She put one foot in front of the other until she made it into the ballroom. Skeezy Steve was standing near the entrance with a plateful of hors d'oeuvres and talking at the crowd of people surrounding him. Oh, super.

"Excuse me for a moment," Steve's booming voice rose above the crowd noise as he walked towards her.

"Oh, arrest him. Please. For the love of all that is holy," Ree said under her breath, and Parker turned in surprise at her whispered outburst. "It's him. It has to be. He's skeezy and he's headed this way. Guilty in the court of my head."

"Skeezy?" Parker said barely above a whisper, amused.

"Yes. You carry handcuffs? A Taser? A sharp stick?"

Parker couldn't help himself. He chuckled out loud and looked at her incredulously. After a few weeks of observing the high-energy professor, she'd seemed happy to see nearly everyone. She greeted her students, other professors, the building staff, and total strangers with a smile and friendly conversation. So at least they were on the same page on Steve. Parker didn't think Steve was smart enough to be involved, but he owed Ree, after everything they had put her through. He slipped an arm around her waist and whispered in her ear, "Just play along." Parker raised his voice. "Can I get you anything from the bar, honey?"

To Parker's surprise, Ree was less than grateful at his gesture. If looks could kill, he wasn't sure who would be dead first, him or Steve. He directed his eyes towards the "skeezy" lawyer while silently willing her to understand his intent. Steve stopped in his tracks for a moment, and Ree's fierce glare softened to annoyance. Seeing the two choices at war in her head, Parker was happy to see Ree determine him to be the lesser of the two evils, despite a few too many seconds of thinking about it.

"Sure, *dear*," she replied. "A glass of wine would be great."

Ree's pulse skyrocketed – lying did not come naturally or comfortably, even when it was for a good cause. Steve paused, clearly surprised by Parker's presence, but not completely deterred from continuing his beeline towards her. Desperate, she made a rash decision and slipped her hand through Parker's elbow. "Actually, I'll come with you. I can't decide what kind I want." She gave an apologetic hand wave to Steve and accompanied Parker to the open bar.

"Wow, you really do hate him, don't you?" Parker grinned.

"Don't start with me, Parker," she said, and then suddenly slowed. Oh no. The strange events of the day had clearly fried her brain. "Parker, we need to talk. Now."

Parker's eyes darted to the left and then to the right. He pulled Ree into an empty hallway and gave her a questioning look. Once again, he stood between her and the crowd.

Ree put a hand to her forehead. "Parker, you are a student of mine. I know you meant well because he's awful, and I panicked. If Skeezy Steve catches on, dating a student will get me fired. Unless you want to tell the head of the department about what is going on under his nose as well, you're going to need to drop my class, yesterday."

"Not a problem," Parker replied.

"Just like that? How good is your team?" Ree questioned.

"I was never in your class to begin with. The paper was a ruse so you wouldn't look too closely when I started keeping an eye on you. Our IT team was kind enough to add me to your personal class roster through a neat little security hole in the school's website. But we're going to have to work on our story if you don't want to pose as a couple. I was trying to help you out, and I figured it'd be a decent cover to explain why I'm around all the time. Plus, I know the guy, and I agree with you – he is definitely skeezy. He may not be guilty of anything other than being presumptuous, but I don't want him getting any ideas about you that you don't want him having. It's the least I can do, given that I helped keep you in the middle of this mess. But I apologize – I should have asked before assuming I was doing you a favor."

"Parker, I appreciate the gesture and the apology, but I need you to let me think about this for a little while. I'm still trying to figure out what this all means."

"Ree, your only job right now is to stay safe. We're mobilizing a team to make sure you have the protection you need until this all blows over."

Ree put her hands on her hips. "If you've been following me for weeks and are as good as I think you are, you know I'm not going to sit this one out like a damsel in distress while you and your team go after someone who could destroy the people I love."

PARKER NODDED and pulled back to give her space. Any further discussion here was too risky. At least Ree had the presence of mind to make demands. They'd just have to continue their conversation another time with fewer people around. It was worth remembering that he thought she didn't mind Steve until she told him otherwise. He couldn't assume she trusted him and his team just because she was nice to him.

Parker separated himself from Ree and began walking around to strike up conversations with Ree's colleagues, particularly the grad students from Ivan's lab. It was hardly an interrogation. All he had to do was ask them about their research, and they were more than willing to talk as long as he would listen. Most of them didn't even ask his name. Unfortunately, the conversations didn't do much to narrow down his list of suspects. They all spoke broadly about their work in propulsion engineering, which, as far as he could tell, meant finding ways to make things that should explode go up or forward instead.

Parker watched Ree out of the corner of his eye charming the university donors without making it obvious that she was avoiding Ivan and Joanna. Finally, Alexis appeared at the doorway to the ballroom. Her eyes briefly locked with his and then settled on Ree. Parker dropped by Ree's table to give her shoulder a squeeze and subtly direct her attention to his partner before walking towards the exit.

ALEXIS PASSED Parker as he left, projecting excitement on her face before approaching Dr. Ryland's table. Recognition flashed in Dr. Ryland's eyes, and at a pause in the conversation, she exclaimed, "Dr. Ryland! I'm so glad I found you! That test you were waiting on finally finished up, and I couldn't wait to show you the results. Your new design is showing even better promise than we expected. Do you have time to come back to the lab and take a look? I just didn't think you wanted to wait until tomorrow."

Alexis looked apologetically at the crowd of donors gathered around Dr. Ryland. They nodded with approval. A middle-aged woman in a heavily sequined gown and perfect make-up smiled and leaned in. "That sounds important, Dr. Ryland. Don't let us keep you." Dr. Ryland smiled and thanked the donors before silently following Alexis to the exit.

Alexis led her to a small black car, parked in front of the ballroom in case they needed to make a hasty departure. She gestured for Dr. Ryland to get in the passenger's seat, and she wordlessly complied. The FBI didn't make it a habit to involve civilians in undercover operations, and Alexis was new to this too. No one was really comfortable with around-the-clock surveillance or a complete shift in their worldview in less than four hours, and Alexis watched out of the corner of her eye for signs of a breakdown. The professor twisted her hands in her lap as they drove to her house, but otherwise, she seemed okay. At least she had a good head on her shoulders. She was going to need it.

11

Ree opened her eyes, stretched, and stared at her ceiling before lifting her head off of her warm pillow. Her thoughts were muddled, but that was normal after a gala, and oh no…she dropped her head with a *whump* back onto her pillow. She had taken a sleeping pill before going to bed, since falling asleep without it would have been impossible. Her racing thoughts still managed to cut through the fog of the sleeping medication until past midnight, which meant that today would be rough, even if she hadn't just found out that her life might be in danger. And apparently, other people could be killed too, although she didn't recall Parker – *Special Agent* Parker Landon – giving her too many details about that. It was going to be a long day.

Alexis had spent her first few years at the FBI doing fieldwork and conducting surveillance, but she didn't often play in the world of witness security. Keeping an eye on the professor on top of managing the loose ends on this case was going to be a challenge. On the bright side, they'd had some time to get to know one another after the gala, and Dr. Ryland seemed like good people, if a little nervous after the prior day's ordeal. Alexis had slept well and was glad Dr. Ryland's anxious pacing had stopped around midnight. She pulled her hair back as the professor came bounding down the stairs, in a ponytail, visor, and running gear.

"Alexis! Huge favor. They keep you in good shape in...basic training? Quantico? Whatever it is?"

Alexis did a quick double take at Ree's casual manner of jumping into conversation and decided her enthusiasm was reassuring, provided their suspect-turned-witness wasn't on the verge of cracking. Alexis nodded, still not catching on. "Sure, Dr. Ryland."

"Better call me Ree. Dr. Ryland is a mouthful. Want to go for a run? I'm usually happy to go for a run by myself, but you have to understand the sheer number of spy novels I have read, and now that I know someone is out to kill me, well, running alone seems less...wise. Unless I have a buddy. However, my go-to running buddy is the wife of my friend, who is now a suspect who may or may not be involved in an international missile smuggling ring or terrorist organization. So, I have two choices. I can hide inside, or better yet, convince my new bodyguard to come out for a run with me, because if you can't keep up, we are well and truly screwed."

Alexis didn't know whether to give Ree a hug or a drink. A runner herself, Alexis was familiar with the calming effect that exercise could have on people and, failing a long-term cure, figured running would calm her down. At least long enough for Parker or Mike to be on duty when the dear Dr. Ryland had her nervous breakdown. She agreed and changed into a long pair of athletic pants, baggy enough at the ankle to hide her service weapon. She placed it discreetly while Ree ate an energy bar and washed it down with what smelled like some pretty strong coffee. Alexis had done nearly the same thing, minus the coffee, thirty minutes earlier. At least she was matched with someone who wasn't going to sit around freaking out and being useless.

REE AND ALEXIS ran six miles with Ree setting the pace. After starting too fast and getting nauseous and winded, Ree forced herself to slow down and used the time to get to know her new bodyguard. It was easier than she anticipated to get Alexis talking, and despite having slightly different backgrounds, it was clear by mile two that they were cut from the same cloth. Alexis was the youngest in her family with three older brothers, and working with Mike and Parker wasn't much different than spending time with her brothers. It was clear she respected the two men, which provided a measure of comfort to Ree. While working as an FBI agent was Alexis's dream job for now, she wanted to go into the Secret Service or CIA someday if the opportunity presented itself. By mile four, Ree had confirmed her suspicion that Alexis was in the same boat she was – she had her career path all figured out, but was still trying to make sense of what was next for her and how to get there. Of course, Alexis also had permission to kick ass and take names, while Ree's job was a bit tamer. Until recently.

Ree was noticeably calmer after their run, and Alexis was happy to have done her part. When she escorted Ree to her office, later than expected due to their unplanned exercise, Ree's shoulders had dropped back down to where they belonged. However, when Alexis saw Ree's back stiffen upon entering her office, Alexis tensed and tried to look around Ree.

"Excuse me, Dr. Ryland," Alexis said loudly, as she dropped her pen. She cut in front of Ree as the pen clattered towards a figure standing in front of Ree's desk.

"Stand down. He's the dean of engineering. Good thinking, though, Alex." As Alexis's earpiece vibrated with the good news, Alexis picked up the pen and nodded to them both. "So sorry. I'll just be back in the lab, Dr. Ryland."

Ree took a deep breath, fighting her nerves while trying to figure out why the dean of engineering was in her office. She didn't think she had done anything wrong, but why else would he be there except to fire her? Really, finding out she was in the middle of an FBI operation and getting fired in the same week? And he was standing between her and her break-in-case-of-emergency chocolate.

Dean Wiley did absolutely nothing to ease her anxiety. He lingered in front of her desk without speaking, and he shifted his weight from one foot to another. He pushed his glasses up on his nose and looked everywhere but directly at her. He was slender, which drew more attention to the wrinkled jacket and baggy, pleated khakis hanging off of his frame. He wasn't a terrible human being, but he wasn't known for having much backbone when it came to sticking up for the professors in his department. Ree's stomach turned. This would probably go well.

Ree plastered a smile on her face and looked at him expectantly. After a long ten seconds of silence, Dean Wiley began speaking. "Dr. Ryland, you have done an excellent job here. We are very pleased with your work. However, we have something important we need to talk about." When Dean Wiley trailed off to ponder his next words, Ree looked towards Alexis, who stood just past the doorway to the lab. Alexis turned her head a fraction to the left and then the right. This was not about the case, whatever it was.

"Dean Wiley, I appreciate your positive feedback, but in my limited experience, good news rarely starts with 'however.' I'm afraid you're going to have to let me know why you are here. Please understand that whatever it is, I won't take it personally."

The dean seemed marginally more relaxed as her dark humor lightened the mood enough for him to explain. "Dr. Ryland, you understand we're a public university and we receive a limited amount of funds, which have recently become more limited. As a result, we've had to realign our priorities." He continued to explain in the most long-winded way possible that "her" lab was going to be able to keep Dr. Moran for the time being but no one else, even though Dr. Moran was hardly ever there.

"Is this my notice?" Ree asked, forcing herself to choke back her emotions. She'd spent years gaining the experience and credibility to do this job. And it was gone. Just like that.

"Heavens, no, Dr. Ryland. You are an asset to the university and we'd like to use your skills elsewhere. Dr. Nobelkov's lab recently received a large anonymous grant. In addition to purchasing new equipment, they are going to be able to bring you on."

"Oh. New equipment. Great." Ree looked everywhere except at Dean Wiley. Her eyes landed on Alexis. The investigation. Ivan's lab. Missile parts. "Um, can I bring my lab assistant with me? She's unpaid but does a lot of meaningful work."

Dean Wiley's eyes lit up. "Of course. We want our students to have great experiences here."

"Yes. That's what it would be. A great experience." Ree nodded and swallowed hard. Alexis gave her a thumbs-up from behind the dean's back.

"That's great, Dr. Ryland." Dean Wiley beamed. "I really appreciate your flexibility."

After answering an endless stream of questions about the work that still needed to be finished before she transferred to Ivan's lab, the Dean finally left. Ree used the quiet time to sit in her desk chair and mindlessly click through emails. She'd networked. She'd gotten critical experience. She'd done the hard work. After all of that, she was being pushed out because of university accounting technicalities. On the other hand, she was still employed. More importantly, she was still alive and now had a personal FBI bodyguard when she could have easily been caught in some sort of bizarre criminal crossfire instead. So, getting upset over moving jobs was a little melodramatic. A tear slipped down her cheek and she wiped it away. Sinking her chin into her palm, Ree barely noticed Alexis finishing up the menial labeling task that had been her cover for the morning. Alexis gave her a small wave when she left an hour later. Ree blew out a deep breath, grateful for a little alone time. It wasn't much, but she appreciated the small slice of privacy to wallow in peace.

When Parker entered Ree's office, he stood just inside her door, careful not to invade her privacy. She only looked up from her task of packing office supplies into a plain cardboard box for a moment. Ree wiped at her eyes with the back of her hand and blinked several times before setting her mouth in a line and plunging a tape dispenser into the box with a solid *thunk.* Parker was the leader of his team and trained to go into dangerous situations, so he took a few careful steps closer before asking, "You okay?"

"Fine. Absolutely freaking fine. Did you have something to do with this?" Ree's head whipped up. Her steely green eyes shot him a look and she pointed her finger at his chest. Parker was glad he had already skimmed her work clothes for bulges in her outfit that might indicate weapons out of habit. She was petite, but he wasn't one to underestimate an angry woman. Her purse was out of reach, so he was likely safe, at least for the moment.

Hands up in surrender, Parker said, "Not my fault. We looked into it. The budget cuts are legitimate, and your position was being funded with unrestricted funds. They don't want to make Dr. Moran angry since he does a lot of publicity for the university. The large donation to Ivan's lab is suspicious, and we have a team working on that. I know this sucks for you. However, maybe with you in Ivan's lab, we'll have a better idea of what's really going on."

Ree rubbed her forehead. "Do you realize how hard this is going to be for me? It was hard enough to see Ivan at one work event and now I have to see him every single day."

"I know. But you are doing a great job. Thanks for making sure Alexis could come with you. I appreciate your quick thinking and cool head. You sure you don't want to quit the university and come work for us?" Parker shot her a wry grin, hoping it would lighten her mood.

Although his tone was half in jest, he'd take her in a heartbeat. She was handling it better than some of the newbies that actually knew what they were getting into. She had a gift for analytical work and had kept her cool so far with no training. Well, she wasn't entirely untrained, considering she had a black belt and was a regular at the shooting range. In any case, it was worth remembering that she had a reasonable chance of dropping him on his ass if he made her mad and subsequently turned his back. He took a step back and waited without speaking, giving her some time to cool down while she angry-taped the lid of the cardboard box shut.

. . .

REE'S MIND was still spinning and trying to find a way to blame it on Parker when she heard a knock on her office door. Ivan Nobelkov came into the room and gave her a big hug. Over his shoulder, she saw Parker's jaw tighten and his hand drift to his belt, which she chose to ignore. Ivan couldn't be involved. And Joanna was absolutely not involved. Even if the neighbors of spies never suspected anything because the spies were smart. Which Ivan and Joanna were. Smart, not spies.

"I hear I am getting a new office mate! This lab's loss is my gain, and we are thrilled to have you on board. I know you have to wrap up your work, and I support you tying up loose ends, but we can't wait to have you in the lab as soon as possible." Ivan seemed to just notice Parker, although how he had missed an entire person in her office was a mystery to Ree. "And who is this? A student? A boyfriend? Both?" Ivan looked at Ree, eyebrows wiggling. She looked at him in genuine horror, stunned silent.

Parker extended his hand and answered in a confident baritone, "Parker Landon, sir. I'm a good friend of Ree's. A new friend. But we are quickly becoming good friends. And I'm not her student." Ivan seemed unaware of Ree's cheeks heating as he openly appraised the man, turning his lips down at the corners and nodding knowingly.

"Well, I am glad our Ree has found a good friend. Perhaps you will side with me when my wife and Ree are arguing with me, yes? As her good friend, that is," Ivan continued, his voice filled with innuendo.

"Ivan! Out!" Ree, regaining the power of speech, guided Ivan to the door and shook her finger at him as he left. Once the door was closed, she plopped in her chair, looked at Parker, and pointed at her door. "Bad manners aside, if that man is guilty, I am a unicorn. Haven't you guys put a camera in here by now? Can I have some peace and quiet, please?" Ree dropped her head to her desk and rubbed her temples.

Parker's voice was distant. "I know this is hard. I'll try and give you some space, but I have a few questions first that I'd prefer to ask face to face."

Ree pulled out a small box from her desk drawer. The piece of dark chocolate with a chewy caramel center was there for just such an occasion. "Hitting the hard stuff so early?" A cup of coffee was nudged towards Ree through a narrow opening between the boxes, and her glare softened. It had obviously been there since Parker came in, but she didn't notice while she was hissing and spitting at him.

As he extended his peace offering, Ree growled a little more quietly at him and said around her chocolate, "Okay, sit. Talk. I know this is a bribe to get me to behave, by the way." She moved a box to the floor so she could see Parker when he sat in her guest chair. Resigned, she leaned back in her chair and drew a sip from the coffee. One sugar, with a splash of whole milk in it. The perfect blend of ingredients was confirmation of their surveillance, but at least their attention to detail came in handy, even if it was a little unsettling. And anything that resulted in perfect coffee hand-delivered to her office couldn't be all bad.

Parker pulled out a pen and notebook and began asking questions. Ree rattled off the names of nearly every person she regularly interacted with. Ree studied the man in front of her taking notes. He had dark blond hair and hazel eyes that missed nothing. A scar in the divot of his chin piqued her curiosity but Parker was too focused on his questions to notice her assessment.

An hour passed as she answered questions and second-guessed the motives of the people she saw every day. At a pause in the conversation, Ree blurted out, "I hope this is helping you guys, but what's the plan? You have a plan, right? How are we going to stop this lunatic? And their accomplices? You guys seem to be depending pretty heavily on the untrained civilian at the moment, which isn't giving the untrained civilian a lot of confidence right now."

Before she could continue, Parker raised a hand. "Dr. Ryland. Ree. It may feel disorganized, but we've had a team of agents monitoring this building around the clock since discovering that it is a major hub for weapons smuggling. We've set up 24/7 surveillance in this room as well as in most of the hallways. However, you can do something no one else can. You have access and knowledge of our suspects, of which there seems to be a multitude. You can separate out the things that matter from those that don't, and help us catch the criminal before anyone knows we're here, before it hits the news, and the only people the wiser are you and my team.

"The secretive nature of the operation has kept it small, but not because we don't know what we're doing. We are concerned if the team gets any bigger, we are going to force an extremely dangerous person's hand, and too many lives are on the line. We usually don't ask so much from the people we are working with, but I thought you could handle it. If it's too much, we can keep a security guard close by for you while we sort this out alone. No judgments. No harm done."

Ree sat back in her chair and winced. She had been prepared for a rebuttal, but his reason had deflated her anger. Couldn't the man just let her get good and mad? Ree sighed. "I'm in. But I want all the way in. If you are going undercover, I want to help. If you have a team meeting, I want to be there. If this is that important, I want to be a part of it. All of it. I can't solve any problem if I only have half of the data."

Parker grinned and put his hands on his knees. "Excellent. We'll be in touch in a few hours. The Bureau is going to want you to sign a bunch of paperwork."

"Done."

"And we'll have to confiscate your gun." Parker's look was pure innocence until his lips twitched.

"No way. I have a permit and it's perfectly legal for me to carry it. I promise I won't shoot you. Deal?" Despite her circumstances, Ree smiled and crossed her arms.

"I'll take it. Welcome to the team, professor." He extended a hand, and she took it.

ALONE WITH HER THOUGHTS, Ree finished packing up her desk, moving in slow motion while she assessed what she actually knew about these FBI interlopers. Alexis and Ree had hit it off immediately, cementing their bond by sharing stories during their run. Alexis didn't share every detail of her life, but Ree understood she needed to maintain some secrecy due to her position. If circumstances were different, Alexis would be an easy addition to her friendship with Joanna.

Ree would love to get her mom's and sister's opinions on the matter but couldn't, for obvious reasons. She came from a fairly normal background, insofar as anyone's family is normal. Her family understood her tendency to get sucked into her work for weeks on end, forgetting to call home. Ree was grateful that she had spoken with both of her parents and her sister the previous weekend. She had inherited her uncanny ability to detect bullshit from them, and they wouldn't hesitate to call her on it if she was the one dishing it out. Ree had happily offered to help the FBI even before she fully understood how big of a mess she was in. Her family could be in danger if she didn't hold it together. It was hardly a leap of logic that someone willing to use her to smuggle weapons wouldn't hesitate to threaten her or her family. Falling apart simply wasn't an option right now.

Everyone she'd had even trivial contact with in the last several weeks ran through her mind. Ree flipped through the mental images as if they were a physical photo album. Ivan stopping by her office for chats, and even Dr. Moran's friendly questions about her weekend and her work suddenly seemed more suspect. She'd never liked Steve the lawyer, and him stopping by for evidence mere days before the arrival of "The Package" made her rethink every detail of their interaction.

Eventually, unavoidably, Ree started thinking about Parker. The way he carried himself was casual, even effortless, but his quiet intensity suggested that under the right circumstances, he could be a formidable ally. He didn't seem the type to start a fight, but she'd just bet that he'd finish one if he needed to. She recalled him sitting in her extra office chair the night of the gala and their subsequent encounters with potentially threatening situations – was it just coincidence that he was blocking her from danger, every single time?

Ree was known for her attention to small details. In fact, her grad students thought it was hilarious to shift around her knick-knacks when she was gone and time how long it took her to put them back when she returned. Apparently, this was a source of income for some of her students, who had started a betting pool. So far, it had never been more than a minute before everything was back in its position.

Parker seemed to mirror her sensibilities. Although he appeared relaxed, he was always in the right place to keep her safe. Still, it wasn't easy to trust someone she'd just met instead of friends she had known for years. Friends who were now suspects. Ree's brain continued to process the personalities of her new allies and the actions of her colleagues through the lens of the FBI investigation. As she became wholly immersed in her thoughts, she stopped noticing her surroundings. When she looked up and saw someone standing right in front of her, she screamed.

"Whoa, Ree. Calm down, it's just me again." Parker put his hands on her shoulders to steady her. "You okay? We may need to switch you to decaf."

"I'm fine. Absolutely. You just startled me. You're like a puma. Are those special issue shoes or something?" Ree straightened her back. "Since you're the brawn in this operation, want to help me carry some boxes?"

12

Early enough in the morning to minimize interactions, but not so early that anyone would be suspicious of his presence, Simon entered the propulsion laboratory. He nodded his head in greeting when he passed Dr. Nobelkov in his office and passed through the door that led to the lab. The box was exactly where he expected it. It had surely been there yesterday, but he had refrained from coming to the lab in the unlikely event that someone had caught on to his attempt to mask the intended recipient of the deliveries. He had come so far and would finish this mission, one small, deliberate step at a time. He would get his revenge, but he wasn't inexperienced or stupid enough to get caught.

Simon scowled at the large box and gritted his teeth as the large dent in one corner taunted his willpower. He took a deep breath and willed the box's contents to be undamaged as he pulled back the flaps that someone had already opened. It was normal for the box to be open, but this was the first time one had arrived damaged. His normally faultless self-control had slipped in the face of his imminent success, and he had checked Dr. Ryland's office the day the box had arrived instead of waiting until she brought it to the propulsion lab. He was unable to go into her office for a closer look since she was still in there with a man who seemed to be flirting with her.

Simon hadn't seen the box, but he had only looked out of the corner of his eye, kicking a hacky sack as he passed. It was an odd habit, but an academic with an odd habit made him blend in better with the other students. It was risky to keep using Irina Ryland's office as the drop-off location, but the benefits of delivering his missile components to another lab continued to outweigh the risks. After the Cold War and outing of spies on U.S. soil many years later, the U.S. had never been able to completely trust the Russians. Ree's friendship with Ivan would keep anyone who was sniffing around off his trail long enough for him to get the parts back to where they were needed. No one from his home country would suspect he was doing anything different than what was on his visa, but if the FBI or CIA got curious, he'd probably never see the outside of a jail cell. But, they were busy, and why would they come looking for an academic who was making no effort to hide his components? And in a lab with over twenty students, who would know it was him?

Victory was certain if he played the long game. The long game was hardly a voluntary choice – it took time to design and make the custom technology. He'd accomplished virtual secrecy by making tweaks to the components that did nothing to impact how they functioned but made them look like custom test equipment. His small country didn't have the manufacturing experience to create such intricate components, which made his journey to the United States a necessary one. Add in the small detail that he wanted to overthrow his country's current leader, and acquiring the components at home seemed especially unwise.

While building a weapon was an unfortunate reality, there simply wasn't another way to get what he needed without being implicated. Simon would get his chance to prove himself, The General would take over the presidency, and Simon would be given a powerful role in the new cabinet from which he could enact change in his country.

Simon looked into the box, pulled back the packaging foam, and muttered a curse. The prototype circuit board for the thrust control system, the final part of the brain of his weapons, had been damaged and was now destined for the scrap heap. He dug his fingernails into his hand and the pain took him away from his frustration for a moment. Pulling in a deep breath of air, he forced his body into calm. Getting angry would make him lose control, lose focus. He would have the component remade. Unfortunately, it would take time, and he didn't have much left. He'd have to order the rest of his parts in bulk, without the opportunity to test the design first.

Simon had very little trouble ordering his components through American sources, citing his research if anyone asked and spacing out the orders due to "funding" limitations, as a normal grad student would. His experience with military weapons design kept him from buying off-the-shelf guidance or control systems that might trigger the American government's interest. He thrust the board back in the box and pulled out his phone, since the lab was still empty of students. The donation The General had arranged had started a timer that Simon was powerless to stop. It would be another month before he had a replacement, but after that, he could set his plan in motion.

As his frustration cooled, he felt for his knife with his free hand, relaxing at the feel of the hard lines of the weapon in his pocket. There was a noise in Ivan's office, and Ivan himself appeared in the doorway. His eyes settled on Simon, and he said, "Do you have a moment to spare for me?"

"Of course, Dr. Nobelkov." Simon smiled, swallowed the bile in his throat, and released his knife. He was a professional. No plan was without mishaps, and he was nearly there. There was no way he would be caught. He was smarter than they were and had covered his tracks. Ivan was a hands-off professor and couldn't find his lab notebooks half the time. There was no way the man had noticed that Simon's test equipment wasn't working.

Simon slid his phone back into his left pocket and followed Ivan to his office, placing his hand over his right pocket to feel the outline of his knife for comfort. Crossing Americans on their soil had never ended well for anyone that had been caught. Even if his country would attempt to get him back on principle, not knowing he was on a mission to undermine the current government, it would be years in prison at a minimum.

"What can I help you with, Dr. Nobelkov?"

"Simon, I wanted to let you know that Dr. Ree Ryland will be joining the lab staff and moving into her new office this afternoon. Her position was eliminated, and we have been fortunate enough to receive a grant that will allow her to join our team. It will take some time for her to get cleared to work in the secured lab, and since you are working on a non-security critical project, I thought it would be a great fit. She is a brilliant mind, and I was hoping she could assist you with your research, as you have been having some trouble getting your equipment running, no?"

Simon tried to pay attention as Professor Nobelkov continued to explain Dr. Ryland's background. Working with Dr. Ryland was an inconvenient consequence of the donation he had arranged. No matter, he would adapt. He had seen firsthand that she was distracted. He only needed to add a few dummy connections to the large machine before Dr. Ryland started getting too curious. And if she got too curious, he'd handle that too.

13

It was late morning for most people, but for Joanna Nobelkov, 11 a.m. marked the end of her overnight shift at the hospital. Before going home, she stopped by Ree's office, still in scrubs, to see how her friend was doing after losing her dream job. She was treated to the backside of a man leaning over Ree's desk. That must be Ree's new friend, Parker. She cleared her throat loudly and was rewarded with Ree's startled expression as she looked up from what seemed to be an intense conversation. *Guilty as charged*, Joanna presumed, and she tapped her finger against her lips as she thought of the questions she would ask her friend later, in private. Parker turned to greet her, and Joanna took in his scruffy five o'clock shadow and intelligent eyes. Once she looked at Ree, still staring at Parker instead of greeting her, she knew her friend was a goner.

"Joanna!" Ree said, shakily, as if just noticing she was there. She hesitated a moment, glanced at Parker one more time, and walked around the desk to give her friend a tight hug. Oh yes, she had some questions to ask later.

As Ree pulled away, it became clear her hands were trembling. Joanna asked, "You okay, honey? Ivan told me you were coming to work in his lab. Poor man is oblivious to how upset you are. Look at you. You're shaking!"

"I'm fine, Jo. I'm delighted to give Ivan grief on a daily basis, and his lab is busy and respected. It could be a lot worse, but it was just...unexpected, and it's been a...busy week so far."

"Really? Any more news that you need to share?" Joanna raised her eyebrows suggestively and looked towards Parker.

Parker reached out a hand. "Parker Landon. It's a pleasure to meet you. Ree's told me so much about you."

Joanna beamed. "It's nice to meet you too, Parker Landon. I hope we'll have the chance to get to know each other better. If Ree's not too...busy."

Ree laughed and threw her hands in the air. "You and your husband. Both of you are impossible. I meant, the gala was busy. You know how much I hate those things, and I didn't even have time to say hello to you while I was there. I'm afraid I have to finish up packing, and then Parker and I are headed out to dinner, but I'm so glad you stopped by."

Ree and Joanna made small talk for another ten minutes before Joanna winked and whispered knowingly, "I'll leave you two alone."

Ree shouted "Out!" at Joanna and waved her hands to shoo her away, while Parker looked on in amusement.

BY THE END of the week, Ree had almost wrapped up the work from her old job and was getting used to a strange new normal. Alexis stayed with her for several nights with no major incidents, which should have come as a relief, but the lack of new leads only made the FBI agents more edgy. Mike, tired of being in the van and communicating through texts and earpieces, called a meeting at Ree's house on Saturday morning to meet in person and to strategize.

While Ree and Parker were used to bantering on a semi-constant basis, and Ree and Alexis were becoming fast friends, Ree eyed Mike warily as the trio entered her foyer. He had dark hair and eyes and looked like he spent a lot of his free time at the gym. Ree wondered if a handshake introduction was appropriate when meeting someone who already knew you from watching your every move for the past several weeks. Not knowing the protocol, Ree boldly stuck out a hand. "Ree Ryland. It's nice to meet you."

Mike returned a firm handshake. "My name's Mike. It's nice to meet you in person, Ree."

MINUTES LATER, Parker shepherded his team and their witness to Ree's kitchen table. Parker nudged Ree to sit next to Mike to spend some time getting to know him. She jumped into the task with a level of enthusiasm he usually only saw when she was breaking parts on her test machines. Within the hour, and after some leading questions from Alexis, Mike had given into Ree's curiosity and was sharing stories about his wife, badly-behaved dog, and home remodeling disasters. Parker let everyone chat for a few more minutes and took a few verbal jabs from his team before calling the meeting to order.

"Okay, guys," Parker said. "As hilarious as it is to tell Ree stories about me climbing into a sewer for a stakeout, we're going to have to get to work."

Mike held up his hands to show how big the rat had been, and Ree snorted.

Parker smiled and shook his head. "Here's what we know so far. Our analysts have found the source of the donation to be a retired American mine magnate with a history of charitable work in West Africa. He seems to have done very well for himself and wanted to donate to the university. He felt that Nobelkov's lab was doing great work, and his only stipulation was that the old equipment be sent to his adopted country in order to stretch his donation farther. While it's odd that his donation was so specific, apparently, Ivan has been applying for grants right and left, and this one came across a committee this guy was sitting on. The grant was rejected, but this guy saw potential in Dr. Nobelkov's work and made a private donation. Everything he's done has been above board. He even incorporated a charitable organization in the U.S. and placed a wholly-owned subsidiary in Ghana for ongoing donations. So, it's not being handled as a one-off."

"So, that's a dead-end?" Alexis asked.

"It seems legitimate," Parker replied. "The problem is the timing feels wrong. But the donor didn't specify which equipment would be shipped over, just whatever could be used in whole, or in part, to help their university continue to build up their engineering labs."

"Is it possible that they're just trying to get Dr. Ryland to move closer to the action?" Mike asked. He'd not spent any time with their witness, and Parker cringed. They had no reason to believe she was anything more than a pawn. While they normally indulged some amount of team speculation, they didn't usually do it in front of nervous witnesses.

"Possible, but unlikely. I'd think anyone who had been using her would want to do the opposite." Parker leveled his eyes at Ree. He had no evidence to suggest she was anything other than a minor player and wasn't going to put any more ideas in her head that would keep her up at night.

"Wait a minute," said Ree. "If Mike thinks that they are using me for more than just my address, I need to know it. Mike? What makes you think that?"

Mike took a moment to answer. "Ivan is from Russia and you have Russian ancestry. I don't think that's an accident. Either Ivan is using you, or someone else is using both of you as a cover. They were hoping we'd see your Russian background, think your loyalties lie elsewhere, and stop looking. The work they've done to mask the components alone is above and beyond what most criminals are capable of. Someone is thinking very strategically about every part of their plan. It's unusual to see so many bases covered at once, especially by a lone wolf."

The team froze, looking at one another as Parker began to nod his head. No one spoke for several moments until Ree's voice broke the silence. "Guys? What is it? You guys all got the same weird look on your face."

Parker took a deep breath. "It's not just a disgruntled person out to make trouble. It feels like an operation. Someone with resources is behind this and doesn't want to leave a trail. We always knew it was a possibility but it makes how we handle this get a lot more complicated. On the bright side, it gives us some clues about what to look for."

The mood in the room shifted from curious theorizing to measured action. Parker began to bark out orders. "Mike – look at the surveillance tapes again. I want to know who went by Ree's office and how often. Run a background check on the delivery guy and anyone else who might have touched that box. Alexis – you need to spend some time with Ree and figure out if we need to add anyone to the list she and I worked on. We need to dig into her list of colleagues, students, friends, and anyone else who regularly crosses her path. We also need a background check on every grad student, administrator, janitorial staff member, and undergrad who works in Ivan's lab."

Parker put on his jacket and pulled out his keys. Ree asked, "What are you going to be doing?"

"Coordinating some additional surveillance and then getting what we need set up and approved for the next step of our plan. If we're going to win, we need to play offense. I need to run back to the office to get a report ready for the Chief. I need a whole heap of permission slips to get you more involved." He smiled and squeezed her shoulder. "Unless you want to sit on the sidelines with a bodyguard?"

"Not a chance, Parker."

"That's what I thought, Professor. Ladies, gentleman, we have some work to do. Alexis, you've been here for five nights straight, and I'm going to relieve you tonight. You need to report to work with Ree on Monday, and I want you sharp, so take some time off. Ree, are you going to be comfortable with me on your couch? I hate to butt in even more, but I don't see another way to keep you safe. If we weren't dealing with pros, we'd just set up surveillance outside, but I don't want you here by yourself. I can try and find someone else or Mikey can stay with you if that would be easier for you."

Ree acquiesced. "Yes, you can sleep on my couch, even if you drive me nuts. Do I have to call you sir, now that I'm on your team? Because I'm not sure I agreed to that."

"Pretty sure protocol says sir." Parker's mouth twitched.

Mike raised his head up from his laptop. "With all due respect, *sir,*" Mike looked at Parker then at Ree. "Don't listen to a word he says. I listen to the surveillance feed, and I fully advocate you giving him as much shit as humanly possible. In fact, I would consider it a personal favor."

Parker glared at Mike, fighting to keep his expression even. "Why don't you just stick with Parker, and we'll call it a compromise. Alright guys, back to work. I'll be back at 1900 for shift change."

After Parker left, Ree attempted to finish the grant application she'd been counting on to distract her, which proved easier in theory than in practice. Alexis made a series of phone calls to her counterparts, and Mike became fully engrossed in his task of scrolling through surveillance video. The annoyance of paperwork was non-life-threatening, and Ree's brain stubbornly refused to devote resources to the persuasive explanations required by the application. When Mike looked at his empty water glass and headed to the sink for a refill, she rose to join him rather than continue traveling down anxiety lane.

"So, Mike."

Mike flipped off the water and leaned his back against the sink. "So, Dr. Ryland."

"Ree, if you don't mind?"

"Sure thing, Ree. What's on your mind?"

"Well, I'm trying to get some work done and failing. And I have some questions. Are you at a stopping point?"

Mike eyed her critically. "I can be. How're you holding up, Ree?" Mike didn't seem like the chatty type and she appreciated him humoring her.

"Doing alright, all things considered. Is there always so much waiting in your work? I mean, no offense, but all we have so far is a box. That's it. What do you do to keep things interesting?"

"Trust me, Ree. You don't want interesting. If we can keep you sleeping at night, we're doing our jobs. And my wife prefers it when my job is boring."

Ree grinned. She'd been prying at Mike, trying to learn more about him. Now, she had a thread to pull on.

"I don't think you mentioned where she works. What does she do for a living? Is she okay with you working for the FBI?" Ree rattled off her questions since Mike had opened the door, after all.

"Scarlett doesn't mind that I work for the FBI. She shouldn't anyway, since she is a behavioral analyst, and we met at the Bureau. I thought I was good at figuring people out, but Scarlett blows me out of the water."

"Did you figure that out before or after you were married?"

"Believe it or not, my charming first encounter with my future wife was over a suspect diagram on a whiteboard. She told me I was investigating the wrong guy. I thought she was an intern. Suffice to say, it didn't go well."

Alexis, finished with her phone calls, broke into Mike's story. "Lucky for Mikey, he agreed with her assessment and invited her to come with him on the investigation, since he thought it would be a good experience for her and a reward for thinking outside the box. He had no idea the intern outranked him. Parker and I laughed for weeks over that one. She finally took pity on him and told him who she was."

Mike grinned. "She found me irresistible."

"Don't push it, Mike. I'm trying to make you look good here." Alexis said in a stage whisper, "Scar and I were roommates in college. She had me slip him a case file with her number on it. After Parker and I didn't tell Mike who she was when he was teaching her how to run an investigation, we figured we owed him one, and the rest is history."

Ree's brain, playing from behind all day, finally kicked itself back into gear. "Ok, I may have watched too many cop shows, but isn't a behavioral analyst a profiler? Wouldn't someone with those skills come in handy for us?"

Alexis looked at Mike and shrugged her shoulders. "Her clearance came through. You can tell her."

Mike finished his glass of water. "Actually, she's already weighed in. For what it's worth, she didn't think you were going to turn out to be the one. Speaking of which, it's time for me to say goodnight and tackle the long drive home, even though she'll be insufferable since she was right. Alex, can you hold down the fort until Parker shows up?"

Alexis agreed and checked her weapon, bringing Ree's fears back to the surface. Ree jumped when she heard a knock on the door. Everyone's cell phones went off with a text. *It's me – P.* Mike shrugged into his jacket and peeked through the window.

"As advertised," Mike said. "See you guys Monday." Holding two fingers to his head in a casual salute, he walked out of the door as Parker came in. Alexis and Parker bumped fists, and Alexis gave Parker an update on the work they had completed that afternoon.

"NICE WORK. This'll give the rest of the team something to chew on until we can put together a more solid plan of attack." Parker took in the dark circles under Alexis's eyes. He gestured to the door. "Now get out of here, kiddo, and get some rest."

Parker explained quietly to her that he'd set up a relief team to look at the data over the weekend. Alexis was great at what she did because she cared about the people she worked with, which meant taking a break didn't come easily for her. Parker's job included making sure she got a day off from the constant stress of protecting another person, even if she thought she didn't need it. She looked back at Ree one last time before Parker closed the door behind her.

Parker flipped the deadbolt, and out of the corner of his eye, saw Ree jump. He turned to face the professor, who was standing in one spot in the hallway, arms crossed and shifting her weight from foot to foot.

"We're not alone," Parker said.

"What?!" Ree sputtered. She started walking quickly towards her desk for her purse.

"Whoa, stand down, professor. I mean, there is a small team keeping an eye on the place outside. You seem nervous. So, either I'm making you nervous or something out there is making you nervous. All you have to do is yell and you have a team of bodyguards at your disposal."

Parker ran his hand through his hair. Maybe he should have had someone sub in for him tonight too, if he was already scaring her ten minutes after he walked through the door. He was generally good at reading people, and while Ree didn't hate him, she was also wary, which could be dangerous. He needed her complete trust, so he gestured to her couch.

"You want to talk or do you want me to leave you alone to process everything?" Parker preferred to think quietly when chewing on a problem, but Ree was the type who tended to talk when she got nervous.

REE LOOKED TOWARDS PARKER, then her couch, then back at him, and decided she needed a moment. "Give me a few minutes, and I'll be back down?"

Ree jogged up the stairs to change into comfortable pants and a baggy t-shirt. She let her hair down out of the tight twist she was used to wearing it in. It had some odd lumps and bumps, but she needed her evening routine to soothe her ragged nerves, even if the closest she was going to get to normal was letting her hair down and sitting in her sweatpants while talking to the FBI agent in charge of protecting her. She had some investigating of her own to do if she was going to continue to trust her life to this man who had just recently barged into it. She ran a hand through the waves in her hair one last time and descended the stairs to face Parker.

14

REE PLACED A STEADYING HAND ON THE RAILING AS SHE WALKED DOWN the stairs that led into her living room. Her eyes immediately fell on Parker, who had flipped on the TV and was watching a soccer match. He almost fooled her into thinking he wasn't paying attention, but his head tipped slightly upon her entering the room.

"Wine? Beer?" she asked.

"Sure, a beer sounds great." Ree went into the kitchen and returned with two open bottles. She handed him one and then flopped cross-legged on the couch facing him, with her own in hand. Parker muted the game, but the TV remained on in the background.

"Ask away," Parker said, and took a sip of the beer.

"Excuse me?" Ree looked at him.

"We hardly know each other, and now I'm bunking with you. I'd be surprised if someone like you didn't want to know a little bit more about her new houseguest." Parker waited, but Ree only shook her head. "If you don't have any questions, we'll start with you. What's your life like outside of work? Are you close with your family?"

Ree took a sip of her beer and parried, "Come on, Parker, I'm disappointed. You think I believe that you don't already know?" She tsked at him.

He raised an eyebrow. "Your mom, Kay, is an accountant and your dad, Jim, was in the Army but now works private security. Your sister Stefanie works in San Francisco for a tech startup, and the two of you are close, but don't talk as much as you'd like. I know you have a third degree black belt, so I'll be nice since you could probably hold your own in a fight. I know you go to the shooting range on a regular basis. You're almost as good as I am, which is impressive and a little scary, considering it's part of my job description. You're good at science and love teaching. Am I close?"

Ree smiled. "Close enough."

"Want to explain to me why a professor in a sleepy little college town is armed and ready to kick my butt?"

"Yeah, that wouldn't be in the file." Ree's stomach roiled, even though she had done nothing wrong. Swallowing hard, she placed a hand on her stomach. Closing her eyes, she answered as economically as possible. "Old boyfriend. Cheated. Couldn't understand why I broke up with him and kept calling me and showing up. He got angry if I wouldn't talk to him. It scared me, and I threatened a restraining order. He backed off to protect his reputation, but I couldn't get over how two-faced he'd been and how controlling he became when it was over. I didn't know what to think anymore. I dusted off my gi from high school and earned a couple of extra stripes on my black belt. And I've gone to the shooting range with my dad ever since I was old enough."

"Wow. You okay now?" Parker balled his hands into fists even as his eyes softened.

"It's been a long time. I'm over it." Ree cleared her throat. "So, do I get to peek in your file, Agent Landon?"

Parker's fists relaxed. "Depends."

"On?"

"My FBI file or my family file?"

"The FBI stuff is probably off-limits. I get that."

Parker nodded. "My mom is a biomedical engineer, and my dad works for a renewable energy company out in California. I have a younger sister and older brother. My sister, Mary, is a high school science teacher, and my brother, Cameron, rides a desk in the Navy. He joined up right after high school. They worked pretty hard to recruit him once they found out his language skills were off the charts, and it wasn't too long before he became a SEAL."

"Wow. That's impressive. So, he's not a SEAL anymore?"

"No. He lost his left leg below the knee to an IED when he was visiting a village in Iraq. I graduated with a degree in engineering three weeks after it happened and applied for a job at the FBI shortly thereafter. I like beer, as you can tell, and my favorite color is purple."

"Really, purple? I didn't take you for a purple man. Not judging, just an observation." Ree raised her hands in the air.

Parker grinned at her. "Just seeing if you were paying attention. Although my sister did get me a purple shirt for Christmas and I still don't know if she was kidding or not, which she thinks is hilarious. You'd like her."

Ree tried not to get attached to Agent Landon, but he wasn't making it easy. She took another sip of her beer, and continued, "Anything else I need to know, Agent Landon? Besides your affinity for purple, of course. How did you meet up with Alexis and Mike?"

Parker debated how much of the story to tell her when his phone popped up a message. *You've got a prowler outside. West side window shades open. Headed your way.* Parker tensed and surveyed his situation.

Parker tilted his phone towards Ree. She skimmed it quickly, eyes widening. "What do we do?"

The phone vibrated again. *10 seconds.*

Parker placed his beer on the coffee table and felt for his Glock. "First, don't panic. I want you to walk calmly to the kitchen and try and stand next to the refrigerator, keeping it between you and the window in your dining room. Is the window closed?"

"Yes, and locked."

"Good, the glass will change the trajectory of anything that might go through it, but be ready to move on my command. Go. Now."

Seconds passed. Quiet, tense seconds of nothing. Ree leaned against the wall in her kitchen as instructed, listening for signs of danger. She prayed silently that somehow this would end well and wondered how bulletproof her refrigerator really was.

The doorbell rang and she let out a yelp. She quickly covered her own mouth to muffle the sound. She heard Parker's phone vibrate again. He called, "Honey, doorbell! Do you want me to get it?"

Ree, puzzled, took a moment before yelling back, "Sure, I'll be right out."

Parker opened up the door and said loudly, "Joanna! So great to see you again. Ree was just running to the kitchen, and she'll be right out. Let me go get her for you." Parker walked to the kitchen, his black t-shirt casually untucked over his jeans and holster. There was no sign of his Glock.

"Babe? It's your friend Joanna," Parker said loudly. In the doorway of the kitchen, Parker wrapped his hand around her waist, pulled her close and nuzzled his nose in her hair, whispering, "We have NOT cleared her yet, and you are not to be alone with her." Ree was momentarily stunned as Parker leaned his forehead against hers, looked her in the eyes and quietly said, "You've got this."

Adrenaline pumped through Ree's veins as she walked away from Parker to greet her friend. She could have kicked him in the shins for not warning her before pulling her close, even if she had technically given him permission earlier, and it was probably a good idea. Damn him, she hated lying to her friends, but they didn't have much of a choice.

"Hey, gorgeous." Joanna gave her best friend a hug and kiss on the cheek. Ree self-consciously ran a hand through her hair, still in disarray, and looked down at her pajamas. Her face flushed as she wondered what Joanna would think.

Joanna, clearly thrilled to see her friend in a relationship, continued, "I didn't know if you had plans, and Ivan was working late, so I thought I'd stop by." Joanna turned to Parker and then back to Ree, looking slowly up and down to take in Ree's outfit. "Since it seems like you two are in the middle of an evening in, I will just give you another hug, steal some of your chocolate, and be on my way."

Ree smiled at the small reminder of normalcy despite the absurdity of her circumstances. She and Joanna had long since agreed that any chocolate in their houses was considered community property. Jo popped open the box on Ree's coffee table, grabbed a chocolate, and turned back to Ree, who remained frozen from the one-two punch of embarrassment and uncertainty.

Joanna gave her a hug goodbye and whispered, "When you two come up for air, we are going out for dinner, and you are going to tell me about this hot little secret you have been keeping from me." Joanna gave her a knowing look, filled with the promise of digging for details later. "Bye, you two – don't do anything I wouldn't do."

Ree flipped the lock after closing the door behind Jo. She leaned against the door and closed her eyes. Parker was back on the couch, typing on his phone to whoever had sent the warning. He looked up as she sank into the cushion next to him and laid her head on his shoulder. He sat stunned for a moment before threading his arm around her back. He patted her shoulder awkwardly.

"We're doing what we can, but it's probably going to take some time to clear those two. With you clear, they look even guiltier than you did, and clearing you took some work," he explained.

"I assumed. Doesn't mean I like it."

"For what it's worth, the information you've been giving us is helping. You've been a real asset so far. I'd love to have you on my team."

"Parker, no offense, but we haven't caught the bad guy yet. And I'm not even sure I like you," Ree said, still tucked under Parker's arm.

"Liar." Parker hugged her a little closer.

"Alright, I like you enough to let you sleep on my couch so I don't get killed, and I haven't broken your ankle for getting grabby in front of my friends. But don't push it."

"I'm confiscating your gun."

"Don't even think about it." As she stood, Ree gave Parker a little shove and a grin. "Don't let the bed bugs bite." She tossed a blanket to him and walked up the stairs to her room.

15

"We need a cover." Ree turned from stirring eggs a little too vigorously in a pan on the stove to point the spatula at Parker. He wasn't a morning person, but clearly, the professor was, and she'd been waiting for his arrival to pounce. She pointed the spatula at a cheerful yellow daisy mug, filled with fresh coffee, on her kitchen table.

Parker raised his eyebrows and took a small sip of the coffee. "Thank you. We have a cover. One in which you pretend to date me and I don't do anything that makes you want to kick me."

"I don't do needy."

"Excuse me?" Parker stared into his coffee cup for answers.

"I don't do needy. I need a reason for you to be around the lab other than you hanging around me. I can't handle clingy men – they annoy me."

"Well, I seem to annoy you, so that works." Parker rubbed one hand down the stubble on his face and blinked hard. "For the record, you're right. I can't show up all the time if I'm your boyfriend, and I'm supposed to have a day job. You have Alexis for twenty hours a week, but I need a job that will explain my odd hours and maybe even give me some reason to be in the lab. I already told Ivan I'm not your student, and he's seen me in the building."

"What if you're my biographer?"

"No offense intended, professor, but why would you have a biographer?"

Ree feigned insult. "Why wouldn't I have a biographer? Science careers and women in science are a pretty hot topic right now. What if you were writing a book or research paper? You could interview everyone in Ivan's lab, and I could act like I am doing my boyfriend a big favor by asking the students if they'd be willing to talk to you." Ree pitched her idea with genuine enthusiasm. She probably wanted to have as much company in the lab as possible, given the elusiveness of their suspect and the very real probability that he or she was one of her new coworkers.

"Not a bad idea, Professor. Let me call it in and see if I can get some cover information going in case anyone asks. If we're cleared, I'll need you to help me prepare some good questions. My sister, the science teacher I told you about, has talked with me about this, so I can fake it a little, but I'd still appreciate the help. After I finish my coffee and I'm among the living again." Parker took a large gulp of the coffee. "Are you always this *awake* in the mornings?"

TRUE TO HIS WORD, Parker sent information to his colleagues within the hour. Before getting down to the business of helping Parker flesh out his cover, Ree led Parker to the trendy part of the city to get lunch at a small cafe. It was an odd combination, to feel so alone, afraid, and reassured at the same time.

"Lost in thought, Professor?" Parker waved his hand in front of her eyes and she refocused her attention on the present moment. They sat on the outside patio in the cool fall air at "The Whole Enchilada," a local Mexican café swarming with college students, many still in their pajama bottoms. She ran her finger along the cheerful summer scenes painted on the round table and took a moment to appreciate the vibrant energy around her before digging into her plate of freshly made tacos.

"Just coming to terms with the fact I actually like you guys. Well, Mike and Alexis, anyway," Ree teased.

Parker placed his fork on the table. "A compliment? You better start eating your lunch before you go soft on me. And this may get worse before it gets better, so you might want to withhold judgment until you're sure. We'll have to get back to work after this."

"Any better ideas than work?" Ree asked, half in jest.

"I'd teach you self-defense, but I've read your file, and I'd rather not go toe to toe with you, if it's all the same to you. What made you get the first black belt? And how did you become such a good shot? Were you preparing to be a spy your entire life, or were your parents just really protective?" Parker's tone was teasing, but he was probably curious after their conversation the previous evening got cut short.

Ree smiled a genuine smile. "Protective parents are what started it all, but I fell in love with both sports on my own. I learned coordination from karate and confidence from target practice. My dad would love to hear that you approve, although he would have loved it more if I'd chosen to work for the CIA. I considered it pretty seriously, but I didn't think I had the stomach for it. I was worried that I wouldn't do a good enough job and someone might get hurt. I've always wondered what would have happened if I'd joined up. Isn't that ironic?"

"VERY. Ready to go back home and get to work?" Parker ended the conversation before it could go any further. Ree was getting close to the investigation details in public and the tables around them were beginning to fill up. He wiped the crumbs from their lunch off the table and casually scanned the area to see if anyone had been watching or listening. He saw no one.

"Of course. But I'm dragging you out on a run later. Since you won't spar with me, I'll have to see what you're made of in a footrace. And I saw that, by the way. Anyone?" Parker shook his head no and took her hand for the walk home.

Later, at Ree's house, Parker stood with his hands on his hips in front of his notes on Ree's whiteboard while she worked on a grant application. Parker asked, "You at a stopping point?"

Ree lifted her chin up from her hand. "Sure, what's up?"

"How well do you know the students in Ivan's lab?"

Ree looked up at the whiteboard and took a few moments to answer. "Not really at all, yet. Some by face, one or two by name. He's incredibly popular and always has a herd of grad and undergrad students rotating through. Are sociopaths charismatic?"

"Off-topic, Ree."

"Is it off-topic?"

"They can be, it just depends on what they want."

"Do you really think Ivan is behind all of this?"

"He could be. Our profiler thinks the person behind this is relentless, driven, and calculated. Someone like you, except they don't care who gets in their way in the process."

"Oh, that's just super. You really know how to compliment a girl."

"Did you hear the last part? Last time I checked, you put your life on hold because a couple of agents from the FBI told you it was important. Couldn't be more different. The point I was trying to make is that the smart, driven, calculated ones are the most dangerous. They're cautious and aren't likely to act on impulse or emotion. And if you haven't noticed, just about everyone in the lab could fit that description. So we can't just watch for action – we have to figure out intent from someone actively trying to hide it. Everyone in that lab is a suspect, and I can't be your shadow every minute of every day, as much as I'd like to."

Parker dug for details for a few more minutes until Ree's shoulders hitched up to her ears and Parker had to mock her taste in coffee mugs to get them to relax. Out of questions and unwilling to push her any harder, Parker drafted a quick report for Sandy. Work complete, Parker flipped on a soccer game while Ree pretended to read a novel. There wasn't much he could say by way of reassurance, but he didn't hear her pacing in her room after she went to bed, so that was at least a positive.

16

Ree arrived on campus just before her first class on Monday morning. While they'd canceled her position in the lab, her coursework would continue as planned. Per Parker's advice, she'd skipped going to the lab early in the morning and was going to gradually change her habits so that she wasn't the first to arrive in the lab on any given day. A small adjustment to her schedule for safety was a compromise she could live with. Ree skimmed her small class and saw only familiar faces, some of them still groggy from sleep. She took a deep breath, took a fortifying sip of her coffee, and began her lesson.

At the end of class, Ree always left some time for questions, and today her students seemed especially eager. The minute her lesson was complete, a hand shot up in the back of the room, and she went through her normal process of engaging the entire class in solving the problem. She watched for fear on student's faces as she scanned the crowd and chose the people who seemed most confident. It wasn't so long ago she was the student silently willing the professor not to call on her if she wasn't certain she knew the answer. Upon exiting her classroom, she saw Matt Brown at the end of the hallway.

Matt also worked for Ivan, and she knew a fair amount about his background and family from their casual conversations. He'd been collaborative and friendly in their prior interactions, but that was before she stepped onto his turf. Under the circumstances, it was worth taking a few minutes to make sure he didn't mind sharing his office and work with another professor. He flashed a dazzling white smile her direction and raised his hand in a wave. While he was a good-looking man, with dark skin and hair inherited from his Puerto Rican mother, it was his approachable disposition that made him stick out in a crowd.

Matt paused in the hallway to wait for her to approach. "I heard you're coming to work with us, Ree. We're honored to have you in the lab."

Ree's responding smile was genuine. "Thanks, Matt! I'd love to hear more about what you guys have been up to."

"Of course. It's always nice to have new professors to shake things up. I'd be happy to get coffee or a meal with you to welcome you to the team if your schedule allows."

Ree was pleasantly surprised at Matt's warm welcome. She had learned the hard way to watch out for unhealthy competition or back-biting amongst non-tenured professors, but Matt Brown seemed genuinely happy she was joining the lab. Still, jumping into a dinner invitation when she was watching out for an enemy with a vested interest in cornering her was a red flag.

Cursing her situation, she forced her smile to stay in place and deflected, "What a brilliant idea. What if we got everyone together for a meeting on campus, and I could get to know you all? I'm treading on your turf here, so I'd like to figure out where I could be most useful. Meeting everyone would really help with that."

Matt frowned slightly, but then recovered his smile. "I'll talk to Ivan about it today. It'd be great to get to know you better."

Ree allowed a bounce to return to her step when her phone beeped. *Alex is running a background check right now on all lab employees – no meetings with Dr. Suspicious until we clear him. – P.* She fought her inner urge to smack him through the phone. Really? He couldn't let her have two seconds of excitement over her new job? Maybe someone was happy to see her for reasons other than her utility as a weapons mule. She rolled her eyes and glared down the hallway, both directions for good measure, since she had no idea where they had planted the cameras.

"Was the reminder necessary, P?" Mike raised his eyebrows in Parker's direction, judgment thick in his tone. "Or were you just pulling Dr. Ryland's pigtails?"

"Probably not, but I don't want her getting hurt. Plus, have you noticed when she's glaring at me, she's not worrying as much about someone trying to kill her?" Parker twirled a pen in his hand.

Mike grudgingly agreed. This was why Parker led this team. He wasn't careless or controlling, but he was willing to put his foot down or play class clown when it helped his teammates' mental health. However, in this case, Mike suspected Parker was having a little fun at the same time. Not a lot of women kept up with Parker's dry humor, and his friend was starting to fall in like with the professor. At least Parker was professional enough to keep it to himself. Actually, Parker probably hadn't even figured it out yet. Mike decided not to inform his buddy that he was on to him, at least for a little longer.

Ree's heels clicked against the hard linoleum floor on the way to her new office, and the cheerful sound stood in contrast to her pounding heart. She didn't mind wearing short, practical heels – they made her legs look good, and she was allowed to appreciate that. Ree was less comfortable with the double standard that required the rest of her uncomfortable outfit. Studies had shown that women had to dress up to be taken seriously, so she'd taken care to wear a button-down shirt with a pencil skirt on her first day in her new job, even though it annoyed her, just a little bit. Having a data-oriented brain could be a real pain in the butt sometimes. She could switch to her preferred uniform of jeans and sneakers when she inevitably needed to fix some test equipment, once she knew her new coworkers a little better. Ree adjusted the strap of her laptop bag higher on her crisp gray shirt and approached her new desk. She gave a quick wave to the students who stared at her curiously when she entered.

Ivan swiveled in his chair to greet her. "Irina! Welcome! Now that you are settled in, I know you will want to know your assignment right away...however, I seem to have misplaced my list."

Ree bit her lip to keep from smiling. She'd tried to set a wager with Parker that Ivan wouldn't be ready for her, but he wouldn't take her bet. She let Ivan off the hook and instead of asking detailed questions about her new job, said, "Thank you for putting that together! I was thinking this morning that it would be nice just to walk around and meet everyone. Do you have any idea which students I will be working with?"

Ivan gestured towards Matt Brown's empty chair. "You'll be helping offload Dr. Matt Brown – you two know each other, yes? Truthfully, Irina, he seems a bit overwhelmed these days. He does so much. He's incredibly bright, but I asked him to take on too many students. I'm going to switch a few over to you. I am still deciding on which ones, but I particularly want your help with a student working on a large-scale fatigue test machine. Between us, I don't think it is going to work, even though he spends a great deal of time on it and tells me it's going well. I need you to look over his shoulder and help him troubleshoot. I know you will know how to push him while making him think it's his idea."

"Of course, Ivan."

"Thank you for being willing to jump right in. On that subject, how are you doing, my friend?"

Ree looked towards her mentor and answered honestly, "Professionally and financially? I am incredibly grateful I have a job and I'm thrilled to hear that I'm needed, but the switch has been difficult. I've spent so much time dedicating myself to automotive safety. I don't feel like I can just drop into another lab and be useful."

Innocent until proven guilty, she thought, on repeat. She really needed her friend and mentor to give her some reasonable advice to help her move forward. FBI investigation aside, her career had just taken a hit, and she'd like to make sure it was a detour and not a nosedive. Eventually, Parker and his team would leave, and she was going to need to have her professional life in order.

Ivan's face softened and he gestured to his guest chair. "Irina. Ree. Sit here. You are an excellent scientist and a good friend. I was ready to speak up at the board meeting where they discussed eliminating your position, but I didn't need to. Everyone who had worked with you before wanted to keep you on the faculty, even if it wasn't in your lab. I trust you can take whatever experience you gain here and apply it to your true passion. I have ensured your projects are focused on materials and testing so you can use the knowledge you've gained no matter where you end up. When you have the opportunity, you can move back to your lab and hopefully be even better at what you do. In the meantime, I know you will make a great contribution to my lab, so it's not as if I'm doing you a favor."

Ivan waved his hand at the last part, and his words began to rebuild her now-battered professional confidence. Tears came to Ree's eyes. Unable to speak for a moment, she nodded and kept the tears at bay. At last, she squeaked out a thank you and shook Ivan's hand. It was a formal gesture, but at work, Ivan was her boss and not her friend, and it seemed like the right thing to do.

Ree set up her desk while she waited for the grad students to arrive. She unpacked a box of personal items and strategized on the best way to help a student who didn't know they needed help.

Ree breathed a sigh of relief when the first student who entered was someone she knew well. Ree walked around her new desk to greet her. They'd met during a freshman seminar she helped teach on careers in engineering. Shayla Carson was fun, smart, and confident in a way Ree wished she'd been at that age. They had talked frequently several years prior but had since lost touch. She was tall with curly hair pulled into a tight ponytail with dark skin and black-framed glasses. She wore a brightly colored scarf with trendy jeans and boots. Shayla made having style look effortless. She gave Ree a huge smile and a hug. She was going to be great to work with.

Another student walked through the doorway and startled when he saw Ree. He introduced himself as Josh Goodwin. Ree reached out her hand and he shook it loosely. He had a medium build and wore a loose university t-shirt and khakis that had long been frayed on the bottom. Josh's eyes darted between her and the lab, his torn attention making her wonder if he possessed the same distracted mind of Ivan. He was either distracted or a genius, but given her friendship with Ivan, the scale of probability tilted towards genius. Josh seemed genuinely terrified of her and clicked the end of his mechanical pencil during their entire interaction without making eye contact. He would take some winning over.

The last student of the morning was Beckett Parish. He was a Ph.D. candidate from England with a baby face and a polite disposition, but that could have been his accent playing tricks on her. He stopped at her desk as soon as he walked in to introduce himself. Ree asked him about himself and was able to extract herself from the conversation about ten minutes after her first question. He was friendly and loved chatting about both himself and what he did. She would make sure she had more time before she asked him questions in the future.

Ree settled herself into her chair after greeting the first wave of students and created memos and notes to direct whoever would continue her research at the automotive safety engineering lab. While she had officially relocated, she had a trail of breadcrumbs to create to make sure she didn't leave any loose ends with Dr. Moran. There was a very real possibility that no one would continue her research at all. She sighed at that. He would continue on as the only professor in her lab since propulsion was apparently the more grant-worthy science of the moment.

With a clear task to complete by the end of the day, time passed quickly. The next time she looked up from her work, only Ivan, Matt, and she remained in the lab. She had missed lunch entirely. Matt gave her a bemused wave.

"Did you get everything done, Ree? I was wondering if I couldn't convince you to come out to dinner with me, since you seemed to have missed lunch?"

Before she could answer, Parker popped his head in the door.

"Ree? Are you ready to leave?" He looked at Matt and Ivan. "Unless you're in the middle of a meeting?"

Matt's head whipped around to Parker and a look was exchanged between the two men that Ree didn't completely understand. Ivan seemed to be amused, folding his hands on his desk to unabashedly watch the scene unfold.

Ree unlocked her desk drawer and pulled out her purse. "We're just wrapping up. Sorry, Matt. We'll have to get together another time."

Parker walked over to Matt's desk and stuck out his hand. "Parker Landon."

Matt stood, matching Parker in both stature and disposition, and shook his offered hand. "Matt Brown. Very good to meet you. Do you work with Dr. Ryland?"

Parker looked to Ree and back at Matt. "No, not in an official capacity. I interviewed her for a book I'm writing on female professionals, and we've been dating ever since."

Ivan said, "Female professionals? You should interview my wife, Joanna. She is a primary care physician at Grace Hospital, just down the street. I'm sure she wouldn't mind helping, with you being good friends with Irina. Irina can give you her cell phone number. Better yet, perhaps you could join us for dinner sometime soon, Parker?"

Parker recognized the interrogation for what it was. It might just work in their favor. He grinned broadly. "That sounds terrific. Just let Ree and I know the when and the where." He held out his hand. Ree wavered slightly, suddenly brought back to reality after a day of distraction back at her real job. She grabbed onto his hand like a life preserver, gave a small wave to her two new colleagues, and made her exit.

Parker and Ree exchanged a look on the way out of the building, and Ree asked, "You want me to set something up for as soon as possible, I'm guessing?"

"Affirmative. You learn quickly, young Padawan."

Ree snorted. "Really? You're quoting Star Wars at me, Agent Yoda?"

"For the record, they are great movies."

"I'm not judging."

"Nothing to judge, Dr. Ryland. By the way, are all of your friends freakishly smart?" Parker gave Ree's hand a light squeeze.

"Coming from an engineering major who graduated at the top of his class, that's pretty rich." Ree bumped Parker with her hip and opened the door to his sensible, navy mid-sized car.

"Did you do a background check of your own, professor?"

"Did you expect anything less?"

"Nope. Proud of you, Doc. You must have called Sandy again. Set up that dinner?"

"I'll work on it. It's not easy for me to lie to my friends, Parker."

"I know. But if they have nothing to do with this, they'll understand. Alexis is already at your house. Need to go anywhere before I drop you off?"

Ree directed him to her favorite local sandwich shop, where she ran in and grabbed four sandwiches. She handed him two of the sandwiches when they reached her house. "Give one to Mike for me, will you? Appreciate you guys keeping the country and me safe and all of that," Ree said, her face reddening. She dashed out of his car before he could say thank you.

The next few days passed without incident, even though Ree's nerves were wearing thin while they tried to make sense of what was happening. The FBI team had been unwilling to tip their hand by putting a camera in Ivan's lab with so many people around and a trained suspect who might know they were being chased, so they were back to older, slower investigative techniques.

Parker popped in every few days at the lab, but primarily, he stayed in the van with Mike, solidifying his cover and supporting the analyst team. They would have dinner with Joanna and Ivan on Friday, and Alexis coached Ree on how to handle the interaction. Their lack of progress in any other area was frustrating, but it was part of the game. Parker pushed on Sandy for more information, but he was unable to provide anything actionable. The only new piece of information for Parker was that the CIA had originally delivered the tip that something was happening. However, when Sandy circled back with his counterpart at the Agency, they claimed to know very little else and would not reveal their source.

When Friday arrived, Parker and Mike discussed tactics, but the goal for the evening was simple – to sell Ivan and Joanna on his relationship with Ree and find out what he could about the Nobelkovs. He would bring a bottle of wine and his Glock. Unsure of exactly what they were walking into, they'd keep a backup crew close by. They'd done more with less.

17

REE EXCHANGED MESSAGES WITH JOANNA ALL WEEK TO SET UP THEIR dinner and answer her many questions about Parker. When Friday eventually arrived, Ree spent most of the day working closely with Alexis. Alexis left the lab a half an hour before Parker was due to arrive to make sure their actions didn't appear as coordinated as they actually were. While Ree waited for her ride to the Nobelkov's, she sat on a stool in the lab reading a draft of an instruction manual for the fatigue machine Ivan warned her would never work. She looked up from it to study the equipment when she heard footsteps. Now all too aware that she was alone in the lab with someone coming up behind her, she forced herself to turn around as normally as possible while looking for sharp or heavy objects, just in case. Her purse was in the adjacent office, too far away to be useful.

Simon glanced at the book she was reading before speaking. "Dr. Ryland. I don't think I've had the opportunity to show you my work. May I show you the fatigue equipment I have been working on?" Ree had met Simon earlier in the week. Their interaction had been polite, but his previously butter-smooth tone now held a note of annoyance. He probably didn't want her meddling with his equipment.

"That would be great!" Ree forced her voice into a cheerful register. "I'm on limited time, however. I'm leaving for dinner soon and my ride will be here any minute. I'm new to the lab, and I'm interested in learning about what everyone who works here is doing. What does your machine do?" Given Simon's obvious irritation, she decided to leave off the part where Ivan told her he needed help.

Ree and Simon whirled in tandem at the knock on the lab door.

Parker leaned in the doorway. "Ree? Ready to go?"

Oddly relieved despite the unremarkable interaction, Ree made her apologies to Simon and grabbed her purse on the way out. Parker was wearing a dark gray button-down and jeans. Ree looked down to make sure she was presentable. "One second." She held up a finger and rummaged in her desk, quickly switching out her sneakers for short heels.

"Perfect. Let's go, Doc." Parker slipped his arm around her waist and guided her out of her office.

SIMON WATCHED THEM LEAVE. Dr. Ryland didn't seem suspicious and dropped her interest in his machine as soon as the man had arrived. He felt in his pocket for his knife and kept his hand there until he calmed down. His suppliers were working on the remaining parts, and while he had to tell The General he had fallen behind, he would make up the lost time. Even with all of the deliveries, Dr. Ryland was distracted and oblivious to what he was doing. Yes, she had been an excellent choice. Simon closed the cover to his exposed equipment and grabbed his backpack.

As he left the building, a hand on his shoulder stopped him short. His nostrils flared, and he forced himself to grab the wrist of the person and look at them rather than just kill them on the spot. It wouldn't do to kill a colleague in broad daylight, even if it was an accident.

When Simon realized who was behind him, he flicked the wrist off of his shoulder and began to walk. "You shouldn't be here."

"He's concerned about exposure."

"He has no reason to be." Simon led the man who had been with The General almost as long as Simon into a narrow walkway between buildings. Knowing The General's love of secrecy, this piece of nothing probably didn't even know what Simon was doing. Just that he needed to do it right and something hadn't gone to plan.

"Then why did he send me?" Simon whirled and flicked his knife open, pinning the weasel to the wall. He held his blade against the man's stomach, eyes darting to make sure no one saw him push the man against the hard brick of the building. The man brushed it away and laughed. "You wouldn't dare."

"And neither would you. You don't know what could happen if I died."

"Perhaps I should clean up your mess while I'm here."

"There is no mess to clean up. No one knows what I am doing."

"Or they won't for much longer. Fix it. He won't tolerate another mistake." The man shrugged and walked away with his back to Simon.

Simon gripped his knife and considered the merits of throwing it at the man's exposed neck. Despite the temptation, The General's wrath would be formidable, and it wasn't worth the risk of discovery. His message had been clear enough, and The General would be satisfied that he had made his point. Simon just needed to finish his work and make sure the professor he was using for cover didn't start asking too many questions.

PARKER PULLED his car into the driveway of a red brick home with white trim. He was calm, but the woman to his right was anything but. It was too risky to bring surveillance equipment with them, so they were going into Ivan and Joanna's house with limited back-up. All he had was a glorified panic button on his phone that would simultaneously bring in an armed team and alert whoever might be scanning for bugs that federal agents were in the house. Arresting Ree's best friends while blowing his cover was not a good way to end an investigation, but it was better than getting killed. They'd just have to watch the food and stay alert.

While Ree had paled when he instructed her to let the Nobelkovs take a bite of everything first, she was willing to go along with his plan. He thought Ree would calm down on the drive over, but as they approached their destination, it became clear his assumption was based more on hope than any supporting evidence.

Ree tapped her finger on her leg as he parked the car. Parker reached for the door handle, but Ree stilled her tapping long enough to place her hand on his arm. "Parker, wait."

He pulled his hand back and readied himself for her change of heart. She was certainly entitled to reservations. Careful not to give her new ideas for what might go wrong, he kept it simple. "You okay?"

Ree shook her head quickly. "No. I mean, yes. I'm fine. But you should know. I don't date a lot."

"That's hardly a crime. Some would say you're careful. I mean, you like guys, right?"

Ree raised an eyebrow. "That's what you think I'm worried about? I told you I had an ex-boyfriend."

"It doesn't matter to me who you do or don't see in your free time. You're doing great."

"That's wonderful, but please stop. Just stop. I like guys, I just don't date a lot. There was the guy."

"The asshole ex-boyfriend?"

"No. Yes. Look, please let me talk." Ree wrung her hands and closed her eyes. "It was several years ago, and I'm over it, but Joanna doesn't think I am, because I don't date a lot so she might bring it up. His name was Brent, and yes, he was an asshole. But I was fine after he backed off, and I'm fine now. I've just not found anyone who holds my attention for more than a few dates, and I don't date guys I work with, and I work a lot, so it just hasn't happened for me. And that's not a big deal. To me. They may freak out on you a little, but they're just excited. Don't let their questions bother you. They just care."

"Okay. So Brent was an asshole, but I'm not. You are now a third degree black belt and a good shot, which is somewhat related. You are now okay. Your friends are excited to meet me, but they might be a little protective. Got it. So...we're good, right?" Parker scratched his head.

Ree nodded. "We're good. You are not an asshole, and they're just excited for me."

"Careful. Praise like 'not an asshole' could give me a big head. You ready to go in now?"

Ree shrugged. "As ready as I'll ever be."

"Great. Let's do this."

JOANNA PEEKED through the curtain at her visitors. Ree and Parker were talking in the car, and it seemed serious.

"Darling, no spying," Ivan said over his shoulder, walking past her with a salad bowl in his hands.

"I'm paid to know what people are thinking."

Once he emptied his hands, Ivan came back into the living room and planted a kiss on the top of her head. Wrapping his arms around her waist, he continued, "My beautiful wife, you are paid to diagnose your patients' illnesses, not read their minds. And you are very good, but that does not allow you to spy on your friends." He continued his thought but switched to Russian. Joanna turned to glare at him.

"I did not learn your language to hear you say that I am nosy."

"My love, the evidence suggests otherwise." He patted her on the bottom. "And, if you don't move away from the window, they will catch you spying."

Resigned, Joanna left her post at the window and flopped onto the couch. She fought a smile as she stared down her husband, who looked at her fondly in return. Before he could tease her any more, the doorbell rang, and Joanna bounded to the door to greet her friend and accept the bottle of wine that Parker offered.

PARKER TUGGED REE'S HAND. She had frozen in the Nobelkovs' foyer after stepping through the door. His judgment remained clear, as the Nobelkovs seemed nice enough but were virtual strangers to him. He checked to see if Ivan and Joanna had noticed Ree's odd behavior, but they were already walking towards the dining room. Parker gave Ree's hand a gentle squeeze, and she gave him a grateful look in return. At least she wasn't glaring at him with her eye lasers. The eye lasers earned their name after he suggested that she take it easy on a run because of the stress of her situation. To prove a point, she dragged him eight miles that day and victoriously told him where he could put his eye lasers. His new teammate was competitive. Lesson learned.

PARKER AND REE settled in the open seats across the table from Ivan and Joanna. Ivan leaned back in his chair and waited for the show to begin. Joanna had been talking his ear off all week about what he knew about Parker, which was nearly nothing, how long Ree and Parker had been dating, which he didn't know, and what Parker did for a living, which he also didn't know. When she tossed her hands in the air and dramatically informed him he was "such a man," he knew she would waste no time getting to know Ree's new friend a little better. Particularly after she caught them in their pajamas the previous weekend. This would be a fun night.

REE ATTEMPTED to enjoy spending time with her friends. She tried putting the true purpose of her visit from her mind. However, it was difficult to hold a conversation when she knew that Parker would, at some point in the evening, excuse himself to go to the bathroom and instead snoop around the Nobelkov's house when he felt the time was right.

Even the simple things became jarring. Parker pulled glasses from the Nobelkov's cabinets and offered to fill them up with water. Joanna shot an approving look to Ree when he offered, but Parker's motives were more calculated then they appeared. He was making sure they weren't going to get drugged that evening, since they were, to use Mike's words of encouragement, "playing on a high wire with no safety net." Someone needed to teach that man how to sugarcoat the truth a little bit for the non-professionals in the room.

Before Ree could get too lost in her reverie, Joanna picked up the salad bowl to serve the table. Joanna wasn't one to mince words, and before she even lifted a leaf of lettuce from the bowl, she asked, "So, Parker, what do you do for a living?"

"I'm a writer," Parker replied.

"What kind of writer? And have you always been a writer?" Joanna asked.

"No, ma'am, I have not. I spent some time working for an electrician and then found my calling. I write a mix of things, both fiction and non-fiction. I'm working on a novel right now that's almost finished."

"Interesting. What type of novel are you writing?" Joanna asked, leaning her chin on her hands, ignoring her salad.

"A spy thriller," Parker answered. Ree nearly spit out her water. Fortunately, her friends were focused on Parker and didn't notice.

Joanna leaned closer. "Have I read any of them? I love a good spy thriller when I can find the time."

"No, unfortunately, nothing has been published yet. I have a family member in the business who read my first draft and said he would back my work. Hopefully, you'll be able to read it in a few years."

Ivan, the seemingly absent-minded professor, jumped into the fray. "Parker, if you are writing spy novels, what are you doing on a college campus meeting our Ree?"

Parker took a sip of water. "That's the non-fiction piece. In addition to the thriller, I'm writing a series of articles about female scientists and engineers. My sister is a school teacher in California and wants to have something for her students to read, so I offered to work on it in my spare time."

Joanna made the same face she made when she saw puppies, and Ree knew her friend was sold. Ivan, acting as her unofficial big brother, probed further. "Oh? And are you planning on staying in town or going back to – where did you say home was, again?"

"Here. In town, actually. I grew up around here, but my sister always wanted to move out west."

"And are you guys getting serious?" Joanna asked, raising her eyebrows.

“Oh my gosh, Joanna, it’s a little early to be asking that,” Ree said, heat creeping up her neck.

“Ree – he spent the night. I think that’s a fair question,” Joanna said in a stage whisper.

“Joanna!” Ree shot her friend a look, her embarrassment genuine.

“That’s all the answer I need,” she said smugly and winked at Parker. “I think you may have hooked our girl. Be good to her, or we’ll have to hunt you down like the spies in your books.”

JOANNA STUDIED Parker over the edge of her wine glass. The way Ree looked at Parker confirmed Joanna's suspicions about how serious they were getting. When Ree failed to mention the new man in her life, Joanna had expected him to be kicked to the curb before they had the opportunity to have him over for dinner. However, it looked like it was shaping up to be exactly the opposite of that.

Joanna adored her friend, but between a busy work schedule, obliviousness to the attentions of the opposite sex, and impossibly high standards, she’d long been worried that Ree would never find someone to share her life with. It took a certain kind of person to keep up with her, and Parker seemed to be enjoying the challenge. More than once, he squeezed her hand under the table when she started to get nervous. This guy might actually be a keeper. For Ree’s sake, Joanna hoped so. It wasn’t easy to find someone you were happy to spend fifty years or more with. She rubbed her hand on her husband’s knee under the table and smiled into her glass.

AS THE GIRLS became engrossed in their shared stories over wine, Parker excused himself to go to the restroom. He kept an ear out for noise from the dining room, where there was laughter and conversation, and turned his focus towards the books on the shelf in the hallway. There was an abundance of textbooks, which were expected, and some novels in both English and Russian. Nothing out of the ordinary. Of course, one of the Russian textbooks could be called “How to Build a Missile" and Parker wouldn't know the difference. He continued on, his brief scan of the bookshelf barely adding any time to his walk down the hallway. Pausing to listen for footsteps or sounds that Ree was in trouble, Parker looked over his shoulder and didn't see anyone. He stepped into the Nobelkov's study and gently closed the door behind him. Spotting a pile of papers on the desk, he sent a text to Ree: *Keep them busy and let me know if there is trouble – P.*

REE KEPT a tight grip on her wine, trying not to spill it as she laughed at Joanna's latest work stories. It wasn't every day you saw a patient with breathing problems because they read on the internet that peanut butter stuffed into their nose would help cure a sinus infection. In the middle of their discussion, Ree's phone vibrated, and she looked down. Usually, she left her phone in her purse when she was with her friends, but given the fact that it was also doubling as a distress beacon, she had it in her pocket.

"Everything okay?" asked Joanna.

Ree's eyes must have conveyed her discomfort as she read Parker's message, and she quickly improvised with the first thing that came to mind. "Yeah, it's just my sister. She's been having trouble at work."

"Aw, what's going on?"

"She's just dealing with a difficult personality at work, and we've been talking about how to approach it," Ree diverted. Everyone had a clash of personalities at one time or another, and she wouldn't have to remember the lie she told later.

"We can call her right now if you want. I haven't talked to her in ages!" Joanna offered excitedly. Ivan stood up from the table and Ree watched him leave. Had he heard Parker?

Ree's palms began to sweat. "I think she has plans tonight."

Joanna's face fell. "That's too bad. You'll have to tell her hello from us."

Ree leaned back in her chair to look down the hallway but saw no one. Had Ivan had gone into the kitchen or followed Parker? It had been less than two minutes since Parker sent her the message, which was not enough time to do whatever he was doing. She hadn't seen him bring in any equipment, but even poking around took more time than that. She quickly improvised, “Ivan! I think your wife could use some more wine. I need more funny stories!"

Joanna's glass was still half full, but it had the intended effect of Ivan popping his head out of the kitchen to shake his finger at them.

“And some for Ree, of course,” Joanna offered. She fought a smile. “You don't have to worry, you know.”

“About what?” Ree asked, her head still slightly tilted towards the hallway while trying not to make it obvious that she was looking for Parker.

“What else?” Joanna looked at Ree as if she should already know the answer.

Ree paused, searching her friend’s bemused expression until realization dawned. “Oh, Parker! Yeah, he’s great, right?” How much longer was that man going to take?

IN IVAN and Joanna's study, Parker snapped on a pair of gloves and looked towards the closed door. He didn’t hear anything that concerned him, but sound traveled both directions. He would need to be hyperaware of his surroundings and the noise of his own actions. It’d be tough to explain his way out of this one. There was a dark mahogany desk in the center of the room, clearly an antique. Sitting on top was a short stack of papers that caught his attention when he entered the study. He flipped through them, phone out, ready to snap pictures of anything incriminating, while hoping there was nothing to be found. It would devastate Ree if he confirmed her friends were criminals, but he'd seen stranger things in his time at the Bureau.

There were mostly bills in the small pile, some receipts from donations to local charities, and some journal articles, none of which yielded any conclusive answers. He gently pulled open the middle drawer but closed it quickly when it only held pens, pencils, and other office supplies. Given the state of Ivan’s desk at the lab, Joanna was clearly in charge of the office at home.

Parker glanced quickly at his phone to confirm he'd only been gone four minutes and pulled open one last drawer. Files filled the drawer, some in English, some not. He flipped through the folders and saw tax returns and some correspondence. He quickly snapped some photos of the letters in Russian but didn't see anything that piqued his interest. However, it was his job to get pictures, not to determine whether they contained anything that mattered.

One more look at the clock told him he'd been gone five minutes. He snapped his gloves off, stuffed them deep in his pocket so they wouldn't fall out, and sent a message to Ree to let her know he was coming back. Parker approached the door and listened for footsteps. Upon hearing nothing, he swung the door open quietly and walked across the hall to the bathroom, flushed the toilet, turned the water on and off, and then walked back to the table.

REE LOOKED DOWN at her buzzing phone. Parker was almost done. She forced a smile and shook her head. "I'm sorry. I'm being a terrible friend. Let me go put this in my purse." She walked slowly, trying to buy time. Ree placed her phone in her purse and discreetly wiped her sweaty palms on her pants. Why wasn't he back yet? Ivan joined them at the table with an open bottle of wine and put his arm around his wife. Out of the corner of her eye, she saw them exchange a look. Hopefully, they only thought she was losing her mind.

Ree returned to her seat and exhaled loudly. "I'm sorry about the phone. What were we talking about?"

"You are so adorable. Rest easy. We like him." Joanna gestured her head in the direction Parker had gone. "He's a much better choice than Brent. Ugh, but let's not talk about him. So, you blew me off earlier, but now that Parker is out of the room...it looks like things are serious?"

"That's none of our business, is it, dear?" Ivan gave Joanna a look that suggested they had discussed her prying – or something else – earlier. Parker returned to the table and placed his hand on Ree's shoulder.

"Did I miss anything?" Parker asked good-naturedly while Ree covered his hand with her own. His calm was a welcome oasis in a sea of nerves, fear, and confusion. He released her hand to rub her shoulders. "So, should we let these guys get some sleep? It's going to be an early day for us tomorrow." Parker smiled at Joanna and Ivan. "Ree and I are getting up early to hike, so we should get going. Thank you, guys, so much for inviting me over. It was great to meet you both."

Back in the car, after saying their goodbyes, Ree looked at Parker hopefully. "So?"

"Your friends are really fun, and they didn't try and kill us, which definitely counts as points in their favor."

"You know that's not what I am asking."

"I didn't see any red flags. Unfortunately, that was just step one. There were a lot of books and papers in Russian, which I don't speak. The FBI doesn't have enough evidence to do anything beyond what we just did. We already have our hands in too many pies, and I'm afraid restraint is the name of the game right now."

Ree growled under her breath but said nothing further. It had been a pleasant evening with her friends but had been overshadowed by the unfortunate reality of the situation at hand. And she would soon have to explain an eventual break up to the two people currently celebrating her happiness. But if she was still alive and they weren't trying to kill anyone, it would be a small price to pay.

THE FOLLOWING EVENING, Ree sat in front of a movie that neither of them cared about with Parker, recovering from their hike in a nearby state park that Parker insisted was for Ree's sanity. It had actually helped calm her nerves, but they were slowly ratcheting back up from the effort of sitting still. Ree turned to Parker and, without preamble, asked, "Why would the Russians need us?"

"What do you mean?"

"Ivan. The Russians. They don't need our help. They certainly don't need a small university lab to help with whatever it is that they are supposed to be planning. It looks like Ivan is up to something, but if you think about it, under the surface, it doesn't make much sense."

"What about a lone wolf, not a part of the official government?" Without a good counterargument, Ree harrumphed. "I was trying to give you a weekend off, but since I can't seem to find your off button, I can fill you in on the latest."

Ree flipped off the TV and turned to face Parker, who raised an eyebrow. "What if I wanted to watch that, Professor?"

"You weren't paying any more attention than I was, Agent. Don't hold back now. Need a whiteboard?" Ree gestured to the closet, but Parker shook his head.

"The analysts agree with you – it feels like an operation, but there isn't a good reason for a country to be behind this. We've asked Scarlett to spend a little more time on it, to look beyond the obvious suspects. Scarlett is Mikey's wife, you remember. She's been working with her team to build a better profile of our perp. So far, she's given us a list of adjectives to help us narrow down the list of suspects – calculated, deliberate, most likely a male, but we can't guarantee it. This guy thinks he's smarter than everyone around him. We have no intel that suggests he's selling the components. Scarlett thinks he's trying to pull off something big and he doesn't want to get his hands anywhere close to dirty."

Ree crossed her arms. "How do you figure?"

"Well, why build a missile when you could build a bomb? Missiles are a lot more complicated – they have to have a whole separate set of parts just to get them where they are going. Something close range, like a bomb, wouldn't require all the extra parts for guidance and course correction. The fact that he's going to all this effort to make a complex weapon means a simple one won't serve his purposes. We also believe it'll be a short-range weapon since you can't exactly build an intercontinental ballistic missile in your backyard without someone noticing."

"Fair point."

"And what type of personality will stay in the same place for at least a year to make it look like he wasn't involved? There are easier ways to make money and very few dealers will take that kind of risk. This perp is most likely motivated by something other than money."

"Someone who thinks he's smarter than everyone else and believes he's doing something important. Okay, I see what you're getting at. But where is he hiding everything? You can't exactly stash a missile in the lab without someone catching on. Even a small one."

"No, you can't, but you can stash the parts that are small and the hardest to come by."

Ree nodded. "Yeah. Normally, I'd ask Ivan about something like this."

"We'll just have to keep an eye out without him."

"Want me to poke around?"

"Yes, but carefully. Let me think about some rules you need to work under. I don't want you getting hurt."

Ree pulled a piece of chocolate from the drawer in her coffee table and offered one to Parker. "I can live with that. One last question before I try and shut my brain off so I can sleep. Who are they planning on aiming this thing at?"

"That's what we're trying to find out. We figure out who will be at the other end of this thing, we find our guy."

Ree finished her chocolate and walked upstairs, slowing her pace as she found herself once again thinking about the man sleeping on her couch. She wasn't intimidated by his mannerisms or stature, which seemed to both surprise and amuse him. She'd dropped bigger guys when sparring to get her black belts. And underneath his consummate professional exterior was a genuine concern for other people, including her. Parker's demeanor was steady and even-keeled. He was solid, a counterbalance to her bursts of energy. He had proved that he was on her side, even when he didn't know she was looking. She bit her lip. Despite her best efforts not to get attached, she was growing fond of him. She closed the bedroom door and tried not to make too much out of their interactions. She had a lot of work to do this week and didn't have the luxury to think much about it. Finally succumbing to exhaustion, she dropped into her bed and fell asleep.

18

Simon slammed his fist into the hard metal frame of his test machine and let the pain soak into his hand. He closed his eyes and rubbed his throbbing knuckles. The propulsion laboratory was empty, and no one was there to witness his rage. He needed the last shipment of components, and his part supplier couldn't get it to him for another three weeks. Three weeks.

He had precious little time remaining in what he was trying to treat as just another job. Without the controls for his thrusters, the only thing he could do, besides wait, was a detailed inspection of the parts he did have. The inspection would be critical since he couldn't put everything together until mere days before his plan would unfold. He couldn't afford to fail. No matter how many of the big bases he had covered, it was still the small things that complicated a mission. And thanks to the visit from The General's friend, he now had to look over his shoulder in enemy territory.

Worse, his efforts to get the fuel he needed to run preliminaries on the missile's small thrusters were being blocked by security rules. He had only a month left to finish his work here. Then he had to execute a successful mission without access to fuel or the secure labs to test his designs. His choices were to accept failure and disappear so that he didn't get killed by his fickle ally, or eke out success despite his current setbacks. Reaching into his pocket for his knife as a balm for his worries, he refocused his attention on his machine.

With only the humming of the computers as company in the otherwise empty lab, Simon unscrewed his equipment's side panels and checked his inventory. His existing circuitry neatly hooked into connectors that would never work but would look convincing to curious passersby. The fatigue test equipment also had some heavy metal components designed to look like they supported the structure of the equipment, but when properly disassembled, they became his control systems housing and rudimentary nose cones. They wouldn't be perfect, but they would do well enough on their short flight.

Since he was supposed to be testing rocket nozzles, the nozzles that would provide directional control had been easy to acquire. They were too small to power a missile or raise the suspicions of the U.S. government, but they were critical to making sure his weapon stayed on its intended path. The General would acquire missile bodies and fuel from a source bribing his way across some of the softer border crossings. However, the large components wouldn't be available to him until he was back home in Ghana.

The General had decided early that they would not put anything really nasty, like biologic or nuclear weapons, in the warhead that might point a curious investigator in their direction, and that eliminated a major complication. With enough mass in fuel, they could take out their target with less risk of the destruction pointing back to him. So many plans. So many obstacles. Simon rubbed his knife again and turned away from his machine, then back to it. He repeated this a few times, finding comfort in the rhythm, until he settled on a stool and focused his mind once again on the task at hand.

If he could outsmart one of the students to acquire fuel to test his thruster nozzles, he would have greater confidence his design would work. Then he would only need to run limited checks on the thrust control boards when they arrived...if the idiots who packed them could manage to ship them without breaking them. Simon stared at his machine until Josh Goodwin entered the lab. Simon had done his homework on his colleagues and knew that Josh was a graduate student who was just barely paying for school. He slid off the stool in front of his machine and moved silently until he was behind Josh.

"Good morning, Josh. Did you have a pleasant weekend?" Simon asked. Josh shrunk away, as if subconsciously aware of the other man's nature.

"Um, yes. You, Simon?"

"Yes, it was very pleasant. Can you help me with a problem I'm working on?" Engineers loved to show how smart they were.

"Sure, buddy, but I'm not sure how much I can help you."

"I just need a second opinion. I think I have all the parts I need for a research project I've been working on, but I can't get the fuel I need to test it. I don't want my work from the last year to blow up on the launchpad, in a manner of speaking. If I can't get fuel, I'd at least appreciate a second set of eyes on it under the microscope to look for defects."

Josh nodded and took the component to the microscope. Simon willed him to see that he could attach it to his fuel project for testing, but Josh didn't seem to get it. He studied the part for twenty minutes before handing it back.

"Machine lines barely visible without magnification, and no defects I can see. It's good quality stuff. Did you order it or do it yourself?"

"I ordered it. It takes considerable skill to get this right, and I don't have the experience. I just can't get any fuel to put through it. Your homeland security rules and all of that, even though our countries are allies. It has to go through Ivan, and he won't have time to get to it, even though I'm sure he'd approve the request. I need to wrap up my project, but I don't know how it will work without the fuel. I even have funding to buy it if someone has extra."

Josh stared blankly while Simon tried to project a quiet desperation. Josh had plenty of rocket fuel for his testing, but it took a background check to get it. Simon would just steal some from Josh, but it was stored in the secure area. "Good luck, man," Josh said. "Hey, I've got to get to my class before I'm too late. Let me know if there's anything I can do to help, okay?"

Once Josh left, Simon cursed and kicked a table. To rely on people who were barely adults was insulting. To not put the boy in checkmate after thirty minutes of opportunity to do so was inexcusable. He fingered the knife in his pocket to keep himself from doing anything rash.

REE DROPPED her purse in her desk drawer, but before she could lock it, the unmistakable motion of a student pacing in the lab next to her office caught her attention. She'd been working long enough to know the signs and symptoms of a student at the end of their rope. It would be best to give them some time to calm down before checking on the cause of their distress or sending in Matt or Ivan to help them out. The last thing she needed to do was to pop in and offer to help someone who barely knew her. She locked the drawer and kept one ear out for sounds of impending disaster.

Matt and Ivan arrived shortly after Ree. She pulled up her files for the day and began to read the journal articles Ivan had given to her to get her up to speed on what the lab was working on. Since she'd lately been focusing her attention on finding a potential killer/enemy agent/sociopath, she had almost forgotten about getting kicked out of her lab. Or, what did they call it, again? *Optimizing our resources to rectify the disconnect between funding and staffing*. Ugh. She wondered at who got paid to come up with that nonsense and then shifted her focus back to the journal articles.

Hours later, Ree's brain was completely fried. Matt waved both hands in an exaggerated gesture to get her attention. "Ree, you haven't moved from your chair in hours. I'm leaving for lunch in a minute – would you like to come?"

"Actually, that sounds great, but I was going to meet Alexis later today, so let me tell her that I'll be late. What'd you have in mind?" Alexis was due any minute, and she should be able to follow them. Ree was worried about appearing rude or indifferent if she turned Matt down one more time after he had been so nice to her. And she'd told Parker she would try and help with the investigation. Getting Alexis to shadow her while she talked to Matt was the perfect solution. They would be going to a public place if Ree had any say in the matter. It was a win-win, as the business professors would say.

"Just the café in the union, if that suits?" Matt asked.

"Sounds perfect. If you'll give me a second, I'll let Alexis know I'll be late." Ree's fingers shook slightly as she sent the message. Her phone buzzed almost immediately with an approving message from Alexis, and she smiled brightly. "I guess there's nothing to worry about, Matt. Alexis is in the student union already, so I'll just meet up with her when we leave."

"Perfect." Matt waited for Ree to gather up her things, and they walked in between the buildings, both ducking their heads into their jackets to protect their faces from the wind. It was just cold enough today to realize that fall was coming to an end, but not so cold as to need hats, gloves, and the other accoutrements of winter.

Ree's lunch was more entertaining than she had expected it to be. While Ivan had her fully up-to-speed on the technical side of the lab, Matt had a keen eye, a good sense of humor, and a gift for telling stories. Her sides burned from laughing as he told her about catching two students making out like teenagers in the lab. In the process of acting like nothing had happened, they had forgotten their actual experiment and created a small lab fire. It was put out before anyone but Matt was the wiser. He had let them off the hook with a long speech, and they had subsequently been some of the hardest working Ph.D. students he had ever had.

ALEXIS SIPPED at her water while discreetly watching Matt interact with Ree. More accurately, she was watching Matt from his eight o'clock so that he didn't notice she was there, but she could still see some of his facial expressions. Alexis was already certain he wasn't their guy. The team had just received word from Sandy that they were to stop investigating Matt *immediately*. Alexis didn't know Matt's full story, but they didn't get the cease and desist phone call very often, so he was either in witness protection or one of the good guys. Parker remained unconvinced that Matt was one of the good guys until he had hard evidence, which was typical. Parker was a good partner to have on your team despite, or perhaps because of, the fact that he was as stubborn as they came.

Studying Ree and her mysterious lunch companion, she fought a smile. Matt's laughter was infectious, and he was incapable of telling stories without his hands sweeping in large gestures as he talked. His initial background check showed Matt was former military, but the details of his service were classified. Alexis could see it in the way he carried himself. Matt's back was straight and his eyes constantly scanned his surroundings even when he was acting carefree. It was nice to see Ree laughing at his jokes. Things had been so serious that Alexis was getting worried about the strain on Ree. She shook her head as she received another text from Parker, who was in the van fussing about his asset. Worrying about every detail was practically in his job description, and she took a moment to let him know she had the situation under control.

"I could have absolutely killed him," Matt continued, telling a story about Ivan dropping one of his test parts. Alexis lifted her head from her phone at the turn of phrase. Ree froze, her smile disappearing from her face.

"Are you okay, Ree?" Matt put his hand on her arm.

Alexis saw Ree and Matt interacting in what seemed like slow motion and did the only thing she could. Across the room, but not so far away that she would cause a scene, she waved her arm and shouted, "Dr. Ryland!" Jogging over to their table, she continued, "You weren't answering your phone, and I was worried I wouldn't get in touch with you. Professor Knight just let me know that he could finally meet with me, and it's overlapping when we are supposed to meet. Are you okay if we just meet for fifteen minutes and then I go over to his office?" Alexis looked apologetically at Matt, who smiled good-naturedly in return.

"Sounds important, Dr. Ryland. No rest for the weary, but at least we got you to eat lunch today." Ree snapped out of her panic, blinking hard. She looked at her watch for the time, made her apologies to Matt, and left. Matt stayed at the table, rubbing his forehead for a few moments before shrugging his shoulders and finishing his lunch.

As he paid for his lunch at the registers at the end of the café, Simon wondered at the exchange that had unfolded in front of him. It was unusual, and he had been trained to notice anything out of the ordinary. Ree had been laughing with Dr. Brown, but if he didn't know any better, her lab assistant had just whisked her away through some sort of unspoken woman code. But who would be afraid of Matt? Unless she knew there was something going on in the lab and thought Matt was responsible? Impossible. He shook the thought from his head. Too much paranoia could paralyze a mission. That was how amateurs lost focus.

"You okay?" Alexis asked, keeping up with Ree as she beat a quick retreat back to the mechanical engineering building.

"I'm not sure. He was just kidding, but before that even registered, fear just hit me and I froze. I'm so sorry. I could have ruined everything. I'm so sorry." Ree's voice cracked slightly.

Alexis wasn't surprised by the intensity of Ree's remorse. Alexis worked with a lot of data-focused perfectionists who didn't handle failure well. Ree was the embodiment of a perfectionist whose carefully crafted exterior was starting to show wear and tear from the constant stress of the investigation.

"Ree, that's why we work on teams." Alexis's voice was low and soothing. "You let me know where you were in case you couldn't handle it."

"What if I can't handle it, Alexis? We're no closer than we were before, and I could have gotten both of us killed if Matt was so inclined."

"First of all, I don't think he wants to kill either of us. Second of all, you aren't Wonder Woman, and we don't expect you to be. Remember the part of this conversation where I told you that I was right there? I was there because you had the presence of mind to tell me where you were going, just in case something happened. I want you to go back to your office and just be Dr. Ryland today. Let us do our jobs while you try to take some mental time off. If you see anything funny, let us know, but don't go looking under rocks for missiles, okay?"

Alexis took a circuitous route back to the van where Mike and Parker were in the middle of some sort of absurd debate over spray cheese versus regular cheese, and after pausing a moment incredulously, she signaled a timeout to break up the conversation. "So, we need to write up a situation report." The men turned their attention to her and she explained what had happened. "I was pretty obvious. If Matt is involved in any way, I just gave him a pretty big clue that we know it."

"What happened? What are we doing about Ree? Is she in there with him alone?" Parker stood, checking his weapon.

"She shouldn't be. I checked Matt's schedule with our friends in IT, and he's busy this afternoon. We'll have to keep an eye on the hallway camera, though. We aren't hearing anything, and I'm worried when our guy finally moves, it's going to be big."

"You're sure it's not Matt?" Mike asked.

Alexis sighed. "Sandy told us to back off, and even if he's finding trouble as a protected witness, he doesn't fit the profile. Heck, I already like the guy."

"Really?" Mike responded in the tone spoken by big brothers everywhere.

Alexis slugged him. "Not like that, you perv."

"I could go talk to him for you," Parker goaded her. "If you need a wingman."

Mike held up two fingers. "You mean two wingmen."

"I'm perfectly capable of talking to a man without your help," Alexis shot back. Her cheeks warmed, and she went silent. The two men gave her knowing looks, and she waved a hand. "Okay, children, let's talk about Ree," Alexis said, her tone dripping with authority and disdain, despite the telling heat still lingering on her cheeks.

"We're going to have to divide and conquer. Do you think you can get the other students to talk to you?" Mike offered.

"I'll try. We can see if Ree can talk to a few that she already knows, but I just told her to take some time off. Parker, why don't you go in today to interview some students for your book? That'll give Ree a little bit more coverage without making her ask the questions. In the meantime, we need to make sure she is alone in the lab as little as possible. I've got a team doing some more work trying to figure out if anyone is shopping for rocket fuel. It'll help —" Alexis's explanation was cut short by her ringing phone. She looked down, annoyed by the interruption, but once she saw the number, she put the call through on speaker.

"Agent Thompson."

"Jordan, what's the latest?" Alexis asked. Jordan Sykes was the computer expert extraordinaire back in the Chicago office. He'd been supplying them with intel since she'd arrived. It was no small advantage to have someone with his ability to find buried information in the cobwebs of the internet working on the case, even remotely.

"Alex, we've got some new information. I picked up on some chatter about someone trying to buy missile bodies and rocket fuel off the Russians somewhere in the Middle East. Our people weren't able to do anything but eavesdrop, but it sure sounds like the pieces and parts our friend at the university is missing."

"Are you sure they're related? There isn't anyone in the lab from the Middle East."

"We don't know if the buyer is Middle Eastern – just that it's where the sale happened. Can't be sure if they're related, but it sure fits everything else we've found. Separating out the bits and pieces makes it harder to track. They alluded to another player they called The Scholar, which fits. Plus, what if they want America in the middle of all of this on purpose? Not everyone loves us, as you may recall from reading the news. Buying the missing parts in a country that doesn't exactly love us is a great red herring to pull us away from where the important stuff is happening."

"I wonder if that's why we can't find fuel or missile bodies here.

They're separating the lock and the key. Maybe this is where they got the idea to make it look like the Russians were involved on this side. But what are they missing?"

"Sounds like they bought everything but the brains and small pieces. They're missing guidance systems, thrust control systems, and small thrusters for directional control."

"Yeah, that definitely fits. Good catch, Jordan. Got any pictures for me?"

"In your inbox already."

"Thanks, Jordan. You're the best. Keep us posted, okay?"

"Of course. Any news from your end?"

"Nothing but a bunch of surveillance footage and some jittery nerves from our witness. We'll take all the intel we can get. We can't keep chasing a dead end like this, but I have a feeling the fire isn't out on our side, it's just banked."

"With all due respect, that's a lot of analogies in one explanation."

"Goodbye, Jordan." Alexis rolled her eyes. She was surrounded by a bunch of smart asses. She looked up from her phone at the team. "So you know that whole giving Ree a break thing? We may need her help, after all."

Parker had already pulled up the images and was zooming in on details.

"Got it memorized yet?" Alexis asked Parker. His face was inches from the computer screen.

"Nearly," Parker said absentmindedly. Parker had a near-photographic memory but printed off the picture, presumably to show Ree. He tapped his foot as he focused on the photo. Ten minutes later, Parker hopped out of the van, muttering that he wouldn't keep Ree in the dark any longer than he absolutely needed to.

19

Parker walked into the large, open lab space and recognized three students from the pictures attached to the profiles in the case file. There was Shayla, a Ph.D. student Ree was fond of. Josh, the grad student who appeared to be terrified of nearly everyone, was staring into a microscope. Simon, a graduate student who had fallen behind on his work despite his evident dedication to it, stood in front of his machine and tapped the end of a screwdriver into his palm.

Only one of the students currently in the lab fit the profile of the suspect. The two others that he'd matched to Scarlett's profile weren't present – Beckett, a British student who was likable but narcissistic and Nicky, an American student with a chip on her shoulder who wasn't really friendly to anyone. Of course, they didn't know if any one of the three was creating a weapon – it could be someone else doing a better job of hiding. However, given the presence of at least one strong suspect in the lab, some caution was warranted.

Parker winked at Ree when she turned away from helping Josh to look at the door. Ree greeted him with a huge smile, which was a bad sign. Generally, she was happiest to see him when she was legitimately upset. Given the importance of their cover, he crossed the room to give her a quick hug, running his hand lightly down her back as he pulled away. He had to appear affectionate but professional, as Ree would never allow a boyfriend to paw all over her at her workplace.

"Hey, hon. How is your afternoon going?" Parker asked.

"Good. I had lunch with another professor and now I'm just trying to learn what all the students are up to." She swept her hand towards her students and, in a louder voice, continued, "Although I have to be careful with this group. They may end up taking my job when they graduate. I'm looking at you, Shayla." Shayla looked up to beam at Ree before getting back to work on her project.

Parker handed Ree a large cup of coffee and pulled a small piece of her favorite dark chocolate out of his jacket pocket. She took the cup from his hand and her eyes softened when she spotted the chocolate. The distraction was short-lived as Ree's eyes darted to the file he'd brought in. He glanced at their audience and shook his head slightly.

"Since you're here, Parker, maybe we can ask if anyone is up for talking to you about your research. I mean, if you have time?" Ree looked at the file again.

"No better time than now," Parker replied. He really wanted to spend some quality time with Simon and the two other students who weren't present, but striking up a conversation with Simon the minute he walked in seemed especially unwise.

"Since your article is about women, Shayla would be a great resource if she's willing to talk to you…" Ree offered. Ree tipped her head towards Shayla, who was still focused on her work.

When Shayla heard her name, she turned to look at them, placed her hands on her hips, and asked, "Alright, you two. What are you planning over there?" Impeccably dressed with her trademark bright scarf and boots, she both looked and acted like a woman with confidence in spades.

Parker explained his idea, and Shayla was happy to oblige. Parker didn't have to pretend to be interested in her story and enjoyed taking notes while they talked. She had been encouraged by free-spirited parents to pursue whatever she wanted, and she decided to be an artist and an engineer. She'd been told by a well-meaning guidance counselor that those two professions didn't go hand in hand but refused to believe it. She loved to point people to her favorite professor at the university who had Ph.D.'s in mechanical engineering, art, and music. After their discussion, Parker summarized the handwritten notes he had taken so he could transfer them into an electronic document. Even with the ubiquity of technology, he still preferred to take interview notes by hand, since a laptop or tablet obstructed his surroundings.

While talking with Shayla, Parker noticed that Josh seemed preoccupied, unaware of the other students until he bumped into them while working. He was wearing jeans that were clean and unwrinkled but worn around the pockets and hems. He, at first glance, appeared to be less efficient than Simon, who had opened his machine and was drilling holes. However, after glancing over at Simon's workspace every few minutes, he saw less progress than he would have expected. That was certainly one explanation for why the other professors wanted Ree to deal with Simon. Telling someone they weren't working hard enough wasn't a job that anyone lined up for.

After Shayla returned to her work, Parker pulled out his laptop to transcribe his notes, carefully angling the well-hidden camera on the front to take in as much of the lab as possible. Though an excellent typist, he pecked at the keys slowly to buy time. He picked up his phone and sent a text message to Alexis to send a message to Ree so that it didn't look like they were communicating. Ten minutes later, Ree was leaning over his computer, asking to read his work and shooing him away so she could read it in peace. He wandered aimlessly around the lab and kept asking her every couple of minutes if she was done yet, as an impatient boyfriend might.

SIMON WATCHED Dr. Ryland's boyfriend pester her and rolled his eyes. Such simple problems these people faced. He would need to wrap up his tools and take a break if they were going to keep this up. Just as he was ready to give up and come back that evening to complete his true purpose, they decided to leave. Finally not under the watchful eye of the professor assigned to help him, he could inspect his components.

He was running out of time to make sure everything would be ready when he received his final shipment.

REE AND PARKER held hands all the way back to the surveillance van for the benefit of any onlookers, even though they hadn't seen anyone. Parker jumped into the driver's seat and Ree in the passenger's. The doors slammed shut, and Ree stated, "Well, that was a bust. And I thought I was getting the day off?"

"Yeah, sorry about that. But, I'm not sure it was a bust," Parker replied, driving a few blocks away so they could all sit in the back of the van to discuss at length. He parked the van, and Ree and Parker walked through the small door into the surveillance quarters.

Mike pulled up the feed from Parker's laptop and spoke after less than a minute of watching it at double speed. "That man is pretending to work."

"Wouldn't be the first time someone did that," Alexis added.

"Whoa, slow down guys. Who was pretending to what?" Ree asked.

Mike pointed to the screen. "Simon was acting like he was working when he wasn't. We think it's him, the British guy –"

"Beckett?" Ree offered.

"Yes," Parker said. "Or Nicky. She works odd hours in the secure lab. You haven't met her yet."

Ree studied the video. After a minute, she let out an uncertain breath. "Okay, so we've confirmed that Simon is a slacker. That's hardly news. His project isn't that hard, and with his smarts, it shouldn't be taking him that long."

Ree thought back to the times she'd been alone in the room with Simon. He had clearly resented her intrusion, but was he dangerous? Or just lazy? It wasn't the first time she'd worked with someone who didn't know they needed help. The team kicked around more ideas but didn't have enough evidence to make a conclusion either way. It was only 4 p.m., and without meaningful answers, they dropped Ree off at her house. The team had guessed correctly that Ree didn't have the stomach for more investigation that afternoon.

The following morning, Ree went into the office without any tasks from her FBI handlers, so she could focus her actual job. For the first day in what seemed like months instead of weeks, she could finally relax. Ree hummed while she calibrated some measurement equipment. She looked up from her task when she heard cheerful voices coming down the hallway. When she recognized the woman chatting with Matt as Alexis, her shoulders fell at the prospect of doing FBI work on her "day off," but her disappointment quickly turned to amusement.

Beckett walked away from his workstation and spread his arms wide at Alexis's entrance like they were old friends. "Alex! Another football match this afternoon at two on the quad if you're in." Beckett gave Alexis a high five and kicked the air to make his point.

"I'm not sure, Beckham – you schooled me yesterday night on the last goal, and I have some getting even to do. Sure you're up for the challenge?" Alexis placed her hands on her hips and raised an eyebrow.

"What are you two up to?" Ree asked.

Beckett hooked his arm around Alexis's neck. "Lex here challenged me to a game of football in the quad yesterday, and we had a good match, yeah?"

"Yeah, I think he just fakes the accent so the girls will swoon over him and the guys will think he's an engineering version of David Beckham. Good thing I know better." Alexis hip checked Beckett and used her free hand to poke him in the ribs.

"So, 2 o'clock, then?"

Alexis sighed as if humoring him was a huge chore. "Fine Becks, but beers are on you if I get a goal. Two beers if it's a nutmeg."

"What's that?" Ree asked.

Alexis shrugged. "When you kick the ball between your opponent's legs and score a goal. You know, a nutmeg."

Beckett clutched his heart as if wounded and basked in her attention. "Do you hear this girl? My ears hurt just listening to her foul mouth. For that, Lex, I'll have to take you to school today." With a wink, he turned back to his work.

Ree bit her lip to hide her surprise at the new personality Alexis had adopted. She had gone from Ree's focused student to the vivacious girl competing with a guy who clearly wanted to get to know her better. Impressive.

After Beckett left, Ree looked at Alexis, eyebrows raised. Alexis grinned, unwilling or unable to say more. If their narcissistic soccer player was guilty, he was toast. Alexis had him practically eating out of her hand. Mike had taught Ree how they looked for signs of someone using a cover identity, so if Beckett was faking his jock persona with any skill, it would take some time for Alexis to crack it. Somehow, Ree felt like Beckett was exactly as he seemed, but it was Alexis's job to prove it, not hers.

AFTER A SLOW MORNING of menial lab work, Alexis checked her watch. It was showtime. She grabbed her duffel bag and ran to the bathroom to change into athletic pants and a loose shirt. She figured Beckett for the type of guy that would "accidentally" run into her various girl parts, but the previous evening when she'd dropped in on their soccer match, he'd been entirely appropriate, which was a pleasant surprise. Scarlett had singled him out based on the narcissism and told her a few other red flags to watch for as she spent time with him. So far, he actually just seemed like a guy with a decent moral compass, a healthy ego, and a big mouth. Beckett thought she was coming out to play soccer and talk trash, but in reality, she was headed out to play a little mental chess. Good thing that was actually her favorite game. Flipping her head over to pull her hair into a ponytail, she checked the mirror to make sure she was put together, left the bathroom, and jogged out to the quad.

As she approached the field, Beckett was juggling the ball and cracking jokes with his buddies. When he spotted her, the soccer ball flew a little further and he juggled the ball more quickly, throwing in a few headers for good measure. He hadn't made a pass on her, but

Alexis got the feeling that if she told him she wanted to change teams away from the boyfriend she'd fabricated, he wouldn't try and convince her otherwise.

"Save it for the field, Becks," Alexis said as she jogged past him. She looked over her shoulder to catch him staring at her backside.

"If I intimidate you, you may concede anytime. I'll take that pint whenever you are ready to admit defeat." That was about all he had time to say until she darted in, stole the ball and passed it to another one of his friends across the quad. Then the game got started in earnest. It was a friendly game with plenty of trash talk, a lot of easy jogging between plays, and a few goals from both Alexis and Beckett.

Alexis's phone chirped a few times during the game. As they were wrapping up, she jabbed at it angrily until Beckett approached. "What do you say in England? My boyfriend is an arse. You still up for that pint?"

"Absolutely." Beckett dropped his arm around Alexis's neck, pulling her close as he recounted his heroics from the game.

Alexis broke contact to grab her bag from the sidelines but stayed close to Beckett until they reached the bar. She ducked into the bathroom to send a message to Parker and Mike. Reaching into her bag, she popped in her earpiece and went back to play her part. So far, this guy was fun to play soccer with, but he was otherwise boring her out of her mind.

An hour later, Beckett was still talking. And talking. Alexis spun a bottle cap on the bar, willing him to stop. Initially, the thrill of the chase kept her interested in his conversation, but as it became obvious that he wasn't their guy, the game began to grow old. She'd been ready to ask the questions Scarlett had given her, but Beckett's personality had rendered them unnecessary.

When he picked up some change for the waiter who dropped it, it was the last straw. Too polite and willing to help other people he didn't know. Despite his obvious desire to make a move on her, he had enough self-control not to push the issue. He didn't fit their profile at all. If those observations weren't reason enough, he simply didn't possess the attention span to be ruthless. She tapped her ear absently, and her phone beeped on cue. She made a fuss over typing a message to her boyfriend, dropped some money on the bar, and slugged Beckett on the shoulder.

"Thanks for the company while I cooled off. I'm going to go meet up with Jordan so we can work things out. He's an idiot, but I love him." Alexis grinned, knowing Jordan Sykes, her favorite analyst, would probably be reading a transcript later. It was a little game she played to keep herself on her toes and Jordan would pull some prank back. It really was the simple things in life.

"Congratulations," Mike said dryly, as Alexis got back in the surveillance van. "I don't think I could have stayed awake. When does that guy take a breath?"

Alexis laughed. "Don't think it's him?" she said sweetly.

"No," Mike replied, blinking hard. Alexis made a call to Jordan to provide an unofficial assessment on their subject. She'd fill out the paperwork later but wanted to keep him focused on their most promising leads. Ree stared at the van door, lost in thought.

After Alexis ended her call, Ree turned to Parker. "That was quicker than we thought. Is there anyone else we could maybe try to clear? Like Ivan and Joanna?"

PARKER WINCED. "The problem is, Ivan is in charge of all three of our suspects. We can't evaluate the likelihood of his knowledge until we know who or how many of them are behind this. Sorry, we just can't let your friends off the hook yet."

Ree's face fell. As a peace offering, he pulled out the file he'd intended to show Ree back at the lab. Ree studied the missile bodies and photos of typical control and guidance systems, running her finger along the details and asking questions until it was time for her and Alexis to go back to her house.

With Beckett off the list, the team of analysts back at the Bureau was getting more information on Simon and Nicky. Alexis hadn't had any luck getting close to Nicky Steadman. She had a prickly exterior and would barely acknowledge Alexis's presence in a few of her attempts to socialize with their suspect. As an authority figure in the lab, Nicky would at least be willing to talk to Ree. Despite Parker's discomfort with the plan, he'd agreed to let Ree approach Nicky the following day alone so that they didn't spook her.

As extra insurance, Parker asked Alexis to spend some time that evening coaching their newest team member on how to ask questions from a hostile party. They were way outside of a typical investigation, but Ree was holding it together so far and assured them she could handle it. Hopefully, she was right.

20

After weeks of arriving on campus later than usual, Ree went into the lab at sunrise, as was her preference. The FBI somehow knew Nicky would be there and felt there was a good chance she would be there alone. Ree was dreading meeting Nicky on a number of levels. Professionally, Nicky had a reputation as being tough to work with. Her attitude and defensiveness whenever someone offered to help her were both ever-present and counterproductive. In the context of trying to find the person in their midst who was willing to hurt other people, her personality traits transitioned from a professional annoyance to potentially dangerous.

Ree sighed, then pulled on her big girl pants and walked into the lab, hoping to see Nicky and get this over with. At first, she thought that Nicky wasn't there until she heard a loud pounding noise coming from a machine in the back of the lab.

Ree approached Nicky with her purse still hanging on her shoulder, taking slow steps to give her time to figure out if Nicky was as angry as the banging suggested. It was hard to gain respect as a new hire or student in any field. You could take one of two approaches – you could understand that this was reality and stick with it until you wore down your skeptics, or you could get bitter. She suspected Nicky took the latter. However, unlike Simon, Nicky seemed to be doing hard manual labor. Of course, she also could just be beating the crap out of a machine. Perhaps she was doing both. While Alexis and Mike had coached Ree on how to talk to a potential suspect, their advice on what to say was quickly forgotten as she focused on the other part of the interrogation they warned her about – making sure she wasn't backed into a corner. In addition to banging on the machine with the large wrench and hammer, Nicky threw in the occasional colorful nickname for the piece of equipment she was trying to fix or destroy. Between clangs, Ree cleared her throat to get Nicky's attention.

"Excuse me, Miss Steadman? Do you have a moment?"

Nicky sent her a withering look as she pulled up from the machine with the wrench in her hand, hooked her finger into her belt loop, and said, "Not right now."

Her anger hit Ree like a physical wall. Ree took one involuntary step back. Okay, Nicky wasn't going to make it easy for her. Normally, she would have let her cool off or intervened on her attitude problems, but given the circumstances, she would have to plod forward.

Ree stuck out her hand, and said brightly, "I'm Dr. Ryland. I'm new to the lab and have heard good things about you. I wanted to come to introduce myself." It was only a small fib. She had been told that Nicky was smart, it just was always followed by a "but".

"Nicky Steadman."

"What are you working on, Nicky?"

"Fixing the machine that the last grad student broke, since apparently, I'm the only adult in the lab. Look, it's nice to meet you, Dr. Ryland, but I work with Dr. Nobelkov, and I can't take on any more work right now."

"I completely understand. You seem to have a full plate." Ree thought it best to agree, since she was now experiencing the full Nicky up close, and the full Nicky was wielding a wrench and a hammer.

"What do you mean by that?"

"Just that you're busy, and I'm not here to add to your workload."

Nicky laughed. "Okay – if you say so."

Ree bit her tongue. "I just wanted to stop and introduce myself. I've been in your shoes and wanted to let you know that if you ever want to chat, I'm happy to do what I can to help."

"Been in my shoes? Okay." Her tone was hard, but Ree wondered if she didn't see Nicky soften a fraction. Ree turned her back and heard a quiet voice say, "Thanks, I guess."

Ree was almost to her office when she realized she was still alone with one of their suspects. She'd assumed one of the other professors or one of her bodyguards would be there by now. She kept her purse on her desk, just in case. She sent a quick text to Parker to let him know she was ok but still alone. Nothing in her manner should have spooked Nicky. In fact, her offer to help was actually legitimate, provided Nicky wasn't going to try and kill her.

"Dr. Ryland?" Ree turned around to see Nicky startlingly close.

Ree swallowed hard and took one step closer to her purse. "Yes, Nicky? Did you need something?"

"You know what, never mind."

"No. It's okay. Is something bothering you?"

"I didn't want to say anything to Dr. Nobelkov or Dr. Brown. I'm not sure they'd believe me. But since you're new and don't have any alliances or favorites, I overheard something and didn't know who would be willing to do anything about it."

Ree doubted Ivan and Matt would ignore a student's concerns just because they were difficult, but they were human after all. She had met people like Nicky before. They always had an excuse, assuming their problems were worse than everyone else's or that someone else was at fault. But, perhaps they were. She gestured for Nicky to sit. Instead, Nicky crossed her arms and began to pace in front of Ree's desk, focusing everywhere but on the professor in front of her.

"I overheard Simon talking to Josh, and it sounded like he wanted him to skirt the rules about getting rocket fuel without a background check. They didn't know I was in the office, and I'm sure I didn't hear everything. I talked to Josh alone about it after and made him promise he never would. I'd feel better if someone knew what Simon was trying to do. I mean, if he gets caught, it could shut us down, and I thought someone should know. I've worked too hard and this is all I have. I won't have another student keep me from graduating by thinking they're a special snowflake who doesn't have to follow the rules."

Ree forced her mouth to stay closed but her eyes widened before she caught herself. She blew out a breath. "Thanks, Nicky, I appreciate you telling me. I'm working with Simon, but don't know him that well yet. I won't approach him directly, and he won't know you are involved, but if anyone is trying to break the rules, it's my business and I will fix it. That's a promise."

Nicky's defenses were back up nearly immediately. Her eyes darted towards the hallway door before she retreated to the lab. Ree forced herself to sit down after Nicky resumed banging on the machine. She pulled out her phone to write another message to Parker, her heart pounding. Nicky's story was the break they were looking for – either she was lying and covering her tracks or Simon was their guy. Parker needed to know.

Simon walked through the office door and her pulse skyrocketed. She placed her phone back on her desk and stared blankly at her laptop. When Simon reached the lab, she picked it up again, but Ivan walked in. She eased the phone back on to her desk. It was too risky. Ree considered getting up from her desk and sprinting to the surveillance van, but even as an untrained civilian, she didn't have to be told it was a bad idea to make sudden moves after getting key information from a suspect. She needed to wait until Alexis arrived for the day, then pull her aside for a private conversation. Ree tapped her index finger on her desk and eyed her purse. She placed it in her desk drawer and for the first time in years, she didn't lock it.

CONFINED TO THE SURVEILLANCE VAN, Parker passed out coffee and muffins to his crew. An update from Ree kept everyone in relatively good spirits, but their energy was starting to flag. He'd set up a small table in the van with all of the evidence they had, pictures of the components they were looking for, and some blank paper for writing down notes and questions. They had a call with their analyst team later that morning, which gave Parker and the team two hours to sort out the questions they needed to ask. They needed to make some tangible progress in the investigation, and soon.

Alexis and Mike accepted the food and coffee silently, focused on the evidence in front of them. Alexis flipped rapidly through all of the visuals Parker had provided. Mike spent more time on each page than Alexis, and he was grouping them together according to his own system. Parker popped a piece of muffin into his mouth and gave them a few more moments to study the information before calling the meeting to order.

"Okay, folks, you ready? I'd like to do a rundown of what we have. Jump in if I miss anything important." Alexis and Mike looked up from their work, and Parker continued, "We have five suspects. Ivan Nobelkov – Russian native, well-liked, smart, forgetful, married to a physician. Doesn't fit the profile, and everything I found at his house was a dead end.

"Matt Brown – I know Sandy told us to back off but I'm not crossing him off the list until I know he's clean. What we've figured out is he's originally from Jersey, former military, and a methodical achiever. He's been successful enough to present at conferences at least once a year, holds a few patents and is ambitious enough to talk to his management about working up to an assistant dean position. He opened up to Ree right away. We can't prove that Dr. Nobelkov and Dr. Brown aren't involved, but they don't seem like our guys. We are confident that neither of them is in the driver's seat since our other agents and tech teams have been keeping an eye on them and have come up with nothing.

"Now for the interesting ones. Nicky Steadman – rude but ambitious, defensive but talented. Ree didn't report anything suspicious but we can't cross her off until we talk to Ree to be sure. She sends up some red flags.

"Beckett Parish – Alexis spent some time with him, and he seems to basically be a harmless tool. He's smart, but he's too lazy to be our guy. I think we can cross him off the list for now.

"Simon Kakra – he's quiet and generally keeps to himself. He gives the appearance of keeping his head down and working hard. He's been cordial but has resented any sort of intervention in his work. I don't want to jump to conclusions, but after observing him doing busy work first hand, I think it's fair to consider him our most likely suspect."

Based on the nodding from his team, they were all in agreement that the odds tilted towards Simon. However, narrowing down your suspect list was only half the battle, and they already thought they'd found her once.

Alexis placed her stack of paperwork back on the small table. "It sounds like we might be able to skip the 10 o'clock with the analyst team if they don't have any new information, but we do need a heavy-duty background check on Simon Kakra. Our initial check," Alexis's eyes darted down to her notes, "indicates he's from Ghana. Doesn't that seem a bit off to you guys? When has Ghana ever had a problem with us or us with them? We're friendly."

"You're assuming a country is behind this – your other alternatives are Russia, England, or New Jersey," Mike said dryly.

"England, obviously a no," Parker said. "This seems too small scale for Russia. They wouldn't need to come over to the States to get this stuff. Honestly, Ghana doesn't make any sense. They aren't exactly having biweekly flag burning parties over there."

"So, assuming our perp is Simon, what does that mean? I think we can assume it's not a nationally-sanctioned mission," Alexis said.

"But do we know that someone high up isn't behind it?" Parker asked.

"What, like someone trying to overthrow the U.S. government? No way. The only thing that would make sense is if they wanted to overthrow their own," Alexis responded, throwing her hands in the air.

Mike stared at the profile his wife had created. He said quietly, "It fits. But it's wildly speculative. We can't go to the Chief with that without evidence to back it up."

Parker said, "Okay. We keep that theory to ourselves for now. Let's have the team dig into Simon, and unless Ree discovered a bigger problem with Nicky, we'll plan on moving in on him tomorrow to see if we can get enough information to make an arrest."

Alexis called Jordan to explain the situation, minus the only theory they'd come up with. They didn't have all the facts, and their team had a good reputation – one that could be spoiled by drawing sweeping conclusions based on insufficient evidence. Jordan promised to get back to them before the day was out.

A FEW MOMENTS after 10 a.m., Simon received the message that his parts would come in early. He would have everything he needed the day after tomorrow with a few days to spare. Apparently, his allies had pulled some strings. The General would help him orchestrate the shipment of his equipment the following week. It would all be over soon.

The only remaining piece of his plan was to convince Dr. Nobelkov to let him accompany his equipment to Ghana. He would use this self-created opportunity to make something of himself in the new government. Sure, there would be a necessary casualty, or several, but it had to be this way. Their plan would never work if President Minkah was still in the way. Simon's conscience had long been silent and was therefore not a hindrance. The only thing that mattered is Minkah stood between Simon and the power that he deserved.

AN OCEAN AWAY, The General sat in front of President Joseph Minkah's desk and steepled his fingers, pretending to listen to his ideas for his next piece of legislation. President Minkah was not a stupid man, unfortunately, and former General Korku Acare couldn't risk him picking someone else to share his seat of power at the next election. He had long considered himself a man of action and had planned for such an occasion. Soon, all of this distasteful subservience would be a distant memory.

As Joseph Minkah droned on about policy matters, General Acare reviewed his plan one last time. He had been trained by the best and learned caution the hard way. In addition to his agent in America, two additional agents were working for him a little closer to home. These agents had been trained to take orders from him alone. The young ones were easily manipulated, and he had a gift for telling each one the right story to keep them motivated.

Akua, an especially skilled sniper, was told her work was for a top-secret government mission and that only he had clearance to discuss it with her. She had no reason to go over his head to verify his story. The other agent wasn't needed yet, but he would think of a convincing lie that would suit his purpose. His security officer was enforcing orders and keeping an eye on Simon when The General could not, but he knew nothing of The General's plans. Given his position in the government, obedience to his orders was not in question.

Simon was more difficult, but he had always been a little unstable, that one. Still, The General had no doubts about his loyalty. Simon's parents died when he was a teenager, and he joined the military soon after. The General knew that, with no surviving family, the boy could be very useful to him and had taken him under his tutelage. He mentored the boy and waited. It wasn't until several years into their camaraderie that he began to suggest Simon's orphaning had been at the hands of President Minkah. The fact that sometimes cars went off of roads in the dark of night to avoid animals was less compelling than his lie to a son searching for answers. After that, Simon had been very easy to mold into an intelligence agent that listened only to him. Yes, Simon would be very useful. Perhaps, he would die or get arrested, but in war, casualties were expected.

JOSEPH MINKAH WATCHED every small motion of the man in front of him. While Korku Acare preferred to be called "The General" to "Vice President," a nod to his time in the military, privately, Joseph called him a snake. His party had insisted on him partnering with someone with more rigid views that fit the party line, and it wasn't until he was in office that he realized the danger his next in line represented. In darker times, President Minkah would have feared for his life. In the current day, he tried his best to humor his colleague and wait for time to pass. He would implement the least dangerous of his ideas to keep The General from causing trouble and counted the days until the next election. Soon, he would announce a new running mate. If General Acare knew about it, it would only be from guessing, as the only person Joseph had told about his plans was his head of security and long-time friend, whose loyalties lay only with him. One could never be too careful in his position.

21

Ree looked up from her computer as Simon entered her shared office from the lab, hefting a bag over his shoulder. Alexis had mercifully arrived in the morning and stayed for several hours. However, when Ree pulled her aside and whispered Simon's name, Alexis shook her head to stop Ree from saying more. Somehow, Alexis knew something was off with Simon. That wasn't safe to talk about in public. And now he was coming into her office. Ree forced her trembling hands steady by placing them on her keyboard. It was impossible to be unaware of his entrance, but Ree was at least able to keep her eyes focused on her computer as Simon approached Ivan's desk.

"Excuse me, Dr. Nobelkov?" Ivan held up a finger and finished typing. She trained her eyes on her screen but still saw some movement in the periphery. Simon absently rubbed his right pocket as he waited.

"I'm sorry, young man, I'm answering an email from an eager donor. These are emails I am always happy to receive, but I find them so hard to finish unless I type it in one try. May I help you?"

Simon did his best to look nervous and apprehensive, even though his adrenaline was soaring. He felt victorious, filled with the satisfaction that only besting his opponents could provide. He forced his eyes to the floor and made his confession sound as genuine as possible. "It's my equipment, sir. It's just that I have not yet finished, and I know I can complete it. But, I just received word that my grandmother is very ill and needs me to go back home to Ghana to take care of her."

Simon looked up from the floor into Ivan's understanding eyes. "I am so sorry. I lost my grandmother just last year. You must go to be with her. Your equipment and this lab will all wait until you get back."

The conversation was not going in the direction that Simon expected, and he quickly amended, "I don't know how long she will need me, and I don't have employment back in my country. Since we are sending equipment as a part of the donation to the University of Accra, I was wondering if we could transfer both my machine and me to the university. I can finish it there and help my grandmother at the same time."

Ivan's eyes darted back to his computer screen. Simon was happy to see that Ivan was putting together the email their accomplice had sent with Simon's request to move back to his home country. While not a trained agent, the donor was friendly with The General and easily led. He'd been considering making a donation to an American university to both improve his image and for tax purposes. It wasn't difficult to persuade him to donate when and how they had wanted him to, believing their fabricated story about why the funds were needed. While not a large amount for the university, it was a large amount for the lab, and answering the donor's emails would be at the top of Ivan's priorities.

"Your timing is better than you realize, Mr. Kakra. We just had a request come in for someone to stay at the university for a year to help with the transfer. They are having an open house soon. I know things are moving fast, but if you are willing to pack up that quickly, it would really help me. I thought to ask you but didn't want to pressure you to leave here just because it is your home country, especially if you wanted to stay in the United States a little longer."

"Yes, I am willing. That would be just right. Thank you for the opportunity, Professor Nobelkov. I am more grateful than you know."

. . .

REE FOUGHT to keep her jaw from going slack. It was impossible that this was a coincidence – but what did his machine have to do with anything? Or was he just getting out of here before the whole place was going to blow? Simon was still lingering in front of Ivan's desk, less than ten feet away, and she didn't dare contact the team. Alexis was in the lab next door and out of earshot. Even after he was gone, the tension stayed at the back of her neck. When Alexis passed by her desk to leave, she dropped off a notebook from her tasks for the day and Ree opened it to see what she had done during her time in the lab. A small sticky note was in the front of the notebook. *We'll talk tonight at your house. We're watching the hallways but all suspects have left the building.*

The minutes passed slowly as she waited for the end of the day and safety in numbers. Matt stopped by to regale her with more stories as she nodded and muttered responses with feigned interest. Once she realized that accomplishing anything else productive would be impossible, Ree pretended to work while listening for any more information from the conversations happening between the remaining students in the lab. Particularly now that what she had previously believed was a case of overactive imagination had morphed into a very tangible enemy.

REE HAD JUST LEFT the office to meet the team in the van when Matt offered to walk her to her car or home since it was getting darker out as the days grew shorter. Ree, unable to find a way to decline without admitting she was working with the FBI and they wanted her to be careful, accepted Matt's offer. She didn't sense any nefarious motive from him, and the team seemed disinterested in pursuing him as a suspect when she'd asked. Perhaps his desire to be a gentleman had been hyper-developed for some reason. There were worse qualities to have in a friend. In case she was wrong, Ree made it a point to pass the surveillance van on her way home.

. . .

EXPECTING to see Ree at any moment, Parker looked out the window of the van and saw her walk by with a tall man at her side. He could spot Matt Brown from a mile away. While his laptop bag, polo, and khakis blended in with other engineering professors, Parker's trained eye saw a quiet strength in his mannerisms and build that didn't quite fit in on campus. Parker waited until they turned the corner and then sprinted down a side street to keep them in view. Even if Parker wasn't allowed to consider Matt a suspect, Ree shouldn't be alone with him until this case was solved.

NOT FAR FROM HER HOUSE, Ree spotted Parker carrying a messenger bag and approaching at a casual pace from the opposite direction. He reached them and leaned over to give Ree a quick kiss on the cheek. "Hey, babe. How was your day? Oh, hey, Matt. Thanks for walking Ree home."

"No problem. I get to work with her every day, so I thought it would be a nice way to return the favor," Matt said, his smile amused rather than annoyed.

Ree narrowed her eyes at both of the men standing in front of her. Ree was usually the last to notice any wordless messages expressed in her presence, but she was pretty certain by their postures and the tone of their exchange that things wouldn't be too different if they were two dogs and she was a fire hydrant.

Ree turned to Matt. "Thank you, Matt. I appreciate the company." Turning towards Parker and shooting her eye lasers, she said, "Come inside, *dear.*"

Parker followed Ree inside. She shut the door behind him before placing her hands on her hips. "Seriously, Parker. You need to tone it down. He's a nice guy."

"Yes, he probably is. Or he's helping one of his students commit murder. I happen to agree with your nice guy assessment, but I'm not willing to risk your life on probably."

Ree wrinkled her nose at him. "Can't you just let me have a good mad once in a while?"

Parker grinned. "Don't want you getting bored. But hey, peace offering – I think we know who our bad guy is."

"Well, hopefully, it's not Simon, since I've been in the lab alone with him." Ree shivered and looked towards Parker hopefully. Her imagination had been running unchecked for the last several hours, and it would be reassuring to find out she was blowing the danger out of proportion.

"Yeah, I hope you were nice to him because the odds are 10:1 that he's not on the same page you are about preserving human life."

"I guess I better fill you in on what happened today. I think it might actually help."

Parker's interest fully piqued, he gestured to Ree's living room, where they both sat on the couch. Her front door opened, and Mike and Alexis filed in, locking the door behind them.

Alexis was talking into her phone and looked apologetically to Parker and Mike. Mike rolled his neck to crack it, tapping his foot impatiently, as if listening to one half of a conversation was pure torture. Alexis accommodated his annoyance by shooting him an exasperated look.

"Yes, thank you, Jordan. I appreciate your work. We'll keep you up to date." Alexis ended the conversation and sat on the loveseat across from Parker and Ree, next to Mike. Ree had retrieved some water bottles from the kitchen, and she tossed one to Alexis.

Ree opened her own water bottle. "Please tell me you guys figured this out today, and you are arresting someone tomorrow. The suspense is killing me."

Alexis rubbed the back of her neck. "We just went from about 50 percent sure to about 90 percent sure in the last five minutes, but unfortunately, the stakes just got raised. We're piecing together the evidence, and this smells like an operation with high-level backing. We've got a big problem here, guys. We can't arrest him."

"Wait. You can't arrest him? So, we just quit? That's it?" Ree asked.

"No," Mike and Parker said at the same time, but then said nothing else. Mike focused on a spot on the ceiling with a disgusted look on his face, and Parker clenched his fists, mouth pressed together.

After a long silence, Parker unclenched his fists and said, "We just have to be more discreet."

Ree jumped up from the couch and started to pace. "How could we possibly be more discreet? I've spent the last several weeks making new friends, avoiding the old ones, not talking to my family in the event I give something away, and overanalyzing every action of every human being I talk to. I fail to understand how we could possibly be more discreet. Obvious, yes. Devious, yes. Discreet, no." Ree paused. "Give me a minute."

Ree walked to the kitchen to get something stronger than water for the rest of their conversation. She had leftover wine and a clean wineglass. It wouldn't solve her problem but would calm her nerves, at least for the next ten minutes. And she was going to need chocolate. There was a large bar of extra dark stashed next to the wine glasses for emergencies, and this definitely qualified.

"Told you she'd be pissed," Alexis said to Mike as soon as Ree was out of earshot. He pulled five dollars out of his wallet and handed it over.

"Seriously, guys?" Parker said, shaking his head. "If she catches you, it's only going to make it worse."

"What's going to get worse?" Ree mumbled from the doorway, holding one hand over her mouthful of chocolate while the other held her wine glass.

"We were going to do an investigation into Simon after hours and wanted to keep you out of it," Alexis offered.

Ree took the bait and swallowed a large sip of wine to wash down her stress chocolate. She sputtered and caught her breath before squeaking out, "I don't know if you need to. This afternoon, Simon told Ivan his grandmother was sick, and he wanted to go back to Ghana. He asked to take his machine with him. Then, Ivan said they needed someone over there within the next month due to a request from an outside donor. It can't be coincidence. Oh, and he was trying to get one of the undergrads to give him rocket fuel on the side, which is not only odd, but also raised some flags with another student I talked to."

"Is it possible that someone could hide these components by making them look like something else?" Parker asked Ree.

"You could do any number of things, Parker. If you're talking about a control system, what is that but a bunch of electronics and some sort of power supply? What if his test equipment is the key to this whole operation? Doesn't it make sense that Simon doesn't have a working machine if it's designed to do something altogether opposite of what he's saying it can? Or, if you weren't even trying to be clever about it, you could build a false bottom and store everything in there. Test equipment can get pretty big." Ree slowed her pacing to take another sip of wine. "And wouldn't that be the perfect explanation as to why the guy has been so unproductive? I would think that if you are distracted, trying to build a missile from the ground up, you wouldn't have a lot of extra time to do your actual job. And, if your boss isn't happy with the work you have been doing, when you ask to leave, they're happy to see you go. Sounds like a rock-solid plan to me."

"What about this outside donor?" Mike asked. "Do you think he's an accomplice?"

Alexis shook her head. "Doubtful. We looked into the guy's emails. He sent a transfer of money after he received a request from an old friend to fund a grant to the lab. Everything else about him seems clean. We'll check it, but he looks like a pawn."

"So, what do we do?" Ree asked.

"The only thing we can do. We need to go talk to Simon and find out what we can without tipping him off or backing him into a corner. Then we need to have a meeting with the Chief and figure out how to stop him without ruining relationships with any of our key allies," Parker said.

"Oh. Well, that sounds simple." Ree said, and took another long drink of her wine.

"All in a day's work." Mike tipped his water towards her in salute while Ree broke off another chunk of dark chocolate.

"Says the guy who sits in the van," Alexis muttered.

"Says the guy who saves your bacon if you get in trouble," Mike corrected.

"One more thing," Alexis said. "I don't know if it's relevant, but Jordan was able to dig into Simon's history. It looks like his parents were killed in a car crash when he was still a teenager, and he joined the military shortly thereafter. Jordan is trying to find out if he has more family or contacts in the area that might help us understand his motive or target. I'll tell him to keep an eye out for a sick grandmother."

"So we'll find out if he's on a mission or just a special kind of crazy?" Mike asked.

Alexis rolled her eyes. "Who says he can't be both? But, yeah, that's what we're hoping."

Before they ended their meeting, the team worked out the details of how they would approach their latest suspect. Parker and Ree would find out what they could from talking with Simon the following day. If they didn't find anything at that time, they would have to take the risk of sending in a search team to Simon's house. The FBI didn't know the extent of the team Simon had in place, and adding more FBI agents to the mix was a big hammer to bring down without tipping anyone off.

As they stood to leave, Parker made a game-time decision. "Hey, Alexis, you mind if I take the watch tonight? I'd like to make some plans with Ree about how we're going to approach Simon tomorrow."

"No problem, boss. As long as you order Mike to stop watching so much football. I got enough exposure to that growing up with three brothers." Alexis rolled her eyes. "I even *like* football, but a girl can only take so much. Replays from earlier championships cross the line."

Parker eyed them both and said in his best parental tone, "You kids play nice and share the remote."

Out of the corner of his eye, Parker saw Ree laughing. Maybe tonight wasn't going to be so difficult after all.

REE RUBBED her forehead and put away the remaining half of her chocolate bar before she went too far. She could barely taste it past the stress anyway. Even the wine didn't touch her nerves, it just made her tired. As Alexis and Mike put their jackets on to leave, Ree's anxiety took a turn to disappointment – after this was all over, she'd probably never hear from them again. When Alexis was hired into Ree's lab, she used a different last name than what she'd heard the analyst, Jordan whoever it was, use for her. Mike had never offered up his last name. When Parker introduced himself as Parker Landon, there was a slight pause between his first and last names the first few times she'd heard him give it. He too was probably using an alias.

Parker ordered a pizza, and Ree's mind returned to the problem of the evening. In the several hours before seeing her FBI friends, she had soothed her troubled mind by convincing herself all they needed to do was find the bad guy. Now Parker wanted to "talk" and "strategize," and Ree really just wanted to throw her head down on to her pillow and sleep off this strange dream. However, much like when she was cleaning the gunk and oil out of the lab equipment, she would just keep chipping away at the problem. She would have her nervous breakdown when her schedule allowed for it.

Parker at least made an attempt at small talk while they waited for the pizza. Despite their inevitable breakup, her curious mind would not behave itself. Staring down into her empty wine glass, Ree began to fidget. When Parker raised his eyebrows, she finally asked, "So, what is your real last name?"

Parker smiled. "You, Dr. Ryland, are the first person to ever ask me that."

"You didn't answer the question."

Parker shifted in his seat. "You are correct."

"That Landon isn't your last name?"

"That I didn't answer the question." Parker winked.

"I think I've earned a little trust at this point."

"Alright – that'll teach me for trying to pull one over on an academic. You're correct – Landon is not my last name."

"Do I get to know?"

"IF I CLEAR it with my boss, yes." Parker wasn't sure why Ree was so stuck on the question, but he chalked it up to her wanting to avoid the issue at hand. The doorbell rang, Parker paid for the pizza in cash and returned to the living room. Parker was pulling a gooey slice out of the box onto a paper plate and paused when the outspoken professor asked softly, "When this is all over, will I get to see you guys again?"

"That depends on you, Ree." Parker talked out of turn. He hadn't voiced his thoughts to Sandy yet, but he wanted to bring her all the way in and keep her as a part-time consultant. Sure, she'd been freaked out, but considering the circumstances, she'd held up. That said something about her. The leader in him had automatically started to recruit her. She'd be a real asset if they needed her skills on future investigations.

"How is that?" Ree asked.

Parker handed her a plate of pizza and sat down beside her. "Look, I have to clear it with the Chief, but if you're willing to work with us on a part-time basis, we can still stay in touch. Given the nature of this case, we've already taken care of nearly everything we would normally do to get your security clearance in order. Otherwise, truthfully, it's going to be difficult. We don't even tell our families what we're doing when we work undercover, so I'm afraid it's not an easy answer. Understand, we don't usually get so close to civilians on an investigation. This has been an exceptional situation, and I'm sorry if you're disappointed that you won't be able to point your eye lasers at me on some sort of regular basis." Parker nudged her with his shoulder. Sure, he had grown fond of the professor and wasn't happy about not getting to see her again either. Still, he'd learned over time that his erratic schedule made it hard to have friends outside of the Bureau.

Ree's lips quirked. "Yeah, not being able to shoot you with my eye lasers or threaten to drop you is really going to cramp my style. But Parker, either way, no matter how this works out – "

"Yeah?"

"Thanks for caring enough to keep me alive."

Parker cleared his throat and shifted in his seat. "Don't thank me yet, Ree. We may be 90 percent of the way there, but it's the last 10 percent that's the real doozy. Speaking of which, can we talk about a certain graduate student we have to approach tomorrow?"

REE SIGHED and looked into her empty wine glass. The full glass of wine had relaxed her at last, but just in case, she retrieved the last half of her chocolate bar. When she returned, she sat cross-legged on the couch facing Parker, and asked, "What do we need to do to catch him?"

Parker outlined his primary plan along with a few contingency plans. Given the high probability that Simon would go off the deep end if he realized he was caught, the FBI had mapped out every detail of the interaction. They would time their questions when the crowd in the lab was smallest, in case of collateral damage, a phrase that caused Ree's eyebrows to shoot up in the middle of Parker's explanation.

Parker soldiered on, Ree ran out of chocolate, and somehow, they made it through all of the intel, planning, and follow-up questions in a little under an hour. When the discussion turned to what could go wrong, Ree found herself turning and getting tucked under Parker's arm as she leaned her head on his chest. If she was going to die tomorrow, and she couldn't have the dignity of companionship with her friends and family, she'd take advantage of the support of her FBI handler, or whatever he was.

To be fair, Parker's job description probably didn't usually include cuddling with his coworkers, but he didn't seem to mind. In the midst of asking more questions about backup plans, Ree started yawning and her limbs got heavy. She would move in just a minute.

. . .

Parker looked down at Ree. She had fallen asleep mid-sentence. Only this woman could fall asleep talking. She needed rest, and he left his arm wrapped snugly around her. It wasn't any hardship for him to stay where he was. Weeks of sleeping on her couch and years of irregular sleeping quarters had made him flexible, and he hadn't really been this comfortable in a long time. He'd send her off to bed shortly.

22

The following morning, Ree woke up more content than she'd felt in years...until she realized there was a weight resting on her stomach. It was heavy and hot. Pieces of the night before fell into place in her head, and a quick glance behind her confirmed her memory. She and Parker had fallen asleep in the middle of their discussion, and things were about to get a little awkward.

Parker stirred, and Ree's heart jumped into her throat, ready to make an apology. She felt his arm tighten, and her eyes went wide as he adjusted in his sleep to hold her closer. Awake now, the seconds ticked by as she waited for him to wake up enough so she could make her escape and pretend it never happened. How embarrassing.

While Ree was ready to admit to herself that she had feelings for Parker, he didn't need to know that, and it was absolutely the wrong time to be thinking about it. Her awake body had clearly been on its best behavior and had done an excellent job keeping her feelings at bay. Apparently, asleep Ree lacked awake Ree's self-control, especially when Parker was probably just trying to be polite. She felt his hold loosen slightly and slipped out from underneath his arm, tiptoeing out of her own living room and into the kitchen. Hopefully, he would be as unaware as she had been, and they could return to normal.

. . .

PARKER WOKE up as Ree crept across the living room, the boards in her turn-of-the-century house creaking slightly in the spot they always did, but Ree didn't seem to hear. He could swear her cheeks were red, and his stomach was still warm where she had been pressed into him the previous night. He was certain there was a brief moment where he was coherent enough to decide that falling asleep was a bad idea, but apparently, his judgment had been on hiatus shortly thereafter. Based on her movements, it looked like Ree was going to act like it had never happened. That worked for him, he thought, as he ran a hand through his hair. He shouldn't have allowed it to happen, but he couldn't quite work up to feeling sorry that it did. He stood and stretched, making more noise than usual as he walked to the shower, buying time for both of them. He passed the kitchen and tried not to glance at the remarkable woman he was absolutely not dating and had no right to think about. He had already caused enough problems in her life.

REE JERKED the coffeepot back into position when water splashed over the edge of the coffee maker. It joined a small pile of coffee grounds on her kitchen counter and wreaked havoc on her efforts to act as if nothing was bothering her. A critical element of their plan for the day was to act normal. Ree had been assigned one simple task, and she should be able to handle it. There wasn't room for anything else to cloud her focus. She just needed to find a way to get Simon to show her the inside of his test equipment. They just fell asleep. So what? Falling asleep in the same place was hardly a crime.

Ree ran a paper towel over the counter to clean up the mess and tapped her foot while her coffee brewed. Mercifully, it beeped right after she pulled her largest mug out of the cabinet. The man she'd been inadvertently snuggling mere minutes earlier scratched his neck as he entered her kitchen, somehow making jeans and a t-shirt look good. She looked past him and asked if he wanted a cup of coffee. Since she'd snuck away while he was still asleep, Ree had nothing to worry about, and they could stay on an even keel.

Parker accepted the cup of coffee and looked at his watch. "Thanks. We need to leave in fifteen minutes."

Ree took a long pull of her coffee before darting upstairs to get ready. In the urgency of the moment, the awkwardness was forgotten. Parker would join her in the lab to shadow Ree for his book, pretending to do research and talking with her students. Having him close was reassuring, but Ree still had to face Simon alone to prevent spooking him.

Before they left the house, Parker checked his gun, knife, and phone methodically. Ree dropped her gun into the pocket on her purse and met Parker's eyes. She preemptively argued, "Not a word, Parker. I'm not going in without something."

"Normally, I'd argue just to drive you nuts, but in this case, Doc, you probably should bring it with you. Keep the trigger lock on it, but unlock it once you get to campus and leave it in your drawer. Relax your shoulders, deep breaths through your nose, and remember, he has no reason to suspect you are anything but what you appear to be." Parker pulled a university lapel pin out of his pocket and helped her place it on her shirt. "This will record everything you see."

Ree raised her eyebrows. "I thought Mike said it was too risky for me to record inside the lab."

"It is risky. But it'll be for a short period of time and I'll be there with you the whole time. Just like when I used my laptop camera. You still ok with this?"

Ree nodded, her throat suddenly tight. She grabbed her keys from the bowl near the door and locked the door behind them before they began their walk to campus. Once they crossed the road that separated the residential area from the university buildings, Ree felt a shiver creep up her neck. Parker said quietly, "Three o'clock. Don't turn your head. Look with your peripheral vision."

Simon was walking towards them, his mouth set in a determined line. Parker put his arm around Ree and slowly pulled her into his side.

Ree was able to keep her cool until she reached the door of the mechanical engineering building. Still rattled after this morning's encounter and Simon's proximity, she missed the door handle as she tried to discreetly look behind her. Instead of meeting the hard metal of the door, her hand whizzed through the air. She heard a light chuckle. She was tempted to stop and shoot her eye lasers at Parker, but that could mean making eye contact with Simon. She wasn't quite ready for that yet. Maturity barely intact, she got a firm grip on the door and led the way into the building, followed by an FBI agent and a man gathering components to blow things up for reasons none of them could fully explain. Friendly greetings were exchanged as Ree held the door open, and a small headache formed at her temples.

SIMON ENTERED the building behind Dr. Ryland and her new boyfriend. Her cheeks were red with embarrassment and she babbled to him on the way in. He would have to come up with excuses to keep the inquisitive professor away from his work. This was not a task to underestimate, since she was forever asking her students about the minute details of their research.

He would have his machine packed this weekend, ahead of schedule. After the last order, he didn't want to take chances and had his supplier ship the remaining circuit boards to an address near his home whose occupants were vacationing in Florida for a month. Simon had the final circuit boards in his laptop bag and would install them today. He reflected on his plan and reminded himself of the near impossibility of being caught as he rubbed the back of his knife. Only an expert could tell by looking at his equipment that it wouldn't work, and even then, they couldn't prove his intent.

"Excuse me, Simon?"

Simon startled and tightened his grip around his knife before turning towards the smiling face of Dr. Ryland.

PARKER SAT across the room from Ree and their suspect, legs spread wide while he typed on his computer with his back to a wall. His gun safety was released and his laptop showed the feed from Ree's lapel pin. Matt was working on the other side of the door that separated the lab from the offices. Nicky was inside the locked door of the secure area and out of sight. To an outsider, Parker looked completely relaxed, although he had just tensed his muscles and was ready to act if necessary. If they'd guessed wrong and more than one person was involved, they were even or outnumbered, but they weren't cornered.

Alexis was on her way to the lab, but per their plan, would not arrive for a few more minutes. Parker could have his gun out and a shot fired in an instant if whatever was in Simon's pocket was a threat. If he had to guess by the size, he would say it was a knife. Despite Parker's hyper-awareness, to an outsider, all interactions appeared normal and not as if a carefully choreographed dance was happening between himself, Ree, and their suspect.

"YES, PROFESSOR RYLAND?" Simon asked, his voice even. His annoyance at her interruption might not have been noticeable if she hadn't been looking for it.

"I was hoping you could tell me more about your equipment. Dr. Nobelkov said it's your own design, which is very impressive." In Ree's experience, people were less threatened when you complimented them. She wasn't sure that held true for killers, but with no better ideas, it seemed like a reasonable place to start.

"Thank you, Dr. Ryland. I would love to show it to you, but you see, I am packing it today and tomorrow to be shipped back home with me. My grandmother is very ill, and I am going to finish my studies closer to home."

"I'm so sorry to hear that, Simon. I'm sure she'll be glad to have you home," Ree said, as genuinely as possible. Thanks to Jordan the analyst, she now knew that he didn't have a grandmother still alive, but her life depended on convincing him otherwise. She continued, "I lost my grandmother when I was about your age, and it was very hard. Let me know if you need someone to talk to."

"Thank you very much, Professor. I think working will be the best medicine for me," Simon said, turning away.

Ree stepped closer to his equipment, and he turned back towards her, blocking her path. "I meant to ask you – one of the other students is working on developing their own control system, and I don't know much about electronics. Did you use quick connects?" It sounded innocent, but she was hoping the basic question would convince Simon she wasn't a threat.

"Of course, Dr. Ryland. I am not a specialist in wiring and soldering."

"How many boards did you need for your equipment? Fatigue test equipment is so complicated and difficult; I would imagine you needed to order most of the boards special for this machine."

Simon's eyes narrowed. Then, they were back to normal. He smiled and said, "Of course. Let me show you." He led her over to the machine, pulling his hand out of his pocket to unscrew the front panel.

Ree tried not to lean away from the equipment. Parker had assured her it *probably* wouldn't explode as they had intel that the explosives had been acquired separately. Trying to ignore the word *probably* echoing in her brain, she looked into the machine after Simon moved out of her way. What she was seeing was equipment that was over-designed. There were too many parts for too few outputs. That alone wouldn't have made her suspicious – inefficiency of design was the hallmark of inexperience – but Simon's glare when he thought she wasn't looking certainly did.

She counted the boards and came up with five unique boards with open slots for another five. Even if he needed two per missile, that was still enough to build five weapons. Of course, for all she knew, he could need ten for a single missile. Upon closer inspection, her poker face twitched. He had placed quick connects on the main board, but he didn't connect them to a power supply. It was such a fundamental and trivial error, any remaining doubts about his guilt vanished.

Faking ignorance, she shrugged and said, "Okay, you have officially gone over my head. Maybe you can talk to some of the computer or electrical engineers if you need any advice before you leave. Otherwise, all I can tell you is your circuit boards look very impressive. And good luck to you. I hope everything works out for the best." The last part was true, but "the best" in Ree's mind involved Simon going to jail for a very long time.

Alexis walked in as they were finishing up and bounded over to Ree. "Hey, Dr. R – you said we could have our mentoring breakfast this morning? We still on?"

"You bet. Sorry, Simon, I'm going to have to let you go. Alexis, do you mind if my friend Parker comes along? He's been working with me and would love to hear your perspective."

"Of course!" Alexis said brightly. Parker packed up his laptop and they left together. As they walked back to the van, Ree grabbed Parker's hand without thinking while Alexis followed. Ree was shaking, the terror of talking to someone who might kill her still raw. What if he'd realized she was trying to get him arrested? What if he'd tried to shoot her? What if the machine had exploded when he opened it? She was generating new worst-case scenarios about every three seconds, a rate an order of magnitude faster than her usual. Parker began to run his thumb over her hand, and she closed her eyes. Her racing thoughts slowed and she clutched his hand a little tighter.

ALEXIS SWEPT the street as she followed her friends. She still wasn't sure if Ree and Parker were aware they had been gradually drifting towards each other, even though she and Mike had a bet on when something would happen. It probably wouldn't go too much farther if Parker got in his own head about it, so she kept her thoughts to herself. However, she had correctly predicted exactly one week ago that he wouldn't be able to resist a damsel in distress who could hold her own in a fight and had a sharp wit on top of it. Mike was going to owe her another five dollars. Ree looked towards their joined hands as if suddenly realizing they were touching and loosened her grip before they reached the van.

. . .

MIKE GREETED his colleagues when they opened the van door. “Okay guys, we’re headed up to Chicago. Time to meet with the Chief.”

“Wait,” Ree asked. “We know he’s up to something now. Isn’t this the part where you cuff the bad guy?”

“You’ve been watching too many crime shows, Ree,” Alexis said.

Parker sighed. “We still don’t have enough evidence. We can’t arrest someone, particularly someone from another country with unknown associates, without evidence. All he has is what may be the brains of a weapon, but nothing that actually explodes.”

“You know he’s guilty,” Ree said. “I recorded what he has, you know he wants to hurt someone, and you still can’t arrest him until he actually tries to do something awful?”

“Technically, we can,” Mike said. “Once we have proof, but all we have are circuit boards. And we don’t have evidence he wants to hurt anyone.”

Ree raised her hands in pure disbelief. “But the circuit boards weren’t even connected to anything. Surely you saw that?”

Mike just replied, “Circumstantial. Incompetence doesn’t prove guilt.”

Ree rubbed a hand down her face. “Does this happen a lot?”

“It’s always a possibility,” Mike said. “But that doesn’t mean we give up. It means we take this information and we use it. Keep in mind, he has to get that machine through customs, and we can take a closer look when it’s getting shipped. It’s too big to go in his carry-on. In the meantime, we have a meeting with the Chief this afternoon, and I think you should come if these guys are okay with it.”

Alexis and Parker nodded their agreement. Ree was in this as much as they were at this point, and hopefully, between all of them, they could come up with a plan.

23

THANKS TO THE BUREAUCRACY INHERENT TO THE FEDERAL government, it took Ree half an hour to get past the administrative assistant at the front desk. There was a missing piece of paperwork, despite the fact she was already cleared for a major operation and had signed more documents and waivers to work pro-bono for the FBI than she had for her actual job. After the no-nonsense look the administrative assistant gave Alexis when she tried to protest, Ree sat down, shut up, and waited until they called her back. Parker and Alexis had both offered to stay with her, but she didn't mind the alone time. She, thankfully, wasn't used to catching criminals and used the time to pull herself together.

Simon could have killed her if he had been so inclined, but he didn't. It should have given her relief, but instead, the "what-ifs" left her shaken. Worse, it still wasn't over. Between the FBI's strategy of identifying everyone involved and the rules of arrest, it was impossible to figure out how this would work out without someone getting hurt. Just as she got herself worked up all over again, she was given a temporary badge and escorted into Chief Sandhill's office to join Mike, Parker, and Alexis.

The office was utilitarian and neat, but before she could study it for too long, Sandy greeted her with a firm handshake and booming voice. "Young lady, it's nice to meet you in person. I'd like to thank you for your help."

"It's nice to meet you, sir," Ree replied. He reminded her of her Army veteran father, not only by his military build but also by the warmth lurking behind his serious expression.

"Heard you've been giving my boys a hard time – thanks for that too." Sandy's eyes twinkled as he gestured for her to sit next to her team. As he settled behind his desk, Ree looked to her counterparts. Parker's jaw was tight – a sure sign he was annoyed, Alexis was grinning, and Mike was leaning back in his chair. Sandy's demeanor radiated calm, but even with her frayed nerves, it was clear she was missing something important.

SANDY FOLDED his hands on his desk. His team told him Ree was frustrated by having to wait for Simon to actually commit a crime. He'd been pleasantly surprised to hear she would want to see this through to the end. If he could convince her to help, her presence would also create an opportunity to get Parker in the middle of the action. If Parker was correct in his assessment of Ree, it would be harder to get her to back off than to help. Sandy slid a report across the desk to Ree.

"Dr. Ryland, we believe Simon is planning on taking his components back to Ghana. There is no known terrorist faction over there, he has no family, and he has a past history of working for their intelligence services. If he intended to aim this thing at us, we believe he wouldn't be pulling so many strings to get it back.

"The problem is, even if we investigate him, we can't prove anything. His trip here was sponsored by someone high up in the Ghanaian government, with whom we maintain a good working relationship. But that relationship will be tarnished if we allow dangerous weapons to be shipped to them with our knowledge. On the other hand, if they find out we've been spying on someone that they insist is innocent, we've created an international incident. And, if we tell the wrong person of our suspicions, he'll slip through the cracks and potentially cause even more damage. I'm afraid we need boots on the ground to stay close to him and his equipment until we figure out what he's up to and how to stop him. Then, we can engage trusted allies in the country."

"That makes sense," Ree said. "And sucks. But I get it. Will you at least let me know how things turn out?"

Sandy steepled his fingers and leaned back in his chair. "No, ma'am, I would like to ask you to continue to help us out, if it isn't too much trouble. For the purposes of this mission, you'll travel as yourself. Since you and Parker have established a cover, we want you to get him anywhere Simon may go on behalf of the university. However, we are going to need to make your travel history disappear, so we'll be providing you with a different passport. It will also help you in case things get hairy and you need to get out."

Ree's eyebrows rose. "No offense intended, sir, but aren't you guys just in charge of what happens in the U.S.?"

"No, ma'am. We have Legal Attachés all over the world, and you'll be working with our Legat at the US Embassy in Ghana and a CIA team familiar with the area. They have relationships with the local police, who can be brought in once we have a better understanding of what's happening. For the safety of everyone involved, only you and Parker will be visible to the suspect. You'll hear your support team through an earpiece, but for the most part, you won't have them with you in the field. We're going to keep Alexis's involvement minimal since our suspect knows her face. She and Mike will run surveillance from the embassy."

Ree placed her hands on her cheeks. "Is that a good idea? What if I make a mistake?"

"It's the best opportunity we have. We aren't asking you to shoot our suspect, Dr. Ryland. We just need you to be our team's ticket to the party."

Ree lowered her hands and blew out a breath. "Okay. I'll help. One request, sir?"

"Yes?"

"I would like to bring a weapon with me. I don't want to go in unarmed."

Sandy chuckled. "Parker warned me you'd want to pack your gun. You can, but you're going to need to use one of ours, which means you need to get some time in on the range. We have a weapon ready for you already and some paperwork for you to read."

"Paperwork?"

Alexis broke in, "Welcome to the government. You need to read a bunch of training documents and go through some basic counterespionage training. No big deal."

REE SWALLOWED. Right. Just a little counterespionage training. No big deal. After checking all of the boxes, Alexis took her to the shooting range. Alexis was as relaxed as Ree had ever seen her and chatted easily when it was time to swap out their paper targets. Ree fought back a smile when she realized this must be Alexis's preferred version of girl time over the more traditional martinis and mani/pedi. It was more fun for Ree too. Hitting her target was a lot more satisfying than getting her nails painted.

While they were loading their weapons for the next exercise, Ree's phone rang. Her mom was calling. She should have expected her family would be wondering what was going on by now. They had exchanged some texts, which kept her concerned mother from calling the police to check on her missing daughter in the short term. However, the all-consuming worry unique to moms had overridden the assurance Ree would call her to have a real conversation when it was a good time.

Showing the screen to Alexis and shrugging her shoulders, she slipped her ear muff off of one ear and answered. "Hey, Mom!"

"Goodness, Ree, where are you?"

"At the shooting range!" she shouted into the phone.

. . .

Ree's mother sighed. Married to Ree's father for over thirty years, she realized early that her husband was raising his daughters the same way he had been raised. While she appreciated that in principle, there was a part of her that wasn't really comfortable with any of her babies shooting guns. Thank goodness it was just practice. The odds Ree would ever use the weapon were slim to none, her husband had reassured her on multiple occasions. The amount of paperwork associated with firing a weapon kept most people that had guns for self-defense from reaching for it unless they were truly in danger. In which case, she would be grateful her little girl was armed. Ree had always walked her own path, and if Kay had learned anything as the wife of an Army officer, it was how to adapt to the unexpected.

She shouted so Ree could hear her clearly, "Are you hitting anything, dear?"

"Of course! You'll have to come join me sometime."

"No, thank you, dear. Your dad and I just went last weekend, and that's quite enough for me. He had to go shopping with me in exchange. He said that I don't have to come with him anymore if this is going to be the arrangement from now on."

Ree laughed. Her mother was a handful, but her father was just as bad. They loved driving each other nuts and would continue to do so for years. She was looking forward to hearing her dad's side of the story, preferably when her mother was in earshot to refute it.

"How is work going, sweetie?"

Ree took a bit longer to answer as she debated between various versions of the truth and settled on, "Better than expected, Mom. Most of my new coworkers are really great, and I'm working on getting to know the rest...better."

"Any nice men, about your age?"

"Mother!"

"Ooh, what's his name? You never get defensive unless I'm right."

. . .

"I HAVE TO GO, Mom! Someone next to me is really loud!" Ree held the phone away from her face and shouted. She was tempted to fire a few rounds to make it sound more realistic but decided not to overdo it. Kay hung up the phone and Ree let out a laugh. Her family was nuts and she loved it.

Alexis looked up from reloading her weapon. "Based on the shade of purple your face just turned, it sounds like your family is just like mine?"

"Depends, does yours ask insanely personal questions and won't take no for an answer?"

"Is there any other way to know that they love you?"

Ree grinned, and they replaced the paper targets for the next round. Ree enjoyed the sense of accomplishment as she transitioned from being intimidated by the new handgun, more powerful than what she typically carried, to shooting it accurately by the end of their practice. There was a neat circle exactly where she wanted it on her paper target. Ree wouldn't carry it unless she felt comfortable, and it was nice to adjust to the unfamiliar weapon so quickly.

Ree had been fortunate to have never used her self-defense know-how outside of the karate dojo. Alexis arranged for Ree to spend a little time with their local trainer on a self-defense refresher course before they went on their trip, which consumed the rest of her afternoon.

By the time Ree was settled into her FBI-approved apartment, Chief Sandhill had pulled some strings to make sure everyone in the lab knew that she was going to represent the university on a network-building trip to a sister school in Ghana in the following days. This would be viewed as a gesture of goodwill as they made a donation of equipment and transferred expertise in the form of one of their students. Ree was happy for the cover story, if only because it allowed her to keep her distance from Simon until they met again on the other side of the world.

24

A FEW HOURS AWAY, SIMON CAREFULLY PACKED UP HIS EQUIPMENT AND circuit boards while the other lab employees and students focused on their work. He wasn't worried about getting the machinery through customs, since there was nothing that was obviously illegal in his equipment, and he had successfully been hiding in plain sight among highly-regarded experts for the better part of a year. If he could design weapons components under the nose of academics who actually knew how the equipment should work, Simon was confident no one in customs would be the wiser.

The General had sent him his final instructions, which he would carry out upon his arrival in his home country. While they were unconventional, the success of his mission required he trust the man planning the operation to ensure it went well. The General had never let him down before.

EXHAUSTED FROM GETTING her butt kicked by Sensei John, Ree flopped into her temporary bed. The accommodations weren't anything fancy, just a two-bedroom apartment with a living area that she was sharing with Alexis. Ree laid down alone in her own room with her eyes closed, letting the events of the day wash over her as she stretched her aching muscles. Her new instructor used not only the techniques she'd been trained in, but also taught her some new moves that were now causing her pain in places she didn't know existed. When she told him that the point was to keep her from breaking when she got to Ghana, and not kill her before she left, he had just laughed. She pulled up her leg to her chest to stretch her lower back and heard a knock on the door. She rolled out of the bed with a groan just in time to see Alexis spring from the couch, weapon in hand, to look through the peephole. She opened the door, and Ree dragged her body over to greet Parker, who was holding a takeout bag from a Thai restaurant.

Ree's hand slapped her forehead. Alexis raised her eyebrows. "You forgot to eat again, didn't you?"

Parker smiled and held the bag up. "Pad Thai sound alright?" The sweet smell of noodles and peanut sauce made the decision for her.

Ree grinned. "For Pad Thai, I'll even let you stay awhile."

Alexis grabbed a small container from the bag and murmured something about having some phone calls to catch up on before retreating to her own room and shutting the door. Parker handed Ree a container and a disposable fork. He held up a finger and reached into the inside of his jacket. A miniature bar of chocolate with caramel swirled over the top from one of the local designer shops was slid into her palm.

"Thought you might need this."

"You thought right." Ree bit her lip to push away her affection for Parker and focus on the Pad Thai. There was an empty kitchen table, but they both preferred sitting on the couch. After a few weeks of living together off and on, they walked over to the couches by unspoken agreement. Ree reverently placed the chocolate bar on the coffee table to be savored after dinner and sat cross-legged on the couch. She popped open the lid, enjoying the smell before digging her fork into culinary heaven.

As Ree took a huge bite of noodles, Parker asked, "So did you kick Sensei John's butt?"

Ree chewed for what seemed like a minute, then swallowed before speaking. "Hardly. I don't think I'll walk again, so I'm going to have to duck out of this case. I'm lucky I didn't die."

"That's not what he told me. He said you held your own."

"Checking up on me, Agent Landon?"

"In my defense, it is my job."

"Look, I may be more prepared than your average scientist, but I still don't have any idea what I am doing in the middle of this mess, Parker. What if I screw something up?"

"Well, you have the makings of an agent. We all think like that. None of us know what's going to happen, we're just flexible. So we'll go in there, we'll figure out how to catch our guy, get out, and then pretend we were never there. Oh yeah." Parker reached into his coat pocket and pulled out a passport.

"Rita Deckart?" Ree wrinkled her nose. Her grandmother's name was Rita, and while she loved her dearly, well, it wasn't exactly a common name for someone under 30.

"It was the closest thing we had to Ree available in our stack. While Ivan and your lab mates know you are going over to Ghana, we don't want any official record of it."

"Parker, what if…" Ree trailed off, unable to form the words.

"Don't go there, Ree. We'll get you in, figure out what Simon's up to, and then get out. You're right – there's risk. However, we'll do our best to make this all a crazy story before you know it." Parker nudged her with his shoulder. "Bright and early tomorrow, we have a plane to catch. Cover needs to be in place once the wheels hit the ground, so get in your zen zone or whatever it is you do to try and convince your brain that it likes me. You're going to have to fake it for a while." Parker slipped into his jacket, and Ree walked him to the door. He gave her hand a quick squeeze, and she held on a beat too long before locking the door behind him.

"Alright, what's going on with you two?" Alexis asked, and Ree jumped.

"What? Between Parker and me?"

"No, you and Santa Claus. Mikey and I haven't said anything, but you haven't been trying to kill him lately, and he seems to be finding reasons to be around you when he doesn't need to be. Like when he brings you dinner and chocolate. It is our job to notice things, you know."

"You'd have to ask him. I didn't invite him over, and I wasn't going to turn down Pad Thai. He didn't even eat."

"And the fancy chocolate bar?"

"I like chocolate. It was thoughtful. No more, no less." Ree brushed away Alexis's question, not because she wouldn't answer it, but because she couldn't. Somewhere along the line, their cover had stopped being a complete lie for her. However, between fearing for her own life and the lives of her new friends, starting a new job, and getting recruited as an FBI consultant, defining her non-relationship with the agent in charge of the investigation hadn't been penciled into her schedule yet. Alexis crossed her arms and eyed her critically. When she shrugged, Alexis mercifully let her off the hook. Ree resolved to take it one day at a time between fervent prayers for safety as she crawled into a strange bed and drifted off to sleep.

A loud noise startled Ree awake, and she fumbled to turn off the alarm. Her eyes felt grainy and thick, but her small bag was packed, leaving her very little to do except haul her aching body out of bed. She ran a brush through her hair, splashed water on her face, brushed her teeth, and met Alexis at the door. They were meeting the boys at the airplane; it was a charter that would take them all the way to Africa. Ree had always wanted to visit and was disappointed she might not see much of a country that had long been on her bucket list, given the nature of their visit. Maybe someday she would get to go back for an actual vacation.

When they arrived at the airport, a couple of new faces greeted them. Jordan Sykes, the analyst and computer expert that Alexis had spoken with on the phone, and Tim Dunn, his counterpart, would be joining them on their trip. They would all stay at the American embassy to avoid attracting attention while Ree and Parker played tourist. When the time was right, they would spend time at the local college trying to figure out Simon's motive and target. Beyond that, their only plan was to take each day as it came.

Ree, Mike, Alexis, and Parker, out of habit or preference, grouped together into four seats next to one another on the plane, and Alexis gestured to Jordan and Tim to join them when they came on board. They rearranged the seating so that they were facing one another. Jordan introduced himself to Ree and then got right to business. Jordan looked every bit the Silicon Valley techie. Despite his laid-back appearance of a hoodie, jeans, and sneakers, his intensity revealed itself when he began talking about the investigation. "Okay, guys. We've been able to piece together a supplier for the missile bodies and fuel, but we haven't figured out what he wants to fill this thing with. Best case scenario, the Ghanaian government is increasing their military capabilities."

Mike retrieved the case file from his bag and flipped it open. "The last report suggested it was an individual. What's the probability on a scale of one to ten that the government is involved?"

Jordan paused. "That someone in the government is involved, nine. Someone is at least looking the other way. That it's a high-level, sanctioned activity...maybe a two? I don't think their government would risk a relationship problem with us for a handful of missile parts. Since we haven't found warhead material and we keep a close eye on that, our people believe we may have a little more time to figure out what Simon is up to. The damage without a warhead would be limited by the amount of fuel it can carry."

Alexis clapped Jordan on the back. "Looks like all your training is paying off, Sykes. That's a lot of good data. Aren't you glad we pulled you out of the programmer's cave?"

Jordan smiled. "I'll let you know when this is all over." He passed out images that had been taken after the equipment had been placed in the shipping container and inspected by customs agents. It looked like the test equipment they'd all seen before, and everyone put the paper to the side except Ree, who continued to study it. Jordan had begun to fill everyone in on Simon's schedule and whereabouts when Ree pointed to a photo of the bottom of the test machine.

"Wait," she said. "Do you have any more pictures of this? Zoomed in a little?" Jordan handed a stack over and the group waited for Ree to flip through them. Back a few sheets and then forward. Back again.

Ree pointed to the base of the test equipment and said, "There is something else here, guys. Do you see this piece on the equipment? You'd never design them to be two pieces when they could be one. It's just one more thing to break, and there's no mechanical reason it would be in this shape unless you were trying to waste material. That's a way more expensive design than a simple base, and it doesn't need to be that complicated. It seems to go past what should be the floor of the equipment, too."

Everyone leaned in, and Ree held the paper in the center of their group. "See how if you removed a little material here and added some back here, it would be conical?"

"These pieces here," Jordan pointed to another view of the base of the machine. "Are those what you're talking about?"

Ree leaned in. "Yes. I think they're covering something up."

"There's no functional reason for them to be there?" Jordan pressed.

"No. What do you think they are?"

Jordan looked at Alexis. "What if they weren't planning on filling the warhead with anything?" He turned to Ree. "Warheads are usually filled with some especially nasty material, but it could just be a plain cone welded to the top of the missile. Outside of the contents of a warhead, they have all the bits and pieces for a complete missile. What if…"

"They just basically wanted a mobile bomb?" Alexis asked.

"It fits Scarlett's analysis," Mike chipped in. "It's a lot easier to launch a weapon, get out of Dodge, and then pick up the pieces afterwards. It's targeted. Limited damage."

"It's a bomb with a map," Ree said quietly.

The team considered other possibilities, but every time someone pitched something, Jordan poked a hole in it. He began typing an email, getting his team on the ground working on possible launch sites near the shipping address of Simon's test equipment. It was a nearly impossible task, given they didn't know the target and, like many other large cities, the outskirts of town were disorganized at best. They would have to check a radius around the city center and see if anything obvious popped up.

Many hours and a few awful meals later, the plane touched down in Accra, Ghana. The University of Accra was close to the airport, but the team was scheduled to go to the local embassy/FBI attaché and wait to tour the university until the following day. Simon's shipment was scheduled to arrive in three days. The extra time would give Ree and Parker a head start to check out the facilities at the university and establish their cover with the local university faculty.

While the others held a private meeting with the leader of the local FBI team, Ree tried to use the alone time to rest but failed entirely. After an uneasy hour of lying on an unfamiliar mattress, she left her quarters and went to the communal area. Parker had given her the unnecessary reminder after they landed that their situation in the country was precarious at best. As a result, they were not to deviate from their cover outside the walls of the embassy, which meant she would need to convince him to go with her if she was going to get out of the building. As much as she wanted to stay within a known safety zone, sitting still in a building with nothing to do but wait was making things worse. Her jittery nerves were nearly always soothed by running, but that wasn't an option here. Getting out for a long walk would at least help take the edge off.

It was easier than she expected to convince Parker to join her after finding him. Within minutes, she'd persuaded Parker that a tour of Accra would make their roles as tourists more convincing. She was pretty sure that Parker was humoring her, but regardless of his motivations, it'd be nice to get a closer look at the city after seeing the long beach and colorful buildings from the airplane. Some of Ghana's capital city matched Ree's expectations, which were largely set by her limited internet searches and the information that Jordan had provided. What she hadn't expected was the vibrancy of their surroundings. The city was loud and alive, and acting the part of a tourist came easily as Ree paused and pivoted every few steps to take in all of the details. It was beautiful. She would definitely come back someday.

. . .

PARKER HELD Ree's hand as they explored the city for two reasons – one, to protect their cover, and two, to easily pull Ree out of danger if he needed to. To prevent getting shot with her eye lasers for hovering, he informed her it was the former reason before they ever left. She conceded easily and her excitement remained as bright as it was when she bounded over to convince him they needed to go sightseeing.

Parker had been to the area before, but only to visit the African FBI attachés as part of a series of interagency visits. The CIA maintained a presence here as well, but they liked to keep information to themselves and run their own show, so whatever they were doing, he would probably be blind to it. In any case, he was happy to have allies, even if they were reluctant to give away their literal or figurative position. It was the nature of the business, and you just had to be happy with what you could get. Despite his reservations about their impromptu tour of the city, Parker was glad he'd agreed to get out of the building when Ree's eyes lit up as they approached the loud, crowded market.

"Go ahead," Parker said. "I know you're dying to go in."

Ree and Parker squeezed in between the stalls, weaving around other people as they took in the chaos of the market. It was obvious by their dress and appearance that they were not locals. Salesmen and women shouted at them as they walked by, persuading them to buy their wares. As with most street markets, haggling was expected, and Ree held her own as she negotiated with a no-nonsense vendor for local fabrics. She walked away holding the small pile of fabric tight against her chest, genuinely thrilled with her purchase.

AFTER AN HOUR IMMERSED in the beautiful chaos, Ree paused to follow her nose, and it led her to a pile of ornately patterned shells. Thinking it was seafood, she looked closer and was surprised to see live land snails half a foot long poking out from a large basket. As the vendor held one out to her, she laughed and waved her hands to gesture that she didn't want to try them. Perhaps she wasn't as worldly as she liked to think, but after a bad experience trying snails as a child that ended up with the round, chewy creature lodged in her throat until she forced it down, Ree couldn't quite bring herself to embrace this particular local flavor.

Parker gestured to his watch and tugged at her hand. It was time to head back to the embassy. Ree took one last look at the market. She wasn't a pro like Parker, but she saw very little outside of what she would expect from any large city, and that gave her some measure of comfort. They had a big day tomorrow, and they didn't need any more complications.

25

Ree awoke in the pitch blackness. The quiet stillness, characteristic of the morning hours nearly everywhere, was unsettling today. There was a whole slew of officials working at the embassy, but her small team was tucked away in a semi-private area where they had been assured they would see very few people outside of their group. While the FBI coordinated with local law enforcement, the new visitors didn't particularly want to advertise their presence to a broad audience. It was too early to hope someone had made coffee in the small dining area near their quarters, but hopefully, she could find some and get it started herself. Ree slipped on her shoes and padded down the hallway, careful not to wake the others.

As she passed the closed doors of the other bedrooms, she wondered who had stayed here in the past. Surely, this was not the first team of federal agents staying here covertly, even if the stated purpose of their lodging was for ambassadors and dignitaries and was appointed thusly. Staying at the embassy made Ree feel as safe as was possible, considering their objective was to catch someone bound and determined to make something blow up. She grinned when she heard someone snoring, the noise loud enough to be audible through the heavy door. At least someone was relaxed enough to get a decent night's sleep despite the jet lag, even if it wasn't her.

She continued walking until she arrived at the open cafeteria area. As expected, it was empty. A clock nearby glowed 4 a.m. She and Parker would leave to visit the local university once it was a more reasonable hour. Out of place in a foreign country, Ree was looking forward to the comfort of being in the company of fellow scientists and engineers. At least until Simon arrived.

Ree startled when a large woman with a friendly face walked in. The woman threw a hand to her chest and then laughed sheepishly before introducing herself. A fellow American and a woman comfortable in her domain, she waved Ree out of the kitchen and got to work, as if meeting new visitors at dark o'clock was a common occurrence. It either happened all the time or she'd been trained to not ask too many questions about strange visitors. Ree pulled a hand through her hair, and when it got stuck in the tangled mess, she decided to give the cook some time to get situated while she went back to her room and took a much-needed shower.

Predictably, after showering and getting dressed for the day, Ree felt better, and it was now a more civilized hour. Well, it was at least later, now that it was 4:45. She made the same walk along the corridor, but this time, she heard clattering coming from the kitchen. Mike had joined the cook to double the number of members of their team in the dining room. He looked as jet-lagged as she felt, but was eating a bagel and seemed perfectly content to sit alone without talking to anyone – a good personality trait, considering his job description. She gave a friendly wave and he nodded. Ree now knew that was a roughly equivalent response for him. Out of consideration for her teammate, she didn't try to talk to him and instead went in search of her own breakfast.

By the time Ree sat next to Mike with her yogurt and coffee, the remaining members of their team began to trickle into the dining area. Everyone took a few minutes to fully wake up upon arriving, but the volume in the room was steadily increasing. Given that they had company by way of the cook, even if said cook likely had a high security clearance, they spoke only generally about the day ahead. Parker came in last, appearing well-rested, evidently used to frequently changing time zones, or at the very least, grateful that he was on a bed and not her couch. His eyes scanned the room and settled on her. Of course they did. His job meant he had to spend the next several days keeping her out of trouble, and he took his work seriously.

After about the tenth time Ree checked her watch, it was finally time to get their earpieces and cameras in place. Once their surveillance equipment was invisible even to those who had put it on them, they were ready to get to work. The FBI didn't know if anyone at the University of Accra was complicit in Simon's plan. Thus, their goal for the day was to observe and assess if Simon had any accomplices. Ree's cover was that she was meeting the professors at the university for the purpose of developing a long-term relationship between departments. The role was an easy one since she was planning on actually making those connections. Regardless of the outcome of this whole mess, connecting with a university halfway around the world would be a good cross-cultural learning experience for her and her students. She fully intended to use her time wisely and keep in touch with all of the professors she'd soon meet. Well, so long as the professors weren't aiding Simon in whatever he was planning.

When they reached the University of Accra, Ree took in the pretty campus with cheerful red buildings and wide sidewalks. Parker tapped a finger on the steering wheel and glanced her direction. "So, the University of Accra doesn't have as large of an engineering program as Indiana Polytechnic. The engineering program is relatively new compared with the rest of the programs on campus."

Ree crossed her arms. "Interesting. Probably a good way to sneak new equipment into the country, then."

Parker nodded. "Yeah, Simon did his homework. They're in the middle of constructing new labs and buildings as we speak. His knack for strategic timing would be admirable if he wasn't trying to blow something up."

"Yeah, and drag the university's name through the mud along with him."

Parker pulled into a parking spot. "He might. Or this could just be the delivery address. Jordan expects Simon's machine to be here the day after tomorrow."

Ree tapped her finger on her leg. "So, what's our job for today?"

"All we have to do is shake hands, meet other professors, and see if anything pops up as suspicious."

Ree stilled her finger. "Oh, that'll be nice."

Parker raised an eyebrow. "You're happy about poking around, looking for accomplices?"

"Well, not the part about looking for accomplices. But to meet everyone, sure. Not everyone here is guilty, and I'm traveling as myself. I get to meet people from a completely different continent doing the same research as my students! I'll probably grab some business cards while I'm at it."

Parker chuckled. "Business cards. Ree, you never fail to surprise me."

"What? They're fellow researchers." Ree reached a hand into her bag and extracted a notebook and pen.

"True. That means we'll need to make sure our cover is airtight today – scientists are an observant bunch. No telling who Simon might be working with."

"Deal. But let's keep the PDA to a minimum. It is my workplace, even if it's halfway across the world." Not to mention, it was hard enough to think straight without Parker being close – she didn't need a repeat of Joanna's visit to her house.

Parker grinned. "You got it. I'll still be working the observant writer and boyfriend angle. But professionally."

"Perfect." Ree opened her door, and they walked towards the newly constructed engineering buildings in the hot African sun.

AFTER A FULL MORNING of shaking hands and exchanging information with everyone in the small engineering department, Parker ran out of reasons to keep Ree on campus. Ree collected a long list of contacts that she intended to maintain when she returned to the United States.

Parker assured her she could use the list once this was all over, and the FBI had cleared it. His confidence that they had assessed this situation correctly grew when one of the professors warned them about the heavy traffic around the campus in a few days. There would be a ribbon-cutting ceremony for a new lab, the lab that would hold Simon's equipment. A large crowd would almost certainly be present.

While Parker didn't love sitting around waiting for something to happen, the idea that the operation was coming to an inflection point spiked his adrenaline, even as he was just walking on the sidewalk next to Ree with no visible threats. He forced his shoulders to relax and threaded his fingers through hers to calm his fidgety muscles. Ree led the way back to the car in silence. Like most engineers, she had a strong visual memory and needed little guidance on where to go after one look at the map of campus. It simplified one aspect of their relationship, at least.

26

Simon arrived at the University of Accra as soon as was reasonable after his flight. No one here knew his true intentions, but if the plan was to go well, he needed to appear as if he cared for the needs of his people so they would speak positively on his behalf when he became involved in the new government. His knife was back in his pocket, where it had been a trusted friend during his mission in America. However, now that he was back in his home country, he also had a gun tucked into the small of his back with a shirt over it. His operation may not end successfully – a risk with all operations – but his instinct for self-preservation in any circumstance had served him well, and he wasn't going to start ignoring it now.

When Ree entered the engineering lab for follow-up meetings she'd planned the prior day, she saw a stranger in the familiar face greeting her new acquaintances. It may have been their change in perspective, their certainty of Simon's guilt, or Simon's arrival back on his home turf, but something about him had shifted. The aloof scientist was gone, and he was introducing himself to everyone in the lab with the huge smile and friendly personality more characteristic of a politician canvassing for votes than the quiet graduate student character he'd been playing stateside.

Parker stepped in front of Ree, cutting her off, and greeted Simon with a firm handshake. He met Parker's eyes and lifted his chin a fraction. Ree was unsure of how to greet him. She had been prepared to keep her cool after a mental pep talk on the way here. However, casually greeting a potential murderer and smiling in the process resulted in a feeling of disgust stronger than she had expected. Parker kept her calm, wrapping his hand around her elbow as if leading a blind person.

She forced a smile, as sincere as her acting ability would allow, and greeted Simon brightly, waving, but hoping to avoid physical contact. "Hi, Simon! How was your flight over?"

"It was long, but it is good to be home, Dr. Ryland. So good to work with you again so soon."

Ree bristled at the familiarity in his tone. She wondered if he was using her credibility as another tool, making it appear as if they were closer than they actually were.

Per their plan, she said, "So glad to hear it. I'm just planning on getting to know everyone, and they said there was some sort of ceremony on Thursday?"

"Yes, the vice president of Ghana will be coming to a celebration at the college, including an open house for the new lab. That's where the new equipment will be placed, including mine."

"Congratulations!" Parker said, still standing at Ree's elbow. "That sounds impressive. Did it beat you here?"

"No, it won't be in for some time," Simon evaded. The lie was perfectly executed. Had she not been told by Parker that the equipment was scheduled to arrive tomorrow, she might have believed him. "It's nice that your...friend...could come along." Simon eyed Parker.

"You mean Parker? Yes, he is doing some research for a book on women in science, and he thought this would be a great opportunity to learn more by joining me on my trip. And, we've gotten pretty serious, so we're turning this into our first vacation together," Ree whispered, conspiratorially, just like she had practiced. She'd felt ridiculous when Parker asked her to rehearse with Alexis but was now grateful that the words came out automatically. Ree tried to calm her roiling stomach and fought the impulse to place a hand on it.

Now would be a good time to make her excuses to Simon and begin introducing herself to any colleagues she had not yet met. In another lab. As far away from this one as possible. Parker pulled her over to a professor who hadn't been there the prior day. They passed another half hour in the lab before saying their goodbyes and heading back to the embassy.

On the way back to the car, Parker dropped something on the ground next to the front bumper of an old truck. Ree raised an eyebrow, but Parker said nothing until they were in the car with the doors closed. "That truck was Simon's," Parker said, "Now it has a GPS tracker underneath it."

Ree's eyes widened. "Impressive."

"It's a start. We at least know where his truck is headed, even if we can't watch him 24/7."

Ree tapped a hand on her leg. "What if he hands off his components to an accomplice?"

"The tracker won't work."

"Or travels on foot?"

Parker's hands tightened on the steering wheel. "The same."

Ree rubbed her face. "Then what would we do?"

"We'd adapt, try and figure out where he went without it. Tomorrow, Simon gets his equipment. After that, things are probably going to get interesting."

Ree and Parker drove back to the embassy and debriefed the team. However, it was still only two in the afternoon. Ree's stomach couldn't take much more, and Alexis was hovering protectively over her shoulder. Alexis was also showing signs of being cooped up since she'd been sidelined to the surveillance team. If Ree had learned anything about Alexis in their short time together, it was that sitting still wasn't really her forte. The palpable tension was broken by Mike challenging everyone to a game of poker. Ree couldn't resist, even though Parker warned her that Mike was shameless about exploiting everyone's tells and enjoyed winning just a little too much.

Ree retrieved a few dollars from her bag to pass the remaining hours until dinner. She held her own, but her observant new friends didn't buy her bluffing, and she was out first. Alexis swept the floor with Parker and Mike as they focused on beating one another.

After Mike slid his last chip to Alexis and she scooped up her winnings, they ate dinner, and everyone went to their separate quarters. Tomorrow, they would all be at the embassy until word was received that Simon's shipment was in. Once he unpacked it and left the building, the real work would begin. Changing into sweatpants and a t-shirt, Ree slid under the covers and waited for sleep to come.

27

SIMON APPROACHED THE BUILDING WHERE HIS EQUIPMENT SHOULD BE waiting. For the first time in months, it was clear he had the upper hand. The University of Accra was much smaller than the campus in Indiana, and he was counting on few witnesses. It was irrelevant in any case. Those in the lab knew nothing about his equipment, and those with expertise had never suspected his intent. He could take the guidance and control systems and nose cones even with other people nearby. No one would be the wiser.

If his machine arrived intact, he would continue as planned. A little welding, riveting, and soldering this afternoon, and he would be ready the following day. Simon had been warned by The General to expect the unexpected and to proceed regardless of any surprises. It was an otherwise unexplained warning that made him uncomfortable, but ultimately, it was all The General thought he needed to know. His only task was to point the missiles at President Minkah, and Simon had the coordinates for his location at the time the missile would be launched. While The General had tried to weave more details into the story about the President killing Simon's parents, he was likely just trying to ensure Simon's compliance. It was reassuring to know he played enough of a role in The General's plans to warrant special reassurance from the man, but the veracity of the story was irrelevant. President Minkah stood in their way, and that was all that mattered. He would proceed as planned.

Simon made small talk with the employees at the university as he leaned against a building near the loading dock. Presenting different personas was something that came more easily to him than most things. Switching to a more outgoing personality was no trouble as he waited for the package to arrive. The General informed him that the machine was en route, and the trip from the airport to the university was a relatively short one. However, the equipment had cleared customs later in the day than he expected. He would need to work through the night. It was no matter. One long night in exchange for the outcome he desired was more than an acceptable trade.

A few minutes after his arrival, Simon's machine was delivered to the loading dock. He pushed himself off the wall of the building, brushing his pants and feeling for his knife before directing the delivery truck driver to the appropriate lab. Simon allowed victory to seep into his limbs. It was a luxury in his line of work, where isolation was typical and emotional control was essential. Seeing his machine arrive in one piece as if it was a normal delivery was a welcome reminder that his plans were coming to fruition.

Once the delivery truck driver left, Simon disassembled the crate, noted that everything was as he had left it, and began to assemble his machine to continue his charade. It took some time, as his new acquaintances stopped by to see his equipment and ask questions. Before he left, he placed five complete thrust control and guidance systems and the metal pieces he needed into a large cardboard box. Five total nose cones, each progressively smaller than the one before, had masqueraded as a fixture at the base of his machine and would only require a little work to form into their proper shape. They were not perfect but were close enough to suit his purpose. He had more parts than he needed, but the solitary nature of his mission meant he couldn't count on anyone but himself, and back-up components were necessary.

Simon walked to his truck and placed the components in the

passenger's seat. It was a short drive to the warehouse on the outskirts of town where the rest of the parts he needed to create his missiles would be waiting.

WHEN SIMON BEGAN to drive away from the college, Alexis and Mike packed up their gear at the embassy to follow him. It was too risky for Parker and Ree to join them. They would stay at the embassy unless they were needed. If all went well, Alexis and Mike would catch Simon in the act of creating a missile, and the team could turn him over to the local authorities and go home before the night was out.

Alexis stared at a small screen that tracked the location of Simon's truck and gave Mike directions until they reached it. The red dot continued to blink, but the truck in front of them was empty. "We lost him, Mikey," she said. She smacked her hand against the inside of the hard car door. They had trailed him into a busy warehouse district. Because of the narrow streets, pedestrians, and the desire to keep their distance, there was no sign of Simon.

"Alex, the guy is a fully trained intelligence officer. We'll find him – it'll just take longer than finding an untrained civilian," Mike reassured his teammate. But Alexis could spot a bullshitter from a mile away, and Mikey was definitely bullshitting. She sighed and looked out the window. They passed the empty vehicle, parked, and communicated their location. Alexis adjusted her hair under a headcover and ran a hand over her traditional Ghanaian dress. She looked like a tourist trying too hard to fit in, but as long as she didn't look like Alexis Jenson, Dr. Ryland's student, that was just fine. They would have sent Tim or Jordan in her place, but they were techies, not field agents. This wasn't her first rodeo, and she could stay disguised long enough to find their man. However, as they crept into the alleyway, it started to feel less like two FBI agents finding one rogue intelligence agent and more like walking into an ambush.

They communicated their situation and requested backup from the as yet unseen CIA team. A couple of guys were there in minutes, explaining that they didn't exist and wouldn't even have a record of being there. Alexis was so grateful for the help she didn't even roll her eyes. One of them had a slight limp – his face was shaded under a hat, but he seemed familiar. The other was either Ghanaian or a good actor, since his accent matched that of the locals perfectly. It didn't matter who they were, as long as they were armed, and their weapons were pointing at their mutual enemy. They checked around corners and looked into buildings, but after half an hour of searching, they found nothing. But, they also didn't get shot in the back, so it wasn't a complete failure. Minutes turned into hours, and soon the sun began to set. They went back to the car, and Mike called in their situation while Alexis stared out the window in silence.

"Guys, we have his vehicle, and they're not launching missiles from the inside of a building. Get back here, and we'll regroup," Parker said. His voice was clipped, as it always was when he was annoyed. Answerless, they had no choice but to go back to the embassy to figure out what was next.

REE WAS CARRYING a stack of paperwork when two dejected agents walked into the room Tim and Jordan were using as a command center. Alexis and Mike stripped out of their bulletproof vests and joined the rest of the team pouring over satellite photography. After getting a quick lesson in what to look for, Ree flipped through the pages with the rest of the team, the high stakes keeping her focused on what would otherwise be a mind-numbingly dull task.

"Got it," Mike said. Waving a part of the map that looked to Ree to just be desert with a couple of outbuildings, he flipped between images from two months prior and those taken yesterday while the satellite was overhead. "New building, nothing around it but a concrete pad. And it's the right size. Get the team, we're going out there tonight."

"Am I going?" Ree asked, unsure of whether she wanted them to approve or disapprove of her coming along.

"Sorry, Ree. You need to sit this one out. Hopefully, we'll come back, and Simon will be in handcuffs. You can stay with Jordan and Tim and help keep an eye on things from here." Parker took off his shirt and put on a bulletproof vest. Over it, he added a long-sleeved black shirt.

The rest of the team followed suit and checked their weapons. The rip and placement of the Velcro on the vests and click of weapons being checked were the only sounds as the team prepped for action. Ree settled into a seat by Jordan, ready to help if her team needed her. If she couldn't relax, she could at least be useful.

"All right guys, let's move," Parker commanded the rest of the team and pointed to the exit. As the efficient line of agents filed out of the room, Mike lagged behind, plugging GPS coordinates into a device. The door closed, and the room went silent except for the humming of the computer that was Ree's lifeline to her friends.

"They'll be alright," Jordan said without looking away from his screen. While his words were intended to reassure, the fact that they needed saying did little to ease her mind. She rapidly tapped her right index finger on the desk while staring at the computer screen, willing it to tell her that her friends were safe.

AS HE SLOWED the truck to a stop, Parker scanned the surrounding area. They were in the middle of the country with no other people around. The only shelter was the small building that Mikey had spotted on the image. It appeared to be deserted. Parker hopped out of the truck, drawing his weapon. The rest of the team followed in a similar fashion. He gestured to the sides of the building, and they split up. The front of the building was corrugated metal, with only one small window and a heavy metal door locked with a padlock. On the other side of the building was a large closed metal garage door. Finding nothing of value on the exterior of the building, Parker flashed a light into the window, and said quietly, "We need to get in there, guys." Parker handed his light to Alexis and removed his lock picking tools while Mike watched the road. Parker heard a quiet click, and the heavy padlock was removed. Alexis opened the door, and it groaned on its hinges.

Parker shone his light around the room but saw no one and no obvious recording equipment. The bases that the missiles would need to launch successfully were sitting in front of him. There were three bases total. A row of metal storage cabinets lined the wall. Approaching one of the large unlocked cabinets, he cautiously opened the door and found what he was looking for. Shutting the door gingerly, he scanned the room to make sure they hadn't left any traces of their visit and indicated that it was time to go.

"Still good, Mikey?" Parker asked, breaking through the quiet tension.

"Affirmative, Parker, no one in sight."

"Place that camera, will you?"

"Affirmative." Mike placed his flashlight between his teeth and planted the camera discreetly under the building's roofline. He was back to the truck in seconds. They didn't dare place more than one, and this would give them the information they needed, even if it didn't give them as much as they wanted.

Five minutes after their arrival, the team left the building, and half an hour later, they were back at the embassy. It was the first score for the good guys, and the mood in the truck on the way back was one of cautious optimism. It wasn't a win, but it was a start, and they'd take what they could get.

REE MET them at the door, relieved they were back safely but exhausted from the constant stress of worrying about what could go wrong. The team seemed happy with the outcome, which was odd, considering they hadn't brought Simon back with them.

"So, everything go okay?" Ree asked, her voice more casual than she felt.

Parker answered, clearly pumped up and more talkative than usual. "Yes. Actually, better than okay. They can't launch these things without fuel, and we just found enough to light up half the city. Now that we have eyes on it, we know at least that source is secure. The only risk is that they have more stashed somewhere, but rocket fuel isn't that easy to come by. It's dark, and we can't find out much more now. We can get some sleep while Tim keeps an eye on the cameras."

"What can I do?" Ree asked.

"Nothing right now. We'll be sleeping in our vests tonight in case we need to move quickly. Good news is we still have a chance to stop this guy. The vice president will be at the college tomorrow, and our intel, along with Simon's cover, points that direction. We need to be fresh, so do what you can to relax tonight. It sounds impossible, I know, but we need you rested for whatever is going to happen."

28

SIMON WIPED HIS BROW WITH THE BACK OF HIS BLACKENED HAND. HE was covered in sweat and grease from riveting, welding, and soldering his weapons into being. He'd worked through the night in the basement of a warehouse with only a freight elevator and no windows. He had three finished missiles, and his mission was almost complete. The fuel was elsewhere, a necessary compromise considering he was working with heat. The General had arranged for a truck with lifting equipment and another agent who was trained to not ask questions to come help him in a few hours. Soon, no one would stand in the way of their plans.

THE FBI AGENTS and one college professor were all up before the sun, even though the big event didn't start until 1 p.m. Mike and Alexis left shortly after waking up to continue their search for Simon, despite the meager odds of finding him in a busy city if he didn't want to be found. If they couldn't locate him by late morning, they'd drive over to the college for two reasons: Simon still had what was left of his equipment there, and there was a high-profile target speaking to a large crowd that afternoon who might need extra coverage. Parker and the rest of the team would be watching the camera they'd planted the night before in case Simon slipped past their defenses at the university.

TWO HOURS after they'd left the embassy, Alexis looked at her watch and grimaced. They had found nothing, and it was time to change locations. Damn. Mike's eyebrows were furrowed, and he was scowling into another alley. Yeah, he was as pissed as she was. He growled into the mic that they needed to go. Their last chance to catch this maniac rested on finding Simon lurking in the crowd, since the shack filled with rocket fuel still sat empty.

Mike parked some distance away from campus proper to make it easy to leave in a hurry, but as they approached the bright red buildings, Alexis twitched at the size of the crowd. The smell of food hung in the air as vendors sold their wares and eager students gathered. Alexis turned her shoulders to slip through the tightly packed sea of people. At least everyone seemed friendly and most were excited. The environment was lively, not unlike big political rallies in the U.S.

Alexis followed Mike, whose head turned back and forth methodically to scan for threats. The large crowd limited their visibility, and she grabbed Mike's arm, pointing to indicate they should try and get a better look from the roof of a building. They tried to walk up a deserted stairway to get to the top of the building but found a national security team already stationed at the roof door. They were told in no uncertain terms that they needed to find another place to watch the ceremony. At least the government had tight security – they'd take all the help they could get.

Given that their covers required them to act like tourists, they retreated to a second-floor window of a classroom in a building farther away. Mike pulled a pair of binoculars from his backpack, but the crowd was enormous and moving, alive in its own right, which made it difficult to find a specific person. Time passed with no sign of their suspect.

When the vice president stepped up to a podium to welcome the crowd, Alexis tensed. The crowd stilled, and her trained eyes looked for motion. Because she was focused on the crowd, she didn't see where the shot came from before the vice president of the country they were trying to help collapsed on the stage.

"Holy shit!" Alexis yelled. She and Mike ran to the door of the classroom, shouting a situation update to Parker on their mics. As they tried to leave the building, the crowd morphed into a sea of chaos, and they found themselves trapped inside a swarm of terrified witnesses.

PARKER HEARD the expletive in his earpiece and shouted at Jordan to communicate with the CIA guys, who were elsewhere on campus but similarly penned in by the crowd. They needed to find a route to get his team safely out, but they didn't know where the shot had come from or why it was happening. The timing was too coincidental not to be connected to Simon's missiles, but it didn't fit the evidence they had gathered. The building housing the fuel Simon needed was still deserted. Parker's highest priority now was to get his team out of danger. Once they were out, they would reassess the threat. Parker kept Mike and Alexis talking, coaching them and making sure he knew their whereabouts in case more drastic action was necessary.

THE GENERAL COLLAPSED and grabbed his leg in pain. Akua had shot him exactly where he had commanded her to. Good girl. While he had been shot before, it was a lifetime ago, and it hurt worse than he remembered. As expected, his security team swarmed, and he heard the distant screech of an ambulance. Per protocol, President Minkah would be rushed to the presidential mansion to get him away from government buildings and other large gathering places. The president would then reassure his country by holding a press conference within the high cement walls around his compound. The General would watch and wait from his hospital bed, surrounded by security personnel who would vouch for his non-involvement. The tragic death of the president, followed by the vice president's government takeover would be complete just after nightfall. Blood seeped from his wound, and he closed his eyes and smiled.

"PARKER." Tim pointed to a monitor, and Parker leaned in to study it. The video feed from the warehouse showed a large box truck pulling up in front of it. The shooting was a diversion. There was a sea of people penning in Alexis and Mike. Someone had to stop Simon before he did something unspeakably worse. Someone else needed to make sure his team got out safely, and Ree didn't know how to work the surveillance equipment. He couldn't pull Tim or Jordan away. He had to make a snap decision. He didn't like it, but they had no other choice.

Ree leaned against his shoulder, studying the video monitor before she turned to him. "Parker, we have to do something." She was wearing jeans and boots, but her weapon was in her room.

"Get your gun. Quickly. We need to go. You ready to do this?"

Ree nodded and jogged away. Parker grabbed an extra bulletproof vest. He was already wearing one, just in case, and when Ree returned, he handed her a holster and dropped the vest over her head. As he pulled the Velcro tight, he swallowed hard. He'd rather leave her within the protected walls of the embassy, but he couldn't risk the lives of even more people by facing two men alone with that amount of firepower. The decision had been made for him. That didn't mean he had to like it.

"Put this on. Follow my lead, and whatever you do, stay behind me at all times, and don't get shot. You okay with this?"

"If you leave me here and go after him alone, I'll shoot you instead."

Parker grinned, despite the circumstances. "That won't be necessary."

Parker peeled out of the parking lot of the embassy and kept his hands locked on the steering wheel. They traveled without speaking, with only the updates from Tim and Jordan in their earpieces to break the silence. Simon and his accomplice were setting their plan into motion, and the sooner they got there, the better. They had no cover, and the rest of their team was otherwise engaged. They would have to wait until Simon and his accomplice went inside the small building and then take whatever element of surprise they could get.

SIMON AND KOJO, the ally who had been selected for him, unloaded the last missile from the truck. Simon had been trained to cover his bases, and he didn't like that this man had seen his face. Simon initially had a handkerchief wrapped around his mouth and wore a hat to protect himself from identification, but it became impossible to keep in place, given the nature of their work and how much he had to move around.

They used specialized equipment to slide the large bases outside. The bases were portable, but it still took two people to place them and lift the small missiles on the launchers. A few lines of code were required to launch them after they were loaded with fuel, which would take some time.

"OKAY, Parker, they're in the back," Jordan said. "They're staying back there an average of two minutes between trips to the truck, but no guarantees. Make it quick."

Parker and Ree pulled up to the warehouse. They exited the car quickly and quietly, both careful not to slam the doors. Parker had his weapon drawn, and Ree followed close behind, imitating his posture and approach. He tilted his head towards the back, his intention to incapacitate Simon and his accomplice from behind while Ree waited near the front of the building. It might not be a fair fight, but neither was shooting a missile at innocent people. With their only camera pointed at the enemy's truck, they were flying blind, but they had little choice in the matter.

Parker's feet made more noise on the ground than he would have liked. He shifted his weight forward to his toes to help reduce the noise and moved quickly towards the back of the building. Before they reached the men, Parker turned and whispered, "Watch your back."

. . .

SIMON HEARD A NOISE, but his new teammate seemed oblivious. He gestured that he was leaving to go get something. He was no one's fool, and he would not take the fall for this if they had company. He could go around the front of the building and escape while they were focused on Kojo. He crept around to the side of the building, gun drawn in case of trouble, just as he heard a familiar voice he couldn't place. The voice was not Ghanaian, which came as a surprise. It was too quiet, so quiet he couldn't hear the actual words, as if the person delivering the message didn't want his voice to carry. He kept his shoulder against the building and went to find out who he was up against.

PARKER CREPT around the corner and directed his weapon towards the unknown subject, who was kneeling on the ground next to the launch bases. No sign of Simon, he said quietly, "Freeze. Put your hands on your head and walk towards me, silently. If you make a noise, I will be forced to shoot you. Do you understand me?"

The man nodded and walked with his hands on his head towards Parker, anger burning in his eyes as he looked for his missing partner. As Parker clicked the handcuffs on his left hand, the man spun and slammed his fist into Parker's face. Parker's mouth throbbed as he tasted blood, and for a moment, all of his focus was on his suspect. He grabbed the man's other arm roughly, and as he snapped the other side of the handcuffs into place, he sucked on his front lip to keep blood from dripping onto the concrete.

IN THE SPACE OF A MOMENT, a muscular arm tightened around Ree's neck, and her weapon clattered to the ground. She felt the cool muzzle of a gun at her temple. A deadly calm voice said, "Dr. Ryland. I think you are somewhere you do not belong." She began to struggle to breathe and kicked the gravel at her feet to make noise. Parker whirled and froze when their eyes met.

Heat and sweat mixed with the pain of Simon's rough restraint at her neck. Simon moved the gun away from her head and said with a quiet vengeance, "And now, you will watch your boyfriend die."

SIMON, a good shot, kept a firm grip around Ree's neck with his left hand as he moved his weapon into position. He would have to aim for the head because Parker was likely wearing a bulletproof vest if the way he had manhandled Kojo was any indication of his true occupation. It would be satisfying to kill the meddling boyfriend first.

REE FOUGHT for air and planned her next move. Her timing needed to be perfect. When Simon moved, his grip on her loosened slightly, and she inhaled what fresh air she could. He raised his arm to shoot Parker. Ree leaned down and bit his muscular forearm, threw her hip into his side, and used his own body weight to throw him forward over her back. Simon landed on the ground less than a foot from her and twisted to reach for her leg. Ree let out a primal scream and kicked him in the face with her boot. Once his head slammed against the ground, she picked up her gun and turned back to face him. He met her gaze, his eyes hot with rage.

"Freeze! Don't move a muscle." Ree trained her gun on Simon, and Parker began to run toward her. It was done.

STILL LYING ON THE GROUND, Simon timed his actions to Parker's approach. His gun was just within reach. He had one last chance to change his fate. Simon kept his head still to appear too injured to move. He grabbed his weapon and aimed it at Parker, his finger had almost reached the trigger when a sharp pain cut through his shoulder. He simultaneously felt and heard the bullet cut through his muscles and bone. He looked up in shock at his former colleague, who stood with both hands on the gun still pointed at him.

"THE LADY SAID FREEZE, ASSHOLE," Parker said, cuffing Simon roughly. "You okay?" Parker asked more tenderly to Ree, who was starting to tremble but had not lowered her weapon. She nodded but did not change her stance.

"Okay, good. Nice work, professor. Keep your weapon trained on him, and I'll be right back." Parker didn't feel pity for the man in front of him, but he also didn't want Simon bleeding out, so he jogged to the car to grab the medical kit he had packed in case of trouble. On the way to the truck, he filled in the crew that had been waiting for an update.

"We have two men in custody, one with a gunshot wound. Boys, you need to get the Legat and the ambassador read in on the double, and I need a bomb disposal unit here yesterday. We're going to try and get these guys to talk, but in case they don't, we don't need these things going off. We'll get this guy patched up, but then we need to have never been here as soon as possible. Make it quick."

Even after Parker had applied battlefield first aid to make sure the enemy agent wouldn't die, Simon remained silent. Parker didn't want to leave Ree alone, but she offered to keep her gun trained on Simon as long as he needed her to. It gave Parker time to shake down Kojo, which turned out to be a wise decision. Simon's compatriot, after realizing he'd been deserted by his new partner, was offering to tell everything he knew to Ghanaian officials before anyone else showed up. He had only been a secondary player who didn't know the true nature of the mission, but he did know who ordered it, a fact that he shared while glaring at his former partner.

Parker also found out that while the missiles hadn't been activated, Kojo had seen Simon put the coordinates in. A quick check of the code would give them an idea of where they were headed. Parker traded places with Ree so she could find the coordinates and read them to the rest of the team. This information was met with a low whistle and no further information from Jordan or Tim.

About 20 minutes after the Ghanaian government had been contacted, an ambulance showed up with burlier-than-average EMTs. The embassy had a good relationship with a few local agents they deemed trustworthy and who were approved by the Ghanaian president himself. These men would work with the Americans on a joint task force to get to the bottom of this, while overlooking the small problem that the Americans didn't technically have jurisdiction, in return for their help. However, with the information they had gathered already, it wouldn't take them long. The two men were escorted to a local prison for additional conversations.

Hours later, The General lay in his hospital bed with a thick bandage on his leg and medication dulling his senses. He wouldn't be able to hear the explosion from the hospital but had turned on a local news program on so he would have the satisfaction of knowing when it happened. A noise at the door cut through the fog of medication. The General raised his head to see the president entering his hospital room with his head of security.

29

UPON THEIR RETURN TO THE EMBASSY, PARKER AND REE FOUND THAT their bags had been packed, and the team was ready to head to the airport. They were back on an airplane and headed home within the hour. It wasn't precisely a celebratory mood, considering the grueling week they had all survived, but a quiet relief mixed with exhaustion allowed everyone to finally relax on their way back to the U.S. Ree alternated between re-telling her story to the agents, who looked at her with pride and clapped her on the back, and second-guessing every move she'd made. She finally fell asleep on Parker's shoulder when he settled in next to her.

After landing, Ree wanted to go back home, but the FBI had other plans. She returned to the Chicago office for several hours of interviews. The only positive was that she was given permission to associate with her friends again, now that she was out of danger and the culprit had been apprehended. By the time she finished sharing her side of the story, the FBI was confident that none of the other lab employees had been collaborating with Simon. Sandy interrupted one of the debriefing meetings to clap her on the back like a proud father and thank her for her service to the country. It was definitely going to take a few solid nights of sleep before Ree felt normal again. Even if she did get back to feeling like herself, she probably wouldn't ever look at a custom test machine quite the same way again.

Parker walked Ree to the parking garage, where she was strangely nostalgic to see her car again. Before leaving, she sent a message to Joanna to let her know she had landed back in the States, wearily dropped her suitcase in the trunk, and turned to face the federal agent who she now considered a good friend. Ree stood on her toes to kiss him on the cheek, and he squeezed her hand in return.

After everything, this was it. She held his hand for a few extra seconds and ducked into her car before a tear loosed itself from her eye without her permission. She was just tired. Ree turned on the radio before pulling out of her parking space, curious to hear what the reporters would say about the events that had transpired. However, the news of the non-fatal shooting of the vice president of Ghana was only a short sentence repeated hourly on the world news update by a man with a British accent, with no additional detail.

Once back home, Ree placed her keys on their hook on the wall, locked the door, and punched a code into the tablet sitting on her kitchen counter. The FBI had a security system installed in her absence, a nice gesture that she suspected was Parker or Alexis's idea. Hopefully, it would make it easier to sleep without her constant bodyguards. She supposed she should call her family, given the lack of contact they'd had recently, but she was tired to her bones and her bed beckoned. Without changing her clothes, she climbed into bed and slept deeply for the first time in weeks.

Twelve hours later, Ree woke up and saw the clock glowing 3 a.m. Her eyes were dry, and she winced as she turned the light on. Waiting until 6 a.m. to get out of bed would strain her patience to its already fatigued limits. Her first stop was the shower.

After changing into comfortable pants and padding down the stairs to make breakfast in her cozy kitchen, she still felt surprisingly lost. Ree once read an article that said that some astronauts, after going into space, suffered from a sense that everything on Earth was less exciting in comparison and struggled to find meaning in the everyday. Laundry and groceries suddenly seemed less urgent, and just...less, somehow.

She chided herself for being melodramatic, made some eggs, and focused on enjoying the normality of the activity. She would find a way to get over it, she supposed, but it would probably take her more than a couple of hours.

By noon, Ree had washed and folded laundry, called her mom and sister, and was on her way to meet Joanna for lunch at The Whole Enchilada. Seeing Joanna resulted in a surreal combination of happiness to spend time together without pretense and some anxiousness as she fabricated activities to explain what she did on her trip. While Ree had never truly believed Joanna was capable of anything worse than killing spiders, getting the official clearance to talk to her as she normally would was still a welcome breath of fresh air. Despite her efforts to keep it in check, her enthusiasm to see her friend bubbled over, despite her fear that she would be called out on the small half-truths of the events of her vacation.

Given the true nature of her trip and the necessity for confidentiality, Ree focused on her experiences at the college and in the market, giving much more time to those details than she would have otherwise. Joanna, after skirting the issue with other questions, finally asked directly how things had gone with Parker. Ree had expected the question and told her things were going well, but she didn't know if Parker was as interested in the relationship as she was. Ironically, that part was actually true. She had gotten more attached than she intended and had already scolded herself earlier that morning when she realized she missed him. Ree would have to explain a break-up in a few weeks when Parker never came around. It also occurred to her that the cell phone number she had for him might not be active anymore.

After lunch, Ree went back home to continue ticking items off her to-do list before her return to work the following day. Keeping busy would distract her from the temporary, unpleasant side effects of a net positive resolution to a potentially deadly situation. Or something like that.

30

A FRESHLY-MADE POT OF BEEF STEW SIMMERED ON THE STOVE WHILE Ree sipped a glass of wine and dug herself out of the pile of work emails that had accumulated in her absence. A knock on the door interrupted her quiet evening in. She wasn't expecting company since she had already spoken with her family and very few people knew she was back in town. Ree knocked over her glass when she stood up to answer it. Looking to the ceiling, she shouted, "One minute!"

Ree grabbed a towel, and splashed some water and cleaner on the carpet – of course, it had to be a nice red wine rather than the white wine most of her friends favored – and threw a towel over the spill. Ree reached the door and chuckled when she saw Parker through the peephole, looking oddly nervous. Why was she always spilling things right before he showed up?

Ree grinned and opened the door. "I thought I just got rid of you." Parker was casually leaning against the wall outside her door, thumbs in the belt loops of his jeans and wearing his standard black t-shirt. So much for playing it cool if the agent came back to visit her. At least she didn't jump into his arms. That would have been worse.

. . .

"If only it was that easy." Parker walked through the door and closed it behind him. Ree's place felt like home – the beef something wafting through the air didn't help. He'd spent most of the drive wondering if he'd imagined how good it felt just to be in the same place as Ree. He hadn't.

"Did you guys need more information from me?" Ree asked, eyebrows furrowed. Her pretty eyes sparkled, and he fought the urge to pull her close, grateful she was alive.

"Actually, I thought you might want to know how things turned out before you went back to work tomorrow," Parker said.

"Of course I do, but I hadn't expected you would have more information in just 24 hours. I assumed you would still be talking to witnesses and writing reports. Is everything resolved already? Thank you for getting the security system installed, by the way. Oh, and does your cell phone still work?"

Only Ree could manage that many trains of thought simultaneously, and Parker grinned. He seemed to be doing a lot of that when she was around. "First, the cell phone works. That's my personal cell, not my work." Parker had accidentally given her his personal number in case of emergencies out of habit. He actually hadn't meant to, but it did make it easier to get in touch should she want to.

Trying to bring his brain back into focus – there was something about this woman that made all thoughts fly from his head – he continued, "And actually, it was resolved very quickly. It was probably the crazy lady with the gun that scared him into talking," Parker said good-naturedly as Ree shot him a look. "But Kojo – that was the first man I cuffed – insisted that he was on a sanctioned government mission after our Ghanaian counterparts arrived. The coordinates you read off were for the president's residence. That's classified, obviously, but the Chief didn't see any harm in you finding out."

Ree's jaw dropped. She said quietly, "Tim and Jordan. They knew when I read them off. They didn't say a word, but they knew, didn't they?"

Parker nodded. "Yeah, those guys are pretty tight-lipped. I had to get permission to tell you this much, but I figured you deserved to know."

"Did Simon know?"

"Yeah, he knew. He and apparently an official high up in the government were working to overthrow the president, who is actually a really nice guy. His name is Joseph, and he says thank you, by the way."

"Oh, does he? That's nice," Ree said, as if he was passing along a thank you from his sister for sending her muffins rather than passing along the gratitude of a head of state who had recently been saved from an assassination attempt.

"Well, not to us, directly. Obviously, he has no idea who we are, and it's going to stay that way...and off the record. But he was grateful."

"That's...good," Ree said, then went quiet. Parker filled the silence.

"Very good, actually. We were on the verge of a pretty ugly diplomatic situation there for a while. The good news for us – America, that is – is that we turned the suspects over to him immediately. I can't get too specific as to the whys and hows, but Kojo, the one you didn't shoot –," Ree shook her head at him, "will be excused from service in the intelligence forces to avoid embarrassment. He was ordered to do the job, didn't know where the missiles were pointed, and thought it was official business. However, our friend Simon knew exactly what he was doing, and didn't care, as long as he got what he wanted. You were right about our suspect being a sociopath."

"I'm not sure if that's supposed to make me feel better. In this case, being right nearly got a lot of people killed." Ree rubbed her hands along her arms.

"But it didn't. Simon is recovering from his gunshot wound, which the news will be happy to report was inflicted by heroic police officers who had a tip that something nefarious was going on outside of town. He probably won't see the outside of a jail cell for the rest of his life. Oh, and if you hear that any other high-ranking officials in the government retire from service, I wouldn't believe everything you read in the news."

. . .

"Wow, is that all?" Ree asked, half-joking, as they still stood awkwardly close in her foyer. Being with Parker was easy, but right now, it was also confusing. He didn't really need to be there to tell her everything in person.

"You mean, aside from all the paperwork you caused me by shooting someone?" Parker said, crossing his arms.

"You're welcome," Ree said, raising an eyebrow. Heat crept up her neck and she looked past him at a spot on the wall.

Parker took a step closer, unusually tentative. He pulled Ree into his arms, and she startled. When he didn't let go, she wrapped her arms around his neck. His eyes filled with the same hopeful apprehension mirrored in her own. He lifted her toes off the ground and pulled her close. "I forgot to tell you. Thank you for saving my life."

"It was no problem. You buy the next round of beers, maybe, and we'll call it even?" she teased. Parker held her in place for a few seconds before lowering her to the ground. Ree was unable to look away. Parker leaned down and ran his hand into her hair, tilted her head, and pressed a soft kiss to her lips.

Parker rested his forehead against hers and took a deep breath. "How about this? I buy you dinner, and you don't even have to shoot anyone for me. I'll even let you leave your gun at home tonight."

"Parker, I'm not sure going out to dinner is a good idea. I've gotten a little more attached than I had intended to." Ree bit her lip, trying to calm her confused, racing heart.

"Good. Me too. Look, Ree, my schedule, my job, my life. It's crazy, I know. But I'm close by. I mean, I just don't meet people like you every day. I guess I just thought..." he trailed off.

"That you'd be crazy not to see where this leads?" Ree continued his sentence before her mind could talk her out of putting her feelings on the table.

"Yeah. That's exactly it. I mean, I did already take you on vacation."

"To see a wannabe mass murderer. I hope all your dates don't start that way. How about we do this date thing my way? Maybe stick to a local place, free of criminals?"

"I can't promise that, but I can promise I haven't invited any. How's that?"

"It's perfect." And for now, it was.

NOTE FROM THE AUTHOR

Thank you, dear reader, for joining my characters and me on this adventure! If you enjoyed this book…

1. Leave a review on Goodreads, Bookbub, or your favorite book retailer. Even a short review is a great way to help other readers find this book!

2. Sign up for my newsletter for exclusive content and news about new releases at: https://ktleeauthor.com/

3. Follow me on social media:

Twitter: @ktleewrites

Instagram: @ktleeauthor

Facebook: https://www.facebook.com/ktleewrites

4. Check out the rest of The Calculated Series! An excerpt from Calculated Contagion is included at the end of this book.

Calculated Extortion (Prequel Novella)

Calculated Deception (Book 1)

Calculated Contagion (Book 2)

Calculated Sabotage (Book 3)

Calculated Reaction (Book 4)

Calculated Entrapment (Book 5)

BONUS MATERIAL

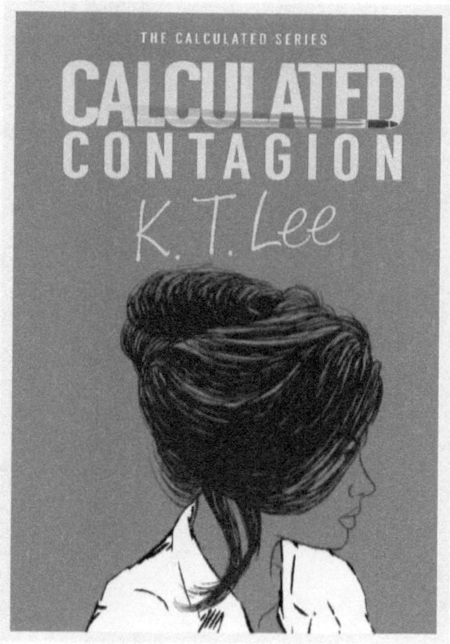

If you enjoyed Calculated Deception, please enjoy the following excerpt from Book 2 in The Calculated Series, Calculated Contagion.

1

DANI CHRISTENSEN CLOSED HER EYES AND TOOK A DEEP BREATH, visualizing air filling her entire body. She exhaled, imagining the air displacing her nervous energy. The makeshift combination of physiology and yoga was normally her tried-and-true method of tricking her body into calming down. It didn't work. She gave an impatient sigh and rubbed the necklace her mother had given her for good luck as she waited for the elevator to reach the lobby of the conference hotel. It stubbornly stopped one floor too early, and the ornate doors opened to Brock Fabian. She clutched the necklace a little tighter before dropping her hands to her sides.

"Dr. Fabian. Hello," Dani said with a forced smile. She'd grown accustomed to her colleague's condescension over the past several years, but he'd been laying it on a little thicker since she'd been asked to present her research at the TED Vienna conference a few months prior. He had not received a similar invitation. She would just keep their conversation professional. And hopefully, brief.

"Ms. Christensen. Are you going to the conference hall?"

"Yes, you?"

"Same place. Good luck with your presentation. They're probably happy to have you as the consolation prize, since the man himself couldn't make it."

Dani's eyes widened and her mouth dropped open before she could stop it. Blissfully unaware, or unconcerned, with his own insensitivity, Dr. Fabian left the elevator when they stopped at the ground floor. The "man himself" was her father and the CEO of VacTech Pharmaceuticals. Even though Dani had dedicated her career–and most of her free time–to vaccine research, there was always someone who believed her success was a result of who she knew instead of what she knew. While most decent people didn't say it directly to her, Brock Fabian had no such inhibitions. Since it had taken a few seconds to get over her shock and make her legs move again, Dr. Fabian was now impossible to see in the swarm of conference attendees. It could only get better from here.

The energy of the conference crowd lifted Dani's spirits, and she smiled and waved at several new acquaintances. Interacting with smart, interesting people between scheduled events was the cherry on top of the joy she'd felt when she received the invitation to speak at the conference. Her smile slipped when she had to detour around a small crowd of vocal vaccine protestors. Upon seeing her badge, they turned their angry words and stares towards her. She put more distance between herself and the tight circle of people, moving towards the staging area with a new determination. The loud chanting that faded as she walked away reminded her why she was there. The best way to ease their concerns was with science, and she would explain the science in very short order.

Despite Dr. Fabian's scrawled review on her journal article that said, "good work putting an old medicine in a new box," and the fact that it wasn't yet ready for full-scale production, Dani had made an enormous breakthrough on a shelf-stable measles vaccine. Ideally, the world would simply learn to get along, but at this point in her life, developing a new vaccine seemed more achievable. That was the beauty of science–it was apolitical.

Once she entered the busy backstage area, she no longer heard the protesters. Dani peeked through the door to the hall to see if they were still there. She jumped when one of them met her gaze and didn't look away. His stare made a tingle run up her spine, and she was suddenly grateful for the security guards scattered throughout the conference hall.

It felt like only a few seconds before Dani heard her name and was directed to the stage. She blinked into the bright lights, took a fraction of a second to compose herself, and began her presentation. Given her family's long history in the vaccine business and the immunization inequality still too present in her mother's home country of India, Dani used her platform to explain the importance of creating solutions that made sense at both a global and local scale. She exited the stage to strong applause, finally allowing herself to study the crowd in detail while she welcomed the calm relief that came with surviving her speech. She locked eyes with a man near the stage and a deep discomfort settled in her stomach. There wasn't anything about him that should cause alarm. He was dressed in a suit, had a notebook and pen, and like every other conference attendee, he had a laptop bag with him. Nothing to be afraid of.

While Dani was most comfortable with data and facts, devoid of emotional attachment, there was still a part of her that respected instinct. If pressed by her peers, she would explain that her brain could probably just comprehend more than could be compressed into a coherent thought. The gut feelings she experienced were merely a manifestation of acquired knowledge that neurologists hadn't quite put a name to yet. In reality, she didn't really know why her gut feelings happened, but they had never yet led her wrong. As Dani reentered the bustling backstage, she made a mental note to avoid crossing paths again with the stranger, just in case. First, the protestor who gave her the heebie-jeebies, now this guy. Maybe her sixth sense had jet lag.

Dani removed her mic and battery pack and was met with handshakes and congratulations. She acknowledged the compliments as graciously as possible. Under normal circumstances, she would be thrilled her presentation was well-received, but it was overshadowed by the deep discomfort still stubbornly taking up residence in her stomach. She shook it off yet again. Her family was unable to make it, and some loneliness was to be expected. It was statistically improbable that two separate people were up to something and focused on her.

It wasn't until she had slipped off her stilettos and laid back on her plush hotel bed later that night that Dani finally realized what was bothering her. The protestor and conference attendee were the same man.

2

"ROMANIA?" CAM MITCHELL LOOKED UP FROM THE SMALL STACK OF papers, tucked into a standard-issue manila file folder, at Morgan Grady. Cam had worked for Morgan in the euphemistically-named Special Operations Group at the CIA for five years, and their interactions had long been stripped of decorum in favor of results. He never knew what to expect when she summoned him to her office, but a quiet country in Eastern Europe wasn't exactly on his radar.

"Yes, Romania. You, of all people, should know crazy isn't limited by geographic area," Morgan volleyed back, arching her eyebrows. Her short, highlighted blonde hair was as neatly styled as her trademark suits. Morgan had fought to get him on her SOG team because she saw his potential in both linguistics and field work, and they'd been tight ever since. Morgan was just over five feet tall and as tough as any Navy officer Cam had ever served under. She was also good people.

"Fair point. But why is the U.S. jumping on this, Morgan?"

"We're getting some unusual reports about a group in the mountains we believe is armed and growing. We have a small presence in the country and have agreed to offer military and diplomatic help if it's needed. Some of our people in the field have sent some issues up the flagpole, so we're going to look into it. How fresh is your Romanian?"

"It's a Romance language, ma'am. Shouldn't take me more than twenty-four hours to brush up if the analysts got the dialect right," Cam said, not looking up from the packet.

"They usually do. A day is about all you have. We don't know much beyond the facts that they're assembling and we've seen weapons in the satellite photos. A small group of men came down from their camp to get treatment at a local hospital, which was when we first got an inkling that something was off. We've gone through the normal channels and haven't come up with much. The satellite images might be useful, but no promises. Obviously, we'd prefer they remain unaware of your visit." Morgan slid a satellite photo across her desk to Cam.

"About 500 men and women?" Cam asked, studying the size of the camp.

"That's our best guess. All of the people we've been able to trace back to the camp have been men. We don't know if they have women there or not. We just want to know what they are up to. If they are just a bunch of Romanian hippies starting a commune, we can leave them alone. If they're building up a small army, we have a slightly different protocol."

"Good thing we got the new leg finished," Cam said, knocking on the hard, composite material, his tone no less objective than it would be if he was talking about a new weapon. Cam had lost his left leg below the knee in Iraq, but thanks to modern technology and some customizations he had insisted upon, he managed well. The injury had been in a previous life, when he was a SEAL trying to locate an enemy hiding among civilians. On his way back to the base, he got hit by an IED. It was a shit-all thing to happen, but he'd been lucky to escape with his life and most of his knee intact. Cam's leg still occasionally caused him pain, but on his good days, it was a reminder of what drove him, rather than a hindrance. Working with the CIA had restored his sense of purpose that had felt too distant during the long and excruciating days of rehabilitation.

"If you hadn't worked so hard to break the first three we gave you, you wouldn't need a new one," Morgan said, beaming at Cam like a proud parent. The Special Operations Group at the CIA had been relentless when he joined up, testing him regularly to ensure he was physically prepared to be in the field. Cam passed the physical exams easily, but the design team for his custom prosthetic hadn't been prepared for his capabilities. Cam invested months with the design team, helping them figure out how to improve the mechanical response system and interface with his actual leg. A few revisions and some expensive material changes later, Cam had a new, stronger lower leg. It was time well spent, since other wounded servicemen and service-women would benefit from their sweat equity. Pushing himself to try and break the design before it was out in the field resulted in changes that made it unquestionably strong.

"You're welcome. Your nerds did a good job. Now it'll hold up in terrain more rugged than city streets," Cam responded, unable to fully mask the pride of ownership in the design.

"Here are the rest of the satellite images," Morgan said, handing him an additional stack of photos. He slid them into the folder, behind the rest of the background information. "You leave in four hours. We're going to drop you about five miles away and you'll have to hike the rest of the way in."

"Is Tyler driving?" Tyler was Cam's best friend, partner and heli-copter pilot. They'd had each other's backs since he started in the SOG, and Morgan kept the two officers together as much as possible. Their results spoke for themselves, and it was rare that Cam worked with anyone else.

"Of course. Take the file, and catch him up when you see him."

Cam placed the file into his laptop bag. "Good. Let's do this."

"Stay safe out there. That's an order, Cam." Morgan raised her hand in a half wave as Cam stood to leave. Cam grinned. She didn't let him get away with much and had no problem kicking his metaphorical ass when necessary, but she didn't want to see him get hurt. It was sweet. But if he told her that, she'd kick him out of her office. So, a salute was probably safest.

Cam raised his hand to his head, both as a sign of respect and out of the habit he'd never broken since he left the Navy. "Yes, ma'am."

3

DANI WOKE UP IN HER ROOM IN A COLD SWEAT, HER BODY CLENCHED into a tight ball from the vivid nightmare. She couldn't remember the details; only the potent mixture of hopelessness and fear lingered as she blinked her eyes open. She was safe. In her hotel room. At the conference. She unclenched her fists and rubbed her eyes. The too-quiet room, still blanketed in darkness, didn't help. Squinting at the glowing numbers on the digital clock, she sighed. Grateful the night was over and 7 a.m. was the same in every language, she ran her hand along the night stand to find the switch for the lamp.

Dani hauled her body upright and threw her legs over the edge of the bed. She pulled back the curtains in her room and took a moment to admire the view just outside of her window before she even left the bed. While the room was average in size by European standards, the quarters were more cramped than a typical hotel room in the States. The early morning light beckoned her to leave the confines of her temporary home for a walk in the brisk Austrian air. If someone really was out to get her, they'd have to be an early riser. Her stomach rumbled. A pastry before the conference began would be just the thing to clear the negative thoughts from her head.

Dani changed into a light sweater and jeans, splashed some water on her face, and laced up her tennis shoes to find sustenance and peace of mind. Once she was out walking on the cobblestone streets, she detoured into tiny alleys separating crowded groups of buildings to take a closer look at the architecture. Despite narrow streets, the charm of her surroundings kept her from feeling suffocated. Dani's shoulders relaxed as she wandered. She took her time before deciding on a busy café a few blocks from the hotel.

After an impossibly flaky pastry and strong tea, Dani returned to her room with a bounce in her step to change into more professional clothing for the conference. She took a shower and brushed out her long, black hair, but was unhappy with the results. She settled on pulling it up into a sensible bun at the back of her head and decided to wear her least uncomfortable dress clothes. Dani eyed the evil power heels she had worn the day before and tossed them into the back corner of her temporary closest so she wouldn't be tempted to choose beauty over sensibility at the last minute. Instead, she retrieved her trustworthy flats from her suitcase, and grabbed her room key, cell phone and notebook. There was one day of the conference remaining, and she was ready to make the most of it.

Time passed slowly in the wake of a poor night's sleep and without the adrenaline boost of presenting in front of a crowd. Worse, she was eager to see more of the city after her brief tour this morning. She dutifully took notes, however, since the foundation had paid her for her travel, and she felt obligated to bring something back in return. Lunch was extremely decent but not memorable. The afternoon made her feel sluggish, and she grabbed a cup of coffee to keep her awake. She usually preferred tea, but the coffee cart was out. Given that she had presented publicly, she couldn't just slip away to find her favorite drink without someone noticing. It would also make both her and the foundation look bad if she was fighting the urge to nod off during a presentation. So, the coffee was necessary. Unfortunately, one of the reasons she didn't like drinking coffee manifested itself forty-five minutes later, when she had to leave in the middle of a session to use the restroom.

Someone else must have had the same problem as she, because she heard heavy footsteps behind her as she walked down the long, empty hallway until she entered the ladies' room. She washed her hands and wiped them on her pants after an inefficient hand dryer refused to do the job. When she exited the restroom and looked down the hallway, Dani startled. The man she had seen the day before was leaning against a wall, studying the ceiling. Had he followed her? No, that would be ridiculous. Her cheeks burned and she forced a polite smile. Still, instead of crossing his path, she took the long way back to the conference hall. Just in case. She didn't make it to the end of the hallway before a large hand closed down on her wrist. As she opened her mouth to scream, she was silenced by a pain in her ribs. A voice she wouldn't soon forget whispered low and deadly into her ear.

"If you say one word, you will die."

ACKNOWLEDGMENTS

Thank you to all of my family and friends. Your support has been my rock. It's not every day that an engineer decides to write a book, and I'm overwhelmed by and so grateful for each and every person who encouraged me along the way.

A few special shout outs: to my mom, for her unwavering support and for the time she took to answer questions and provide opinions. Thank you also to Darcy, who encouraged me and read even the roughest first drafts with an eagle eye – no plot hole was safe from her pen. Also, a thank you to my dad, a retired police officer and veteran, who not only supported me, but also made sure I didn't take too many liberties with the cop stuff – any goof-ups were mine or taken as artistic liberties. Christa, fellow writer and dear friend, thank you for your early reads and for encouraging me to keep chasing my dream. Thank you to my husband – for keeping my plots on their A-game and for being fearless enough to read my manuscript. Thank you to Emily for answering all of my questions and for helping me make my dreams a reality. Also, huge thank yous to Granny, Julie, and Anna for your relentless support!

Finally, big thank yous to Laura Anderson and Bridget Fryman, two fabulous editors who helped me turn my manuscript into a book.

ABOUT THE AUTHOR

K.T. Lee is a writer, mom, and engineer who grew up on a steady diet of books from a wide variety of genres. When K.T. began to write the kind of books she wanted to read, she mixed clever women and the sciences with elements from thrillers (and a dash of romance) to create The Calculated Series.

www.ingramcontent.com/pod-product-compliance
Lightning Source LLC
Chambersburg PA
CBHW031716170626
46808CB00005B/1770

* 9 7 8 1 9 4 7 8 7 0 0 0 0 *